SKIP

By

COREY R. PARSLEY

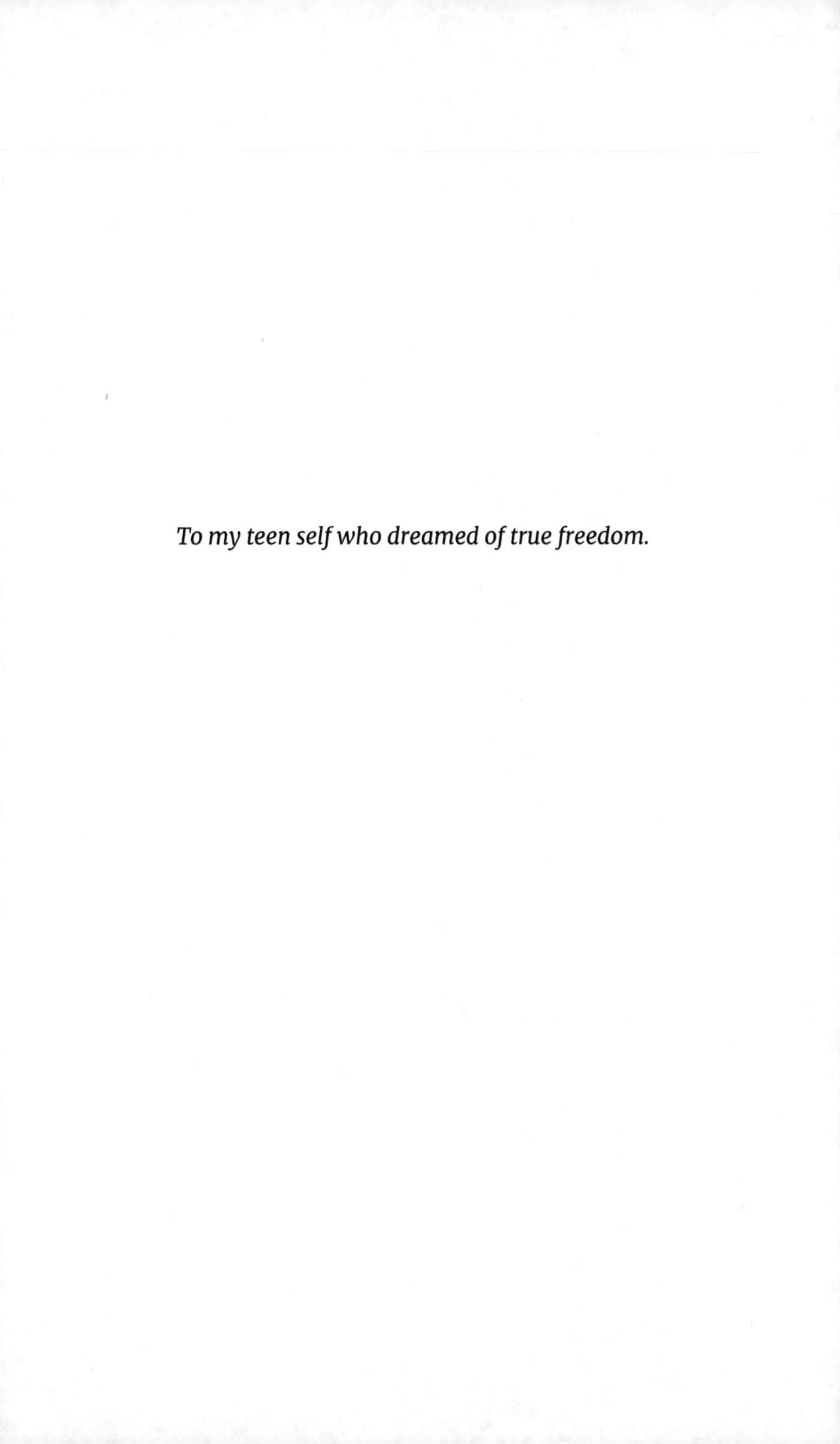

To my teen self who dreamed of true freedom.

Foreword

Hello Dear Reader!

You are about to enter into a thrilling adventure about two best friends falling in love and teleporting around the world. Keep in mind, they are teens. So they are messy, indecisive, impulsive, and full of charged emotions. This book contains discussions or instances about LGBT+ issues, abuse, religious trauma, sexual assault, blood, violence, underage drinking, cursing, bullying, and mild sexual scenes. If any of the aforementioned themes do not sit well with you then feel free to "skip" it, but please pass this book onto someone whom you think might enjoy it.

Otherwise, if you are still intrigued then I promise that tons of cute gay kisses, teleportation, alchemical magic, diverse characters, and plenty of teen angst awaits you! Have you ever dreamed of having supernatural abilities? Have you ever wanted the courage to be your true self? Have you ever wondered what it would be like to go on a grand adventure? Then this book is for you. And so, I give you: SKIP.

Acknowledgments

To my Cover Artist, Mylisha Sexton aka Inkibloo, you captured the true essence and feeling of SKIP. From the endless, wine fueled discussions to the sporadic message/email chains, it was all worth it. You have been there since day one rooting me on every step of the way. You are a brilliant artist. I deeply admire you and thank you for all your dedication and hard work. I'm proud to call you my friend.

To my Interior/Advert Artist, Kairo Binda aka Kryptid Creative, you are an incredible human being. I am consistently blown away at how talented and hard working you are. You have been an integral part of this process and a reliable friend I could always count on. Whether we were just shootin' the shit, running from killers in Dead By Daylight, or brain storming projects, you have always had an open door policy.

To my Editor, Charlie Krank, you are the secret weapon that came out of nowhere. With thirty-seven years of experience under your belt from the board games and book publishing industry, you offered to edit SKIP with such grace and gentle kindness that is rare in a lot of people. With every red mark I knew you were determined to make SKIP shine as brightly as possible. You are truly a diamond in the rough.

To my family and friends, thanks for putting up with my endless jabbering about my story for years. Thanks for reading endless versions and listening to endless anxious whining sessions from yours truly. You all are my foundation and I'm so blessed to have you in my life.

And finally, to you, the readers. Thank you for picking up this book. Thank you for giving it a chance. You are the cornerstone of an authors' livelihood and I appreciate every single person that takes the time to enjoy my writing. I can't wait to bring you more!

Sincerely,
Corey R. Parsley aka King Corey Bear

4 BEST DAY EVER

S

ummer.

No school, no responsibilities. Just friends stirring chaos and cementing memories full of laughter, but that was all going to end soon. A cool, California breeze blew in through my bedroom window as the last streak of light vanished from the sky. There was the scent of moisture in the air from a rare approaching storm. It was a good thing too. This dried-up valley needed it. Three plastic game controllers clacked competitively in unison. Wielded by three friends surrounded by neutral gray walls. They were covered in a variety of memories from over the years; movie posters, a neon sign that glowed blue and green and read, "Game On!", and a wooden plaque above the desk that had an inspiring quote carved into it.

"No one will write your story for you. Only you can hold the pen."

Discarded snack wrappers and half empty soda bottles lay strewn across the floor from our ravenous appetites.

We sat on plaid sheets and played well into the night. These are the kinds of nights I wished never ended.

"I've got you now!" I taunted them.

"Vale! What the hell? You keep spamming that move!"

"Well, Eli? I guess you'd better get good!" I grinned wide and bumped his shoulder with mine.

"Both of you know better than to ignore me."

"Oh no, Lauren. What are you plotting?" I asked.

"GAME!" The announcer in the video game yelled from my forty inch flat screen TV.

Eli and I groaned loudly and flung ourselves back onto my bed, letting the controllers fall out of our hands. "She did it again!"

"How does she keep beating us?!" Eli griped.

"You do remember I have two little siblings who love to play Smash Bros. all the time, right?" Lauren explained.

"Oh yeah, you have all that practice on us." I admitted.

"Exactly! Which means, ya'll owe me ice cream."

We rolled our eyes at her and groaned again.

Just then, there was a knock on my bedroom door.

"Come in." We called, simultaneously.

My dad entered, holding his phone. He wore a furrowed, almost angry, expression.

"Elijah, your dad's on the line. He needs to chat with you." Dad offered his phone to Eli, holding it to his ear.

"Oh...okay? Why didn't he just call me? I have my phone on me." Eli's question was met with silence. Dad held his phone closer to Eli, until he grabbed the phone and walked into the hallway. My dad followed, and closed the door behind them. Lauren and I could hear, through the wall.

"Hola papá, ¿qué pasa?" Eli's muffled voice answered the call. "¿Qué? Pero este es el último fin de semana, antes de nuestro último año y—

Pause.

"¡Mentira! ¡Pues lo es! Bien. Hablaremos de ello cuando

llegue a casa."

Eli stormed back through the door with my dad right behind him. "UGH!" He grunted.

"What happened?" I stood up from my bed looking at my dad for answers.

"Ask your homophobic parents! Oh here's your stupid phone back." Eli lobbed my dad's phone to him, and he barely managed to catch it.

"Hey! That is completely uncalled for young man, and I won't have you disrespect me in my own house. Now we've said our piece about the issue. Despite your insult, you are still welcome here, but you can no longer sleep over. Lauren, you should probably head home now, honey." My dad's face darkened. I clenched my fists and my forehead began to bead with sweat.

"Is this because Eli came out as bisexual?" I managed to say through gritted teeth.

"Vale! Stay out of this." Dad barked.

"Dad! What the hell?!"

"Vale, it's fine." Lauren said firmly. "We'll go. Thanks for having us, Mr. Dagwood. Tell Mrs. Dagwood, the dinner was really good." Lauren put her hand on my shoulder and gave a subtle squeeze after grabbing her bag. She grabbed Eli by the arm and led him out of the room with her, before he could say another word.

My breath was short and my chest tight as my dad stood in the doorway, staring down at me. I hated him. His bias, his obvious bigotry, was poisoning me against him.

I wanted to shove him into the wall.

I wanted to smash that expensive car he loved so much.

I wanted to report him to the IRS for tax evasion.

I wanted to hurt him in some way like he just hurt me.

"Vale, I–"

"Don't. Just...don't, dad. What if I were gay or bi or whatever? What then?"

"Aren't you straight?"

I wasn't, but he didn't need to know that. Not yet.

"Yeah, dad, but my point is you never had to question your way of life in the slightest. People who are different make you uncomfortable, isn't that right?"

I dug into him, every fiber of me demanding an explanation. However, no explanation would ever suffice.

"You need to watch your tone when you speak to me, son! You are seventeen and only once more will I remind you: you live under my roof, you follow my rules. When you turn eighteen you can get your own place and have your own rules. Until then you're stuck with me, bucko!" My dad bellowed and his voice rang through the house. His face was plump and red as a tomato. Before I could get another word in, he slammed my bedroom door.

"What's with all the noise up there?" Mom called from downstairs.

I kicked my dresser as hard as I could, snapping off one of the metal drawer handles and hurting my heel in the process. I flinched and sharply sucked in air as I held my foot. "Ow! God damnit!"

I threw myself on my bed and, after punching my pillow several times and screaming into it, tears streamed down my cheeks. Eventually, the comforting embrace of sleep consumed me.

The rest of the weekend I avoided my parents entirely. I had nothing to say to them and their intentions were clear. The first day of school arrived on a warm Monday morning. I launched myself out of bed, rushed my morning routine, and hurried out the door with barely an apple for breakfast. Instinctively, I paired my earbuds up to my phone, shoved them into my ears, and hit play on my regular playlist. The melancholy songs of the band Daughter were just what I needed on a day like this, the start of my senior year. I walked the old concrete sidewalks that had weeds creeping up from the cracks. White oak trees and ornamental pear trees lined the median of the main road. I wrinkled my nose as I walked further down my street, looking at the white petals as the culprit of a rancid smell. The stench became so heavy I covered my nose with one hand.

"Got caught up smelling the cum trees, huh?" A figure with wavy black hair, tan skin, stocky build, and a cute smile appeared holding a backpack on one shoulder.

"Oh my God, yes! That's literally what they smell like!" I laughed.

"Well, not all cum smells like that! Take it from someone who is an expert."

"Eli!" I gasped, shoving his shoulder with mine while still holding my nose.

"What?! Don't judge me, Vale. Just cause you're Mister Abstinence." Eli teased.

We started walking alongside each other toward the direction of our high school. There was a thick silence between us at first. It felt as if we both wanted to discuss the what happened between him and my dad.

"So...what did your dad say when you got home?" I asked, pausing my music.

"Just that it's not appropriate for me to stay over at a boy's or girl's house anymore. I find ways of hooking up with people anyway when the feeling arises. Plus, you two are my best friends! Why are parents like this?" Eli complained as I stared forward watching the sunrise above the boring gray buildings and lonely streets.

"But that makes no sense. Your dad has known you are bi for a lot longer than me or Lauren. Why change now?"

"He says, because your dad asked him to agree to it. My dad's reasoning was that 'I'm too old to be having sleepovers and that I should respect other people's households!' Or something like that." Eli mimicked his dad's voice in a goofy, inaccurate manner.

"Then my dad is just a homophobe?" I assumed.

"Probably. They did raise you to be Christian after all. My bet is most likely." Eli chuckled.

"Whatever. He'll just have to deal with my silent treatment then. Lauren was surprisingly understanding of that whole situation too." I rolled my eyes and kicked a pebble that flew across the road and nearly hit the windshield of a parked car.

"I think she was trying to be respectful since it wasn't her house or her place to say anything. Not to mention, she wanted to get me out of there before I said anything else I would regret."

"Ah, right. I guess I didn't see it that way. My dad just seriously gets under my skin sometimes." I clenched my fists and dug my nails into my palms.

"Hey, I totally get it, but let's focus on making this year the best one possible. Yeah?" Eli stopped and turned my shoulders to face him. He looked into my eyes, sunlight illuminating the golden brown around his pupils. The skin on his arms was incredibly smooth and his touch sent a shock up my spine.

"Right. Best year ever." I said, unenthusiastically.

"Oh come oooon, Vale! You can do better than that. Best. Year. Everrrr!" Eli howled. I turned bright pink as he waited for me to follow his lead.

"BEST. YEAR. EVERRRRR!" I howled back, reluctantly. We both laughed in unison as we crossed the street to our school.

The big, white and green sign read, "Fresno High School". The campus was a conglomeration of pristine concrete buildings, freshly-shaped squares of grass, and a long black iron gate that stretched down the length of the school. We were met by another figure, taller and darker than both of us, and who wore her best outfit for the day ahead.

"What the heck was all that yelling about? Did you two have too much sugar in your cereal this morning?" Lauren looked down at us over the top of her sunglasses.

"Nah, just an apple today. I was trying to avoid my dad so no time for much else." I lobbed the honey crisp apple half a foot into the air, caught it, and messily bit into it.

"Probably a good call." Lauren nodded.

I wiped my chin and pointed to a book in Lauren's hand. "Whatcha reading?" I said, my mouth full of apple.

"Oh just some fiction about the famous alchemist, Nicholas Flamel. I figured the first week of school would be full of syllabi and nonsense so I might as well have some entertainment." Lauren held the book out to me as I scanned the cover.

"Sounds cool! I always wanted to know more about that kind of stuff."

"What stuff?" Elijah interjected.

"Alchemy, Magick with a 'K'. I kind of wish that stuff was real. It certainly would make school and life a lot easier." I admitted as I finished off my apple.

"Well you can borrow it when I'm done reading it." Lauren smiled.

"I'd love that! Thanks!"

The first bell of the day rang and a horde of students sluggishly began shuffling to class. The three of us straightened up and courageously made our way to our first class of our final year in High School.

"Oh! If you guys could have any magical ability or power, what would it be?" Elijah piped up.

"Telekinesis. Definitely. I could get so much more done in a day if I could just move things with my mind." Lauren said confidently.

"Pfft, lame!" Elijah chorted.

"Okay, genius, what power would you have?"

"Simple. Mind reading. So I could see who is actually straight and who isn't."

Lauren and I stopped in the middle of the hallway and gave Eli an accusatory look. "What? I wouldn't out them if that's what you're thinking. It would be for my knowledge only so I would know which guys were even remotely an option or if I should stay away from them." Elijah shrugged and we all continued walking.

"Ah yes, still thinking with your dick, I see." Lauren commented.

"Always. Have you met me?"

We reached the door to our first period classroom. I thanked God that we at least had the first and last period together as a group. It would make this year a lot more eventful and smooth to say the least.

"What about you, Vale?" Eli asked, taking our seats at a middle set of desks. I thought about the question for a moment as I pulled out a notebook and a pencil. I looked at them sheepishly.

"Probably...teleportation?"

The first day of senior year came and went faster than Elijah failing his driving test. A chorus of squeaking sneakers and slapping flats rang throughout the concrete halls. The three of us met up in front of the school by the low iron fences. Lauren had a sour look on her face as Eli appeared laughing with some other peers and exchanged hand slaps and fist bumps.

"What teacher assigns homework on the first day?! Spawns of hell! That's who!" Lauren complained.

"Oof, lemme guess Mr. Kepler in AP Chem?"

"Yeah! How'd you guess?"

"I had him for Biology in sophomore year and the only other classes he teaches are Chem and AP Chem."

"Hey, what's up guys? Miss me since lunch?" Elijah approached us, adjusting his backpack on his shoulders. His arms flexed slightly and a whirlpool started in my stomach.

"Oh, how could we ever go on without you, Eli?" Lauren put her arm around Elijah's shoulders and acted overly-hysterical. As Lauren touched his shoulders and caressed his chest with her hand my cheeks filled with blood and I stared at the ground, laughing off the moment.

"So what are you nerds up to this weekend?" Elijah asked.

I shrugged at him.

"My parents are actually taking me and my brother to Disneyland this weekend. It's my little brother's thirteenth birthday and he has been dying to go." Lauren rolled her eyes, but I could tell she could hardly contain her own excitement.

"Aw, well bring me back some Mickey ears." Elijah grinned.

"And me a pin!" I gasped.

"Alright you two! We'll see!" Lauren laughed.

Eli shifted towards me. "Well, you're free this weekend right?"

"Yes, actually. What'd you have in mind? I need something to get me out of the house and away from my parents."

"Do you want to drive us to Morro Bay? One last beach trip before the summer heat goes away?" Elijah's tone was soft, like velvet, but strong as leather. I could never say no to him, especially with those eyes that overflowed with sincerity and genuine kindness.

"That sounds like an excellent idea. I'll have to convince my mom to let me borrow the car, but otherwise, let's do it!"

Elijah held his hand up for a high-five which I sheepishly reacted to.

"Great! Let's stay the whole weekend. I have my fake ID so we can get a motel or an Airbnb if we need to."

"Wait, really?" I asked, completely taken aback by Elijah's admitting to having a fake ID.

"Yes, really! Where are we supposed to sleep? The car? No thanks. I need maximum leg room."

"Alright, well you two have fun with that! I'll see you tomorrow for more thrilling classes." Lauren said, smacking her bottom lip and wearing a sly expression that told me she may know more than she let on.

2 STRETCH MARKS

The night before the beach trip I was frantically trying to figure out what to bring with me. I was a procrastinator by nature, so it didn't help that my mind was preoccupied by sudden intense feelings for Elijah. I mulled over the idea of telling Lauren, but she can't keep a secret to save her life, especially when she and Elijah get talking. No, it was best to play it safe until I was ready to express my emotions to Elijah.

Is that really something I wanted? Would that mean our friendship trio would change or is that simply a part of life? What if he rejected me? I wasn't as physically fit as he was. I had a round belly and my chest jiggled. Plus, I had stretch marks on my sides. What if I'm not his type? It would hurt like hell to be rejected by him and I'm pretty sure our friendship wouldn't survive the awkward days to come afterward.

I stood at the end of my bed with a small backpack in front of me and other items sprawled out on the sheets. I packed an extra set of clothes, a towel, two bottles of SPF 75, a notebook, and a pencil. I looked toward my side dresser for about a full two minutes before opening up the bottom drawer and lifted up some papers to reveal a pack of condoms. I snuck them into my backpack when they were giving out boxes for free in

Health Class last year. It was a pack of twenty four and I had twenty three left. One I used because I was curious to see what it felt like to wear one. It was strange at first, but it wasn't so bad. Do condoms expire?

My laptop was open on my desk and music from one of my favorite video games, "Life is Strange" was playing, but suddenly I was getting a video chat request. I looked at the screen. It was Elijah. I quickly fixed my hair and straightened up my room before finally answering the call.

"Hey Eli! What's up?" I said, casually.

"Vale, are you ready for tomorrow? Did your mom say it was okay for us to use her car?" Elijah's background was mostly dark with only white light from his computer screen illuminating him. I could make out his face and broad shoulders. He was shirtless and his tan skin was flawless. He had a little patch of dark hair on his chest that made me start to sweat. I swallowed silently.

"Yeah, she's fine with it. My parents have some errands to run tomorrow, but they're going to use my dad's car."

"What about staying the whole weekend? Are they okay with that?"

"That part was a little more tricky. I sort of...lied and said that you had a cousin that lived there who was letting us crash with them." Guilt was bubbling inside my stomach.

"Wow! Look at you! Little Vale is growing up real fast. Wait... what are you holding?"

I then realized I was standing in front of my camera still holding the box of condoms. I swiftly tossed it to the side and it hit my pillow out of the frame of the camera. "Nothing. Just some new cologne my mom got me."

"Oh, well that was sweet of her. All packed up for tomorrow?

I'll meet at your house at eight so we can get some breakfast on the way."

"Yep, I'm excited! Okay, sounds good. I'm definitely down for some pancakes and coffee."

Elijah's phone started blowing up.

"Who's that?" I chuckled.

"Ugh, remember that quarterback I hooked up with?" Elijah groaned.

"Yeah?"

"He's been constantly messaging me to make sure I don't accidentally out him, and now he's bugging me because he wants to hook up again. Guess the D is just too good." Elijah winked at me and I felt my heart jump in my chest. I laughed along with him. "Anyways, I'm just gonna block him." He sighed and lifted his arms, hands behind his head, revealing his hairy armpits. My heart picked up its pace and my stomach was doing cartwheels. I felt sweat start to collect on my forehead.

"Jeez, where'd you even find this guy, Elijah?" I asked, but I already knew his answer.

"On that app, Rainbow Tunnels. I've shown it to you, right?"

"Oh yeah, I think I remember." I couldn't wait to tell Elijah the truth. I hate hiding like this. I knew very well what the app was, but Elijah, thankfully, never ran into me there since I was anonymous and he was public with who he was. I could easily avoid him. In all honesty, I never even hooked up with anyone. I just like looking and was curious to see who was in the closet at our school. Surprisingly, a decent amount, but most were anonymous like me. Eli was one of three people at our school who were actually out, when, in reality, there were at least ten other queer kids there.

"I'm done with that app for a while though. Tired of the

toxic culture it pushes and I don't need other people's drama." Elijah looked just as ready for the beach trip as I was; perhaps me more than him.

"Do you think you might like someone romantically?" I asked, before I could think too much about my words.

"Huh? Actually, yes. I think I do, but I don't think it would work out. I'm pretty sure he's straight and I wouldn't want to make things awkward at school by making a move." Elijah blushed and rubbed his neck.

"Oh so he goes to our school?" I smirked.

"Shut up. What about you? Any crushes on your end, lady killer?" Elijah poked fun at me. I didn't like the idea of flat-out lying and saying the crush was a "she" and I couldn't say "he", because that would give me away.

"You'd be surprised when I say, yes I do. They go to our school as well, but I'm super nervous to even bring it up to them. I don't want things to change, but I can't help the way that I feel, ya know?" There was a pause on Elijah's end.

"I think I do know. Anyways, it's late. See you tomorrow. Get some sleep, mister." Elijah quickly diverted the conversation while stretching and yawning.

"Goodnight, Eli." I waved to him and he smirked back at me, his eyes lingering just a little bit longer than usual before the video call ended.

I could barely sleep that night, and eight in the morning could not come soon enough. I tried writing out my feelings through poetry, but the blank page had been a daunting sight for a while. I managed to get out something on the page and as I leaned back, stretching in my chair I read it back to myself.

"Will I? Won't I? Will the chill from the unknown freeze my nerves like a sealed meat locker? Will the strain of being seen

seize my muscles into cardiac arrest? Will I let the sun rise on these new possibilities? Or will I hang on the shadow of the moon continuing to shed my solitary, secret tears? If his eyes are the sun then my skin is like ice that needs thawing, a task that is oh so easy in his presence. Will I? Won't I? Will the dreams of hope, of truth, of love come alive? Or will the sinking tragedy of lost friendship fade away into the cold months to come? May the sands of time warm my footsteps. May the ocean waves crash against me and shake away the leftover sleet. I will proceed, prevail, persevere. I won't cower, crash, crumble. Will we? Won't we? Hug? Kiss? Whisper? The sun's light will reveal all."

It was about six-thirty when I decided to stop staring at my ceiling and take a shower. I couldn't stop thinking about Elijah and I was really riled up from that call with him so I "took care of myself" in the shower. At least I could be clear headed on the drive as to not do anything prematurely or something I would regret.

I was all packed up and sat on the staircase in front of the door waiting for Elijah to knock. He lived a few neighborhoods over so it only took him fifteen minutes to walk to my house. Before last weekend, Eli would have just come over last night and slept over. We would leave in the morning together and all would be fine. Thanks to my Dad's blatant bigotry and my Mom's idleness that can't happen anymore. Thankfully they couldn't tell us not to be friends. I would fight like hell for that, if I had to.

"You're staying with Eli's cousin Greg, right?" Mom appeared from behind me, passing me on the stairs.

"Yeah, he lives out in Morro Bay. We really want to enjoy the beach before senior year steals all our attention." I explained.

"Alright, well be safe please. Pay attention to the road and keep your cell on in case we need to get a hold of you." She ordered. "And be home before it gets dark tomorrow."

I nodded, happily. She kissed me on the cheek and gave me a tight hug. Her skin was cool against mine and her rosey perfume filled my senses, comforting me.

"Love you, Mom."

"Aww, I love you too, sweetie. Have fun, okay?" She breathed, earnestly and left toward the living room.

Just then, a figure stood in front of the foggy, glass door and knocked. I almost tripped on the stairs going for the door knob. I hesitated, glancing in a mirror hanging on the entryway wall. My white, Jurassic Park tee and dark blue board shorts tightened around my stomach and thighs. I fixed my short, blonde hair. "Good enough." I sighed.

I threw open the door to Elijah standing there with a back-pack, turquoise sunglasses, light blue boardshorts, and a pink tank top. My throat swelled and my heart thudded loudly in my chest.

"Hey!" He embraced me and we both squeezed tightly. Elijah gives the best hugs.

"Got everything?" I asked, lightly blushing.

"Sure do! You?"

"I believe so." We tossed our bags in the back seat of my mom's pearl white toyota solara after I locked the house up. We both got in and I started the engine.

"Sunscreen?" Elijah asked.

"Check."

"Snacks?"

I reached into the back seat and lifted up a bottle of soda and some potato chips. "Check."

"Condoms?" He smirked.

What?! Did he really see the box last night? Shit! What should I say?!

"I'm just kidding. You're gonna be a virgin forever." Elijah laughed and pushed my shoulder. I laughed along in relief, but also felt slightly offended. He was such a jerk, but a really cute jerk.

Before long we were halfway to the beach. We pulled into an iHop, stretching as we exited the car and sped walked into the lobby. We threw open the glass doors and were immediately greeted with the scent of freshly made pancakes and sweet, hot syrup. It swirled into an enticing redolence that made our stomachs rumble. A young bright-eyed girl, with a brown pony tail greeted us, grabbing two menus as she gestured for us to follow her. "Welcome in! Table or booth?"

"Booth." Elijah answered before I could open my mouth.
She led us to where we would be eating and handed us our menus. "Your server will be right with you." She said just before dashing back to the front.

"What are you thinking of getting?" Elijah asked.

"I'm simple. Just some pancakes, bacon, and scrambled eggs. Oh, and some coffee. I need coffee." I nodded, setting aside my menu.

"I think I'm gonna get a burger."

I must have given him a judgmental glance cause he leaned back and smiled handsomely, his cute canines glinting past his lips.

"What? I'm not much of a breakfast food person." Elijah shrugged.

Just then, a tall, dark, and stubble-patterned young man in a branded apron approached our booth. "Hey fella's, what can I getcha?"

We gave our orders, and the server shot Elijah some sweet smirks and smiles as they made small talk. I felt a turn in my stomach as my blood began to simmer. The server, whose name tag became blurry now, was barely giving me a passing glance. "Alright, I'll have that out to you in a bit."

"Thanks, Taylor." Elijah winked and Taylor smiled, shaking his head bashfully as he walked away. I didn't think watching Elijah flirt with another guy would bother me so much. It never used to, but it did now. Back then, I was so wrapped up in accepting that I was attracted to guys in the first place to notice my feelings for him. Now we're here, I'm gay, and I just want to kiss my best friend.

Our food came out quicker than expected. Then again, the restaurant wasn't that busy on a Saturday morning. If it was a Sunday that would be a different story. Either way, it was to our benefit. We shoved down our food in our eagerness to get back on the road. The check came along with Taylor and his classic good looks. Before I could reach the check, Elijah grabbed it, snapped a picture on his phone, and slapped some cash on the table.

"I got the bill. Are you ready to go?"

"Oh, yeah! Thanks, Eli. You didn't have to."

"Don't mention it." Elijah patted my back as we got up and walked back toward the lobby.

"Thank you for coming in!" The hostess waved and we waved back.

"Can you believe our server gave me his number?" Elijah said as soon as we got out to the parking lot.

"I can actually. The flirting was palpable. Are you going to message him?" I asked, fidgeting with my keys on the other side of the car out of Elijah's view.

CHAPTER 2

"I don't know. Maybe? I'm seeing where this one prospect is heading first."

"Oooh, the mystery person huh? Do I get to know who this crush is?" I prodded.

"Just get in and drive, nerd." Elijah shot back.

"Wow, rude!" I yelled. In a moment we were buckled in and back on the road. I handed him my phone to play some music over the car's Bluetooth. Energy pulsed through me, followed by an immediate need to belt out the song now playing over the speakers. Eli put on 'Into the Unknown' from Frozen 2. Maybe it was because I was gay or grew up a Disney kid or both, but we sang in unison to every song that played in that playlist. By time we reached Morro Bay we were crying from laughter at each other's goofiness and Elijah's inability to carry a tune. We were two peas in a pod, that much was clear.

As soon as we got to the beach parking lot we put on our sandals, grabbed our backpacks, and hit the sandy shores. The sun's glare beat down on my vulnerable skin which tightened under it's intense gaze. Salt and moist sand wafted through the air. I breathed in deep as my feet hit the course shore. We wasted no time laying out our beach towels and applying sunscreen. Ever since puberty hit I just gained weight so easily, but I didn't grow in height after I hit five foot six inches. I was embarrassed to take off my shirt. Elijah on the other hand was carefree and had his tank top off as soon as possible.

"What's wrong, Vale?" He asked.

"I think I'm gonna keep my shirt on. I burn pretty easily."

"Nonsense. That's why you brought two bottles of sunscreen, right? Why do you look so nervous?" Eli saw right through me.

"I just...I have stretch marks." I whispered. That was the truth.

"Pfft! Dude, most of us do. I have stretch marks too." Eli admitted.

"Yeah, but they look...fine on you." I crossed my arms in protest.

Elijah looked at me for a moment and pondered something over. At first, I thought he was mad at me, but he just stood there stroking his chin.

"Fine. Pants me."

"What?!" I laughed. Did I hear him correctly?

"I'm not wearing underwear. If you pants me while there are all these people around then no one will notice your stretch marks. They will just be laughing at me and my junk." Elijah said, confidently.

"And you're okay with everyone seeing...ALL..of you?"

"If it will help you. Plus, we may as well give them a show. Who knows when it will be warm enough again to come back here." He shrugged, passing by me. He faced the ocean with a superhero stance. "Go for it."

"No way, dude!" I giggled. "It's fine. I'll take my shirt off. Sheesh. Thanks for making me feel better." I quickly threw my shirt off and squirted some SPF 75 into my palm. Just as I was finishing applying, Elijah wore a menacing grin over his shoulder that could only mean trouble.

"You know me, Vale. Once I set my mind to something... " Suddenly, Elijah grabbed the side of his board shorts and shoved them down to his ankles. I noticed his butt cheeks were lighter than the rest of his body as he stood proudly in the warm, summer breeze. Some parents gasped and covered their children's eyes. Others giggled or murmured nearby as Elijah flashed the whole beach.

I swiftly ripped up his towel from the sand and wrapped

his waist with it. "Okay! Okay! I get it, Eli! Have some decency!" I yelped and kept my eyes away from everyone's gaze. Elijah must have thought it was hilarious since he was tearfully laughing loudly while he picked up his board shorts from underneath his towel. He hiked them back up around his hips as he locked eyes with me. At that moment, I'm not sure what came over me, but it only took a split second for our friendship to change. Maybe it was the way his skin glowed in the golden rays. Or maybe it was the way his dark stubble made his lips look increasingly more inviting. Or maybe it was the way his hand caressed my arm as if to check on me. All I knew was one moment I was in the car with my best friend coming to the beach for a final summer trip, and the next I was locking lips, half naked in the sand. The world swirled around us as the waves crashed furiously. Electricity shot through my whole body like a thunderous monsoon after a heatwave. I pulled back for a moment to look at Elijah's reaction only to see that his lips curled into a pearly white smile and his hand moved to my lower back, pulling me in for a deeper, longer kiss. I couldn't tell which heat was rolling through my skin. Was it his taste? His touch? Or the rippling rays of sunlight pouring over us in approval?

My stomach did flips and my heart pounded like a jack hammer. I touched Elijah's face and continued to kiss him as if I was drowning, his breath being my only hope of survival. My mind raced with a cyclone of thoughts. Had I always wanted this? Of course I did! I wasn't always honest about my attraction for Elijah until recently. I pushed it down, donning a facade of straightness. I denied my feelings, denied that part of me, but no longer. For the first time in my life I felt like I was right where I needed to be, in his arms. However, it only took a kiss and four little words to shift the very fabric of our lives forever.

"Look at those faggots!"

☄ I HEART SF ⊕

The words seemed to bounce off Elijah, but not me. I instantly yanked my face away from his and turned toward the ocean as if to hide from what I was just doing. It didn't feel wrong, but at that moment I felt caught, as if committing a crime. I quickly grabbed our towels and packs out of the sand.

"Oh, I'm sorry. I didn't know this beach was still in nineteen sixty-five. We'll gladly leave." Elijah shouted back.

I turned around and there were three guys from our school that just so happened to be at the beach as well. I recognized one of them as Brian, a tall, square-jawed, half-brained douche who bullied me and other kids throughout the years. It was the worst last year when him and his two lackeys shoved me and a few others from the GSA club into a broom closet then went on to tell people we were having an orgy. Out of all the places these three dunces could have shown up, of all the moments, it had to be here and now? The universe clearly hated me.

"Whatever." Brian scoffed. "Why don't you go to San Francisco? We don't want to see that shit here."

Elijah and Brian were standing three feet apart, glaring at each other, creating a hurricane of a power struggle. "Look. All I'm saying is that had we known that the Nazi party of America had rented out the beach today, my boyfriend and I wouldn't have intruded. So, my apologies." Elijah motioned his hands in a prayer shape, sarcastically and turned to walk away.

"Hey!" Brian yelled, grabbing Elijah's shoulder, turned him around, and gave him a right hook to his left cheek. Elijah did not fall, but something came over me. I instantly pushed off the ground toward the group of thugs, scooped up a handful of sand, and threw it into their view. Some of them were blinded, but Brian was able to block my distraction. Just as I pushed Elijah out of the way and turned to run with him in the opposite direction I felt someone grab my backpack. Everything was happening so fast I completely forgot I strapped my pack on. Before I knew it, I was flat in the sand, my face throbbing, and my head spinning.

My heart was racing and I was terrified. I wasn't sure what these guys were capable of doing to us. I just knew I had to get away, fast. My vision was blurry, but I could see other figures huddled around Elijah in the sand. They kicked and punched him. I heard him crying out in pain and no one was doing anything to stop it. Fury pulsed through my body, an inner heat that burned from head to toes. I stood up, ran, and leaped into the cluster of homophobes.

As soon as I landed on Elijah I heard a loud, thunderous crack. It was as if a bolt of lightning shot off right above us. I thought for sure I was crushing him underneath my weight, but the sensation of falling never ceased. It wasn't until I opened my eyes that another thunderous clap sounded and we landed roughly on a grassy knoll. I felt something close behind us that was like a powerful vacuum shutting off. Instantly, I smelled fresh cut grass and a passing cloud of marijuana smoke. Music blared from a nearby rattling music box. Cool wind gently caressed my skin which formed goosebumps.

I rolled off of E li. I gasped and realized I was holding my breath. I had the faintest taste of bubblegum on my tongue as I smacked my lips.

Huh, weird.

It took me a minute to regain my balance, but once my head cleared I looked up and was completely bewildered. Somehow, someway, we were in the middle of San Francisco. I recognized the rolling hills and quaint neighborhoods as Dolores Park. I noted a few glazed eyes staring in our direction, but nobody said anything. Over to my right Elijah's still shirtless and unconscious body was laying face down in the grass. I rushed over to him, flipped him over, and sat him up.

"Eli. Eli!" I shook him until he started to open his eyes. He had cuts and bruises on his torso and face. The most noticeable wound was a gash over his right eyebrow that was still bleeding.

"Huh? Vale. Where are those assholes?!" Elijah flexed his fists as he jerked upright. "W–where the hell are we?"

"San Francisco..." I stated.

"What?! But...how...we were just—"

"I don't know how, but the important thing is, we got away from those guys. Let's get cleaned up and get you a shirt then we can figure, whatever this is, out." I attempted to calm him down, but it proved difficult, as I was barely holding it together myself. Elijah just nodded and winced from pain as I helped him get to his feet and handed him his bag.

Oddly enough, we didn't get a lot of weird looks or curious glances as we walked the streets of The City. I supposed the residents of San Francisco see many strange things on a daily basis. We hardly made the cut of strange or weird in their eyes. I was relieved to find that my wallet was still in my board shorts pocket, but both our phones were gone. They must have fallen out onto the sand in the fight with those circle-jerk buddies.

We came across a small convenience store where I was able to buy Elijah a new t-shirt that said, "I heart SF" on it in big red print. I also tracked down some alcohol wipes and bandages for his cuts. Once we paid, I made sure to find a private place near a cute little bistro to clean his wounds, and talk.

"All I remember is you threw sand in their eyes, they hit you, and then bum-rushed me onto the ground. I heard a loud bang, almost like a gun going off." Elijah gasped in that moment. He quickly looked up and down my body. Then, he felt all over his own body. "Did someone get shot, Vale?" His eyes were wide, but he seemed glad that it wasn't us.

"No. No one had a gun, but I do remember that loud bang. I *think* it came from *me*." I was not even sure what I was implying nor did I know what it meant.

"Came...from you? What does that even mean, Vale?!"

"I don't know, okay? I just know one moment we were at the beach getting pummeled and the next I jumped on you..." I paused trying to make sense of what I was about to say.

"And?"

"Eli. This might sound insane, but I think I can teleport."

"Teleport?" He repeated and it sounded crazier coming out of his mouth. "So...What? You have powers? Since when?"

"I don't know, maybe?" I started to pace.

"And what was that kiss about anyway? I was pretty damn sure you were straight and then you go and kiss me? Are you secretly gay too?" Elijah sounded angry. Who could blame him? I had only been lying to him for years. Not about my ability, but about my feelings.

"Well, what about you?!" I reacted.

"What about me?"

"You told those guys back at the beach that I was your boyfriend. Is that true or was that just you cracking jokes?" Rage bubbled up from inside me now too.

"Vale—"

"And so what if I hid that I'm gay from you. Maybe it was because I didn't know if I was, or wanted to be, gay. Maybe I wasn't ready to accept that about myself, but I recently did and you know what?! I like you, Eli." Everything began pouring out of me like the bursting of an age old-dam, flooding a peaceful valley that lay below.

"Vale, I—"

"And you honestly believe I would keep something as big as me being able to..." I looked around in every direction to make sure no one was listening in. "...being able to teleport, from you?" I whispered sharply.

I walked a little way down the alley around the corner from the bistro. There was an empty plastic bottle on the ground and I kicked it with all my might. It bounced against the alley walls and slid out of sight around a corner. My breathing was heavy and my mind was spiraling into a panic. At this moment I didn't care anymore that Elijah knew that I was falling for him. I only wanted to figure out how to get us home.

"Vale, listen to me. I'm sorry that you felt like you couldn't tell me. I'm sorry that I never thought to just ask." Elijah sighed, having followed me into the alleyway.

There was a pause—the sounds of a busy city embracing us. The air smelled of salt, coffee, and sewage. I enjoyed an odd feeling of privacy. Even though we were among the hustle and bustle, it still felt like we were left alone. As if everyone were minding their own business. If only the rest of the world were like that. That would be a dream come true.

"I meant what I said back at the beach. I want you to be my boyfriend. At least, that's what I felt at that moment. Maybe not yet, but soon. It's just a lot all at once." His words filled me with warmth and reassurance. I wasn't losing my friend, far from it. Something else was emerging, and I don't just mean our love for each other. "For now, how about we find out what makes that ability of yours tick and get back to Morro Bay." He looked around and smirked. "I can't believe we are actually in SF."

I looked at him for a moment. Elijah had his hands in his pockets and waited patiently for me to answer. "Alright. We should probably start back at Dolores Park. That's where we arrived."

"Sounds good. Oh, and Vale..." Elijah pulled me back toward him. He grabbed my neck and planted his lips on mine. I was shocked at first, but quickly melted into his embrace. Our kiss ended and I leaned my forehead against his, placing my hand on top of his head and caressing his black locks. "Okay, now we can go." He said.

I smiled at him as we made our way back to the scene of our arrival, firmly grasping his hand in mine.

4 A DAY TO REMEMBER

I was busy people watching and admiring the city architecture around us when Elijah waved his hand in front of my face. "Hey! I have an idea. So, when we..."

"What?"

"Well I don't want to say the 'T' word!" He whispered, sharply.

"What do *you* suggest we call it then?" I asked, bewildered.

Elijah paced for a moment with his hand covering his chin. "How about flashing?"

"No..." I looked at him with one eyebrow raised.

"Oh! How about—"

"If you're thinking about that one film, then no. It was dumb anyway. Samuel L. Jackson was cool in it though." I interjected.

"He's cool in everything. Hm, okay Mr. Writer. Why don't *you* try a word then?" Elijah challenged me.

"Froggering?" I said, sheepishly.

"That's truly terrible, but figures you would pick something based on a video game. Typical Vale." Elijah jested.

"Alright, smart guy. Your turn."

Elijah looked around as if looking for a source of inspiration. He spotted a group of kids running across and jumping rope on a playground. Two kids, who held hands, skipped joyfully across the AstroTurf.

"I've got it. Skipping!" Elijah blurted out.

"Skipping? I suppose that makes sense, because we *skipped* over all that distance to get here." I pondered.

"Does that mean I can call you Skipper?" Elijah chuckled.

"No. Not at all." I shoved him and he winced.

"Ouch, easy. I'm still in pain from the fight."

"Still cute though." I said and even I was impressed with my sudden confidence. I managed to make Elijah blush on top of it. Despite the pummeling and the current outlandish predicament, I could tell that today was going to be a good day. A great day even. Certainly a day to go down in history.

"This should be a good spot." I led us to a more private part of the park and turned toward him. We were near the center of the park under the cover of lush palm trees. I held out my hands and Elijah took them both in his.

"So, how are you—"

"Shh!" I snapped, my eyes closed. "I'm trying to focus."

"Oh, my bad."

I took a deep breath and thought of Morro Bay.

Nothing happened.

I focused on the car.

Still nothing.

Frustration rushed over me and I threw my hands down.

"Dammit!"

"What is it?" Elijah asked, worry spread across his face.

"I don't know how to trigger it." I admitted.

"Well, let's think. When you triggered it the first time it was when those guys were attacking us."

"Right and my heart was racing and I remember just wanting to get you and me to safety."

"What if that's it?" Elijah proposed.

"What? Adrenaline? Panic?"

"No, I can see why that would make sense, but biologically speaking that's not feasible. What if it is linked to your emotions?" Elijah was a science wiz and it started to show. He is so adorable when he gets excited about a topic. I recalled the fourth grade science fair; while everyone else did their projects on volcanoes or plants or carbonated drinks, Elijah did his project on the concept of time, space, and gravity. The adults were dumbfounded, but his dad was immensely proud. "What if it's as simple as just wanting to be somewhere and then believing that you're there?"

"Like mind over matter?"

"Exactly!" Elijah's eyes were wide with giddiness and I couldn't help but humor him.

"Alright. I'll give it a shot. It's the best idea we have anyway. It's not exactly scientific though." I shrugged.

"A few moments ago we didn't even know Skipping was a possibility. Maybe allow traditional scientific methods to take a back seat right now. This is all new territory and we're probably the first people to experience it!" Elijah beamed and I couldn't help, but smile back at him.

Once again, I held out my hands and Elijah grasped them tightly. He rubbed them with his thumbs.

"You've got this." He whispered.

I focused on the beach again. I pictured it clearly in my head. I could hear the waves and smell the air. I was able to see the car in the parking lot a short distance away. I was able to feel the warm sun on my skin. My whole body was tingling and it felt as if I was actually there. My memory flashed back to my first kiss with Elijah and my whole body was instantly warmed.

Just then, there was a loud, thunderous crack like before. I could still feel Elijah holding onto me, but I was scared to open my eyes. I feared that I had failed and that the crack was all in my head. Static coiled up my arms and made my hair stand straight. A cold, metallic scent, I hadn't noticed before, crossed my nose and the taste of gum was present again.

"Vale! Look! You did it!" Elijah yelled and shook me. I finally opened my eyes to the site of rolling clouds and rippling waves.

"I did it?! I did it!" I yelled back and we jumped up and down wooping and hollering. We threw some sand in the air and Elijah tackled me. We rolled onto our backs looking up at the sky still laughing and breathing heavily.

That was insane. I'm able to control it. I thought.

I wanted to see where else I could go. I wanted to take Elijah on an adventure to places we've never been before, and experience everything together. It was all new, all exciting, and I was overwhelmed with the possibilities in front of us. We still had a full day ahead. We could do anything we wanted to and it felt like no one and nothing could stop us.

Elijah propped himself up on his elbow and was staring at me. He had his hand on my chest and I played with his fingers. We smiled back at each other and he leaned in, kissed me and laid his head down on my chest. I was in a daze now. I'm not sure how I would describe it, but the word, "overjoyed" comes to mind. Everything was going my way for once. I'm out to my best friend, who is becoming my boyfriend, and suddenly I have the power to Skip?! I was awestruck and my brain felt like a water balloon about to burst.

I felt something hit my stomach and I flinched. Elijah had gotten up and retrieved what was left of our things from the sand. He managed to find both our phones and tossed mine onto me.

"Oh wow, thanks." I said, surprised. I checked the time on my phone after wiping the sand off it. It was ten minutes past noon. We were only gone for about an hour. My stomach started to grumble and Elijah looked at me. Apparently it was loud enough for him to hear.

"Hungry?" He asked.

"Yeah, I think it's lunch time."

"Agreed. There's a great seafood place near the pier." He suggested.

"We just found out that I can tele- I mean 'Skip' and you wanna go to lunch on the pier?" I questioned. I stood up and dusted the sand off my body. That's when I had the greatest idea ever. "Grab my hands. I'll take us somewhere to eat."

"Aren't you tired? I figured you'd want to take a moment, before Skipping again."

It was nice that he was concerned for me, but I felt fine. I was ready to try it again. I wanted to see how far I could go.

"I'm fine. I promise. Grab on."

Elijah did as I said. "Where are we going anyway?"

"Somewhere I went with my parents one winter break. The place with the best Pizza in the world." I smiled as Elijah squeezed my hands and I closed my eyes.

I pictured busy streets, towering skyscrapers, dozens of passing voices and faces, and the smell of fresh-baked pizza. A familiar crack snapped above us as I grasped tightly onto Elijah and we were off and away once more.

5 FALLING

We appeared in the middle of a bustling crowd. Time Square was crawling with people just as I remembered it. I could smell fresh-baked bread and tomato sauce nearby. Elijah seemed dumbfounded so I grabbed him by the hand and led him across Broadway to, "Joe's Pizza", one of the most efficient and delicious pizzerias I have ever been to. We entered through two big, red doors which were propped open. Instantly, we were met with the sweet odor of yeast, tomato sauce, garlic, and many other condiments. Inside the crowd had hardly diminished. On either side of us were patio tables where customers ate their pizzas as they watched the crowds behind polished windows. I checked my phone and it was about three in the afternoon, but that hardly mattered. It was the weekend in the city that never sleeps in the most touristy spot imaginable. Red tables and bars were filled to the brim with people eating delicious slices and the line to order snaked out the door and around the corner.

"Yikes, look at that line! We're gonna be here all day!" I complained.

"What do you want to do?" Elijah shrugged, his eyes still dazzling.

I lifted myself onto my tiptoes to see over the crowd and

spotted the back area, beyond the registers. Hanging up on metal hooks were a hat, a shirt, and an apron all with the, "Joe's Pizza" logo embroidered on them. I thought about it for a moment. I could easily Skip over there, dress up as an employee, make our pizza, and leave. Of course I would pay for it, but I would have to be a convincing actor. I didn't want to waste our whole day here so it seemed like the best option. Even if it was dangerous and probably illegal.

"Wait here." I quickly told Elijah then exited the restaurant.

"Wait, Vale! What are you planning?" Elijah called back, but I was already out the door.

I made a sharp left turn down an alley and walked all the way to the back door. It was one of those doors that didn't have a knob or a handle of any kind, just a lock. I placed my hand on the warm metal and focused on the back area I had seen from inside. In a flash and a clap, I was in. I could hear all the workers calling out orders and the customers talking loudly in the dining area. I looked to be in an office area where there was a desk and a computer for employee's to punch in and out of their shifts. I spotted the clothes hanging on the hooks, yanked them off, and put them on in the employee bathroom before anyone noticed. I looked just like the other workers, except I had board shorts and sandals on. As long as no one looked down at my feet and I kept moving they wouldn't notice. I took a deep breath and stepped onto the floor behind the front counter. I kept my head down and moved swiftly to the pizza dough station. I grabbed a pizza that was already formed then moved onto the next area, being careful to avoid bumping into any of the other workers. I spread the tomato sauce, the cheese, added pepperoni, and mushrooms. Just as I was placing the pizza in the brick fire oven one of the workers approached me.

"Hey, you must be new. I don't recognize you. Where's your name tag?" A scruffy-faced, bald man with flour dust speckled across his apron asked me. I looked down at his name tag which said, "Jonnie" in black letters.

"Oh, uh, I wasn't given one yet, but I'm learning pretty fast." I answered with a nervous smile. He mulled over my words for a moment.

"Alright, finish up that pizza you're workin' on then we'll get you learnin' register." Jonnie bought it. I nodded at him and did as he said. I placed the pizza in the brick oven and moved over to where Jonnie was standing next to one of the registers. I made sure to write Elijah's name on a pizza box with a stray sharpie I found in the apron. I caught Elijah's eye while I was behind the counter and he looked shocked while working to hold back laughter. I nodded at him and then turned back toward Jonnie.

"I just, uh, need to use the restroom before we get started." I made up an excuse to get away.

"Okay, but hurry up. It's busier than a shoe sale on a Sunday." Jonnie remarked.

I nodded again and rushed to the restroom to change back into my regular clothes that I stashed behind the toilet. As soon as I was done, I concentrated on the alleyway behind "Joe's Pizza". Just like before, I disappeared and reappeared where I wanted to go. I was surprised that no one took notice of the sound of my Skip. Had they not heard it over all the commotion in the restaurant?

I rushed back around the corner to the front entrance where I knew Elijah would be waiting. I peeked inside through the glass and saw one of the workers handing the pizza I made to him. It was then that I realized I had forgotten to pay for the pizza. Before I could do anything, I saw Elijah pull some money out of his wallet and pay for the food.

I met him outside and we jogged down the street a ways until there was a gap in the crowd. "I've got to hand it to you, Vale, you've got some huevos doing what you did." Elijah commented, patting me on the back.

"I'm just sorry you had to pay for it. I meant to do that myself."

"Don't mention it. You got us here and you risked your ass making our pizza back there. Where do you want to eat this bad boy?"

"What do you mean?"

"Well, we can't just eat this supreme pie, this *King of Pizzas*, just out here on the streets. No, we have to go somewhere amazing." Elijah exaggerated his words to make it sound like a serious mission. I was into it and agreed. This meal had to be shared somewhere special, but where?

"Like...Niagara Falls?" I suggested.

"Perfect! We'll eat on one of the rocky ledges overlooking the falls."

"Only one problem. I've never been there before." I stated. I suspected that I could only travel to places that I had physically been too. At least, that's how it was in the movies. I was still figuring out this whole Skipping thing. Not to mention my mind was flooded with so many other raw emotions. I almost didn't want to go home later. Home is where my parents are and eventually I'd have to come out to them. That's something I wasn't looking forward to, especially considering the way they reacted to Elijah's coming out. It was all still fresh in my mind.

"What if you saw a recent video of the place? Could you get

us there then?" Elijah tried to come up with another solution, but it didn't seem likely.

"Maybe?"

"Here." Elijah took out his phone and typed something into it. He turned it around to reveal a crisp video of Niagara Falls during the day time. He turned the sound up as loud as it would go. "Okay, now focus on the moving picture. Just listen to the water rushing. Does that help?" He instructed. I attempted to focus and listen to the waterfalls, but nothing seemed to be happening.

I wracked my brain. There had to be a way other than physically being there before. I continued to look at the video, but this time I closed my eyes after a moment. I visualized it in my mind, listening to the water. I smelled moisture fill the air and heard the birds singing above. I saw the tour boats in the basin below. I felt the cool mist on my face. A tingling sensation surged up my spine.

"Hold onto me, Eli." I gasped.

"Oh!" said Elijah, and I felt him grasp my forearm. Instantly, the thunder cracked above us. We were soaring, falling through space until I opened my eyes. I landed with an, "Oof—". Suddenly I realized that Elijah was no longer holding onto me. The sound of water crashed around me. My eyes fell on the landscape in front of me. Everything the sunlight touched glittered and glistened as if the surfaces were made of trillions of tiny crystals. The cliffs stretched out wide on either side of me and the great falls roared with immeasurable strength, flowing into the rocky pool beneath my feet.

"Eli! We made it!" I screamed out in excitement.

"Vale!" He yelled, but his voice seemed far away. I glanced toward the edge of the cliff. There was the pizza box. As I peered over the edge Elijah hung onto the ledge with all his strength. Below him, jagged rocks and a cloud of mist waited hungrily to engulf him.

"Oh shit, Elijah!" I jolted toward him, grabbing his hand and with all my strength, pulled him up onto the ledge with me. He lost his balance, pushing me over, and toppling onto me. We both let out loud grunts as we hit the damp rocky surface. Elijah rolled over onto his back. Both of us breathed heavily. He started to giggle and laugh toward the sky. I looked at him in disbelief, but his laughter was too contagious to resist. Elijah continued until we both were crying and holding our stomachs in gleeful celebration.

"I think we've earned that pizza now." I struggled to say through my remaining chuckles.

"You can say that again."

Both of us finally were able to settle down and sat up together. As we looked out over the falls we let out a collective, "Wow.". Elijah was the first to grab a slice of hot, cheesy goodness and as he took a bite I scanned all of him. The way he chewed on mostly the left side of his mouth, the little hums of approval with each tasty bite, his defined, muscular arms holding his thick legs to his plump chest, the tuft of dark hair peeking out from his armpits, all of him sent my heart into full-on gymnastics. That's when I fully realized what had changed, and what was happening in real time. I was completely and unreservedly falling in love with my best friend. I was allowing myself to dream about being with him, and what our lives would look like. I never thought I would be Elijah's type, but he proved me wrong. Now we are on this incredible, impossible, journey together. Just like the Falls, my love for Elijah was continuously flowing and our time together now felt endless.

🪐 EQUATOR

After finishing our pizza, and belching together at the top of the Falls, we wiped off our hands and mouths with napkins that Elijah, thoughtfully, remembered to grab. Several fluffy white clouds floated overhead and provided us with dappled shade. Rays of light rippled along the edges of the lone nimbus' drifting by. Elijah had his feet hanging off the edge of the cliff and I was leaning back, just taking it all in.

"Ya know, you're kind of like Peter Pan." Elijah said, staring out toward the horizon.

"What?"

"Yeah, and I'm like your Wendy! You are whisking me away through magical means. This isn't Neverland, but...close enough."

"But Wendy is a girl. Plus, I'm not sure green tights would be flattering on these thick thighs." I joked as I slapped my thighs with both my hands.

"Then call me...Wendell! Oh, and trust me, green tights would definitely look hot on you." Elijah winked. My cheeks felt warm as I looked away, hiding my face.

"I still can't believe you almost died. I'm so sorry about that, Eli. I'm still getting used to this ability." A surge of guilt hit my heart.

"What fun is an adventure if there isn't life-threatening danger involved. Plus, you were able to pull me up, weren't you? So we're all good." Elijah winked again, reassuring me of our purpose of being here in the first place. He was so amazing. How quick he was to forgive and look past my faults. It only confirmed my decision to be his boyfriend. Elijah's raven hair wafted in the wind and I could smell his shampoo in the breeze. I smiled at him and he smiled back, his eyes shimmering like pools of gold in the daylight.

"What?" He asked, bashfully.

"Nothing. You're just so handsome."

"Alright lover boy, so are you. Now where do you want to go next?" Elijah stood up and reached down to me. I grabbed his hand and he pulled me to my feet.

"Elijah, I don't know if I want to go anywhere else but home, if I'm being honest." I hesitated.

"What do you mean? I thought we were having fun?" Elijah frowned with concern stretching across his face.

"We were, but isn't this all...I don't know...just a little insane? Like where did this ability even come from?! Why do I, Vale Dagwood, have it? Also, you almost died, Eli!" My thoughts overcame me. My emotions flipped from the laughs we shared seconds ago to a sour, nagging fear. The thought curled around my brain like barbed wire slowly tightening.

"Listen, Vale..." Elijah held my neck and rubbed it with his thumb. The fog on my mind was so thick I hadn't even noticed him step closer. "I don't have any of the answers you want, but I'm fine. I'm still in one piece. We just have to be more careful. I promise you will find the answers you are searching for. I want to know just as much as you do, and I'll be right next to you the entire time, until then and onward."

I steadied my mind, breathing in and out slowly a few times. Elijah kissed my forehead. That was the first moment I felt scared about Skipping. I suppose after the initial adrenaline wore off and we had a moment to reflect it all came crashing down like a stack of books. "Alright...I trust you." I sighed. "Let's figure this thing out together, but no more high places."

"Fair enough. That would have been a crazy drop!" Elijah said, peering back over the edge of the cliffs. "So then, where to next?"

"Hmmm...New Zealand?" I suggested.

"Why there?"

"Why not? Haven't been there. Pull up a picture of the capital city and let's give this another try." I said as I gathered up our belongings and handed Elijah his bag.

"Alright, but this time try not to send me hurling off a cliff." He jabbed.

"I said I was sorry!"

"I'm joking, dork! Now here. Take a look and focus."

Elijah pushed his phone toward me, having pulled up a photo of Wellington, the capital city of New Zealand. The skyline shined with short towers of varying colors, rolling green hills lined the horizon, pleasant beaches lead to a reflective harbor, and colorful trams carried commuters to their destinations. I shut my eyes and thought of city noises, crashing ocean waves, howling winds, the name of the capital, and the low groan of a fog horn. Elijah must have taken that as his cue to take hold of me as I felt his hand clasp my shoulder. A tingle crept up my spine and thunder rolled. Now the taste of mint was strong on my tongue. Intense cold, like a blizzard, clung to my exposed skin and ignored any layers I wore. Before I could stop, we had arrived.

Seven inches deep in snow, we sank in wearing only summer clothing. The cyclone howled and snowflakes pelted us from everywhere. It was pitch black, but I heard Elijah yelp next to me.

"Holy crap! I-I-It's f-freezing!"

"What the heck happened?! I thought I was taking us to New Zealand!" I was confused. I dropped us into a blizzard in the middle of, what I thought was, a tropical city.

"Of course! It's w-w-winter right now!" Elijah explained.

"W-what?!"   I shivered and hugged myself with arms crossed.

"Just get us out of here!"

"Where?!"

"I don't care! Anywhere warm!"

I shut my eyes and I felt Elijah wrap his arms around me. I focused as hard as I could while my body shivered violently. I let my mind flood with memories of warm beaches and the sun hitting my face, palm trees waving gently until I could feel it and my skin began to thaw. I opened my eyes to find we were standing on a beach I recognized as the lush island of Honolulu. I once came here with my whole family for a reunion. I was much younger then, but I still vividly remember the time I spent here.

"Are we in Hawaii?" Elijah asked while wiping melting snow off himself.

"Yeah, I came here once when I was a kid. What did you mean it was winter there now?" I asked, noticing I also had snow clinging to me. The warm sand surrounded my feet and I let myself sink a little bit to thaw my poor toes.

"Well Vale, if you paid attention in Geography you would know that because New Zealand is below the equator they have a different season cycles. Currently, we are in summer here in the States. So, over there…" Elijah explained it again to me, but this time more thoroughly. He paused waiting for me to finish his sentence.

"Over there it's the opposite?"

"Ding-Ding-Ding! We have a winner!" He snarked.

"Tch, well wise-ass, you were the one that handed me the video so I'd say it's both our faults." I pointed at him and he rolled his eyes.

"Yeah, yeah. Are we gonna go see the shops in town or what?" Elijah warmed his feet in the sand too, before putting his sandals back on.

"Sure. Let's go."

At that moment, when Elijah turned away to walk off the beach, I got the strangest feeling that we were being watched. This part of the beach wasn't too populated, and everyone seemed busy with their own lives, but I still couldn't shake the feeling. Glancing around, I couldn't see any obviously suspicious figures. Mostly pale white, nuclear families with fake tans or sunburns.

"Hey, you okay?" Elijah asked.

"Huh? Yes, I'm fine, but I was thinking, with all this Skipping, do you think the car is okay back in California?" I questioned, worried about my mom's car being messed with while we were hundreds or even thousands of miles away.

"I'm sure it's fine. Let's just focus on having fun, okay?" Elijah put his arm around me and squeezed gently. I leaned my head into him and wrapped my arm around his waist as we headed into town. He gave me a swift peck on the head. At that moment, I thought this day couldn't get any better.

7 ANOTHER

City streets were clogged with busy locals and tourists, like us. Well, maybe not exactly like us.

I could feel my skin tightening from the sun's rays, so I stopped to apply a layer or two of sunscreen. I turn as red as a lobster otherwise, and I didn't recall applying any before. Oh that's right, because we were interrupted by Brian and his lackeys. Then, all *this* happened. That all felt like it was days ago. Even my face stopped throbbing from the beating and Elijah's wounds already looked better.

I had Elijah apply some sunscreen on my back, and I relaxed at the feeling of his touch. He gave my shoulders a little squeeze when he was done and I turned to face him, giving him a peck on the lips. I put my shirt back on and looked around at our buzzing surroundings. I wasn't sure if it was just my imagination or the excitement rushing through my veins, but the air smelled sweeter here.

"What shop do you want to visit first?" I asked, seeing all the tourist traps that dared to lure us and our wallets inward. I pointed to a surf shop that didn't only supply surfboards, but also jewelry, shirts, and other knick-knacks. Elijah shrugged and I took that as the sign to lead the way. As we meandered through the surf shop I spotted a rack of bracelets. One that caught my eye was made with dark brown leather. It was wide, and carved on it were a mixture of Hawaiian swirls and Celtic knots. I found it strange that something like that would be in a shop in Hawaii, but that's what made it stand out. I looked at the tag and it was forty dollars too much. I frowned, shrugged, and walked away.

As I headed back to Elijah, I noticed someone else move over to the same rack I just shopped. I gave them a glance. It was a short girl, with black hair and a pink stripe going down the side of her bangs. She definitely stood out from the crowd. She wore a gray jean jacket covered in decorative patches with black skinny jeans and sneakers. She also had a plethora of rings on her fingers and I thought I could see the edge of a tattoo from just below her left sleeve. The girl grabbed the bracelet I looked at only a moment ago. She glanced around, as if to see if someone was watching. That's when she spotted me looking over at her. Her eyes got big, but then she smiled and waved at me.

There was a feeling in the air, almost like an increasing pressure. Just then, there was a crack like the sound of someone snapping a whip, and she was gone. My heart nearly jumped out of my chest. I couldn't believe it. *Did she just Skip?! I'm not the only one? I have to find her and get some answers. Who is she?* I thought, my mind being thrown into a hurricane of questions.

Quickly looking around for Elijah, I spotted him looking at some decorative mugs. "Eli!" I grabbed his arm and he smiled at first, but it dropped from his face once he saw how frantic I was.

"What, Vale? What's wrong?"

"I...saw...someone." My mind was so scattered that I stum–

bled over my words. I pulled Elijah out of the shop with me and looked in every direction for the girl, but she was nowhere to be seen.

"Um, okay? Was this person trying to harm you?" He asked, concerned and grasping for my attention.

"Uuuugh! No! I saw someone...like me." I grunted, annoyed and confused.

"What?! Are you ser—"

I shushed Elijah as I heard someone whistling in our direction. Not a tune, but as if to get our attention. I peered down a small alleyway I had missed before as there was a food cart blocking my field of view. All the way at the end of the alley I could see the same small girl wave at me, but this time she had the same bracelet in her hand.

"Hold onto me, Eli."

"Why?"

"Just do it!" Just as Elijah grabbed my shirt, I focused on the end of the alley way and we Skipped to the same spot where I saw the girl vanish. I released Elijah and ran further down the path.

"Vale! Wait!" He called out as he chased behind me, but I dared not slow down or stop. She could've been my one chance to figure out what I am and why I have this ability. I couldn't stop, not even for Elijah.

I took some old stone stairs downward and rounded some corners all the while following the pestering whistle of that other Skipper. *Ugh, no. Still hate that name.* It was as if she was leading me deeper and deeper into an unknown part of this tropical island; a labyrinthine trap made of ancient stone, metal, and wood set for someone like myself, or perhaps a trap specifically meant for me alone. I only prayed Elijah wouldn't get caught in it with me. He needed to stay safe. I needed to keep him safe.

The mysterious girl entered what looked to be an abandoned factory. The walls were made of brick and the doors made of thick, heavy steel—like I were about to enter onto a cargo ship set out to sea. Rust and moss covered the edges of the doors and windows. Elijah caught up to me, out of breath.

"What's your deal, Vale? Who are we chasing?"

"I saw a girl and she Skipped right in front of my eyes. She just went into that building. She knows I'm coming. She led me here." I panted, my eyes sharply focused on the steel door hanging ajar, inviting me forward across its threshold.

"Whoa, whoa, whoa! Hold up. You see a random girl who can also Skip, so you Skip after her yourself, not to mention putting us at risk of being seen. Now we are just gonna follow this random girl into a creepy abandoned building? No thanks!" Elijah stood in front of me, sweat glistening off his face and arms.

"I have to get answers, Eli. She is the only one I've seen who is like me; What are the odds that within a few hours of discovering this ability, I run into someone else who shares the same ability?" I tried to move Elijah with my words, but he would not budge.

"That's exactly why we should *not* go in there! It seems super suspicious that all of this is happening so fast, don't you think?" Elijah warned. He was right. I was being too hasty. I needed to rethink where I was and what I was doing. I must have shown disappointment on my face, because he spoke up again. "Look, I get that you want answers, but let's just be prepared before we go in there." Elijah yanked his backpack off and set it on the ground. He unzipped it and dove both hands in. I could hear some rattling and metal clicks as if he were assembling something. "I wasn't planning on bringing this out or even thinking of using it, but you can never be too prepared." Elijah pulled out a handgun and then pulled back the metal sleeve to load a round into the chamber.

"Holy shit, Eli! Why do you have that? You couldn't have known all this was going to happen. We were just going to the beach!" I stepped back, my eyes wide with adrenaline. What the fuck was Elijah thinking bringing that? We've been to the beach before and nothing even remotely bad happened to us. Why would he feel the need to bring it this time? Or has he always brought a gun with him?

"I was never planning on using it! I just said that! It's just so...I feel safe. My dad got it for me and taught me how to properly use it and clean it. So don't worry I won't accidentally blow anyone's head off." He joked.

"Not funny, but I guess I'm glad we have some sort of protection. We're in over our heads here. Why would your dad get you a gun? That just seems very unlike him." I felt myself calming down a little as we talked it through. All the while I could still hear the hollow wind howling through the doorway into an unknown bunker.

"It was. I was surprised too, but after what happened I guess he wanted me to be more prepared." Elijah explained as he pulled a gun holster out of his bag and strapped it onto his waist. "This holster was my idea. If I'm going to carry a gun I might as well do it in style. And yes, before you ask, I have a license to carry a firearm. Dad had to finesse a friend to make that happen since I'm not over eighteen yet."

"Wait...after what happened?" I was not aware of anything happening to Elijah that would warrant his father buying him a firearm.

"Huh? Oh it's nothing. All in the past. The important thing is I've got your back if something goes wrong, or if this is a trap." He holstered his weapon, shouldered his backpack, and headed toward the steel door. I wanted to press further, but I felt it best not to right now. Whatever it was I was certain he would tell me on his own when the moment was right. I needed to focus on the task at hand. Whoever or whatever awaited us on the other side of that doorway was doing so knowingly. Whether a treacherous trap or a pleasant greeting, I welcomed it curiously and willingly. At least now I have a bodyguard. Not too sure I was okay with it being Elijah, but it was his choice to make and I respected him for that.

🪐 THE PULL

The steel door was cold to the touch and rough from all the years of rust. The opening was big enough for both of us to slide through. Before going completely in, I looked back at Elijah and put my finger up to my lips. He nodded at me as he patted his gun still sitting in his holster. I heard a tiny click as he switched off the safety. There were no other lights illuminating the room except for the daylight pouring through the dusty windows and the cracked doorway. A thin layer of water covered the ground beneath our sandals. The strong stench of something that molded or rotted filled the room.

The door slammed behind us and we glimpsed figures up in the rafters spray painting the windows black so no light could peek in.

We were trapped.

The way was shut.

I felt Elijah's back press against mine. I was about to yell out to whoever our captors were when a mechanism turned on above us. Spot lights sprang to life one by one, bringing a blinding resonance to the room. I could no longer make out shapes since, in every direction, glaring light stunted our vision.

"Who are you? What is this?" I broke the silence.

"You are trespassing. We will be the ones asking questions, Boy." A raspy, male voice responded.

"Um, well we followed a girl here. We don't want any trouble." I stated.

"You followed a young girl down a dark alleyway, and your friend there is packing. Yeah, neither of those things help your case, bro." That time it was a younger-sounding male voice.

"Look, it wasn't like that, okay? As for the gun it is just for—"

Before I could finish my sentence the room burst into laughter.

"Alright kids! I think we've had our fun. Time to rescue this poor boy." The same raspy, gruff male voice rang out. That's when the spotlights shut off and fluorescent overhead lights were activated with a metal creak in the distance. We could finally make out figures in detail. Standing around us in the rafters were a group of seven young faces, three girls and four boys. They were all different ethnicities, backgrounds, and walks of life. Standing up on a staircase landing was a much older man. He wore a tarnished, dusty gray trench coat with a black bandana covering the bottom half of his face. His hands were covered with pristine white gloves. From the small amount of skin I could spot there were blue veins bulging out and there was calluses forming around his scalp where gray, slicked-back hair sat. His most noticeable feature was his steampunk-ish goggles fastened to his face. He gave off the vibe of a mad scientist and a business man wrapped in one.

"Who are all of you?" I asked again.

They climbed or jumped down from the rafters. The older man limped down the steps clutching onto the railing and a chromatic cane he had concealed under his coat. They lined up in front of us; our backs toward the door. I was able to see the rest of the room then. There wasn't much around us. but it looked as inhospitable as it smelled. Why would they stay in a place like this? It couldn't be comfortable.

"You can call us the Travelers, but it looks like you're one too." One of the other girls spoke. She had tan skin, black braided hair, wore light colored, wispy clothes, and had a multitude of rings in her hair and bangles on her wrists. Her accent was Hindi and her eyes were kind. She seemed out of place considering our surroundings.

"Like a group of nomads?" Elijah asked, his voice a little shaky.

"Something like that, but first tell us about yourselves." The older man ordered. The tension in the room was thick and palpable.

"I don't like this, Vale. Let's get out of here." Elijah whispered to me, but it was clear they heard every word.

"My name is Vale and this is Elijah. We are just visiting from California."

"Oh? And how did you get here?" The Man inquired.

"I—"

"That was a rhetorical question, bud." A taller, lanky guy spoke up. He had dark skin and his accent reminded me of someone from New York. He wore loose, comfortable clothing as if he were getting ready to go for a run. Then, a high pitch, like a tiny spinning firework being lit, reverberated off the walls as he disappeared into thin air and reappeared behind us. Elijah gasped as the sound startled him, but I grabbed his wrist to put him at ease. His shoulders relaxed and he glared at the face smiling back at us. "We know what you can do."

"So it's true then. I'm not the only one who can Skip."

"Skip? That's what you call it?" Another boy of Latino descent chuckled.

"I like it. It's cute. Almost...whimsical." The girl I chased from the marketplace stepped forward. She snickered at me and then gave us both a wink. "I'm Liv." Her English accent was thick and suddenly her style made sense. It reminded me of Punk meets Post-Grunge. Each person introduced themselves then.

"I'm Ember." The girl with the wispy clothes said and waved.

"I'm Eliza. I'm just your average Aussie." She was the second in the line. Her red hair flowed over her shoulders topped with a blue baseball cap, a Hawaiian shirt loosely buttoned, and tan cargo shorts. I nodded and looked over to the third.

"I'm Kaito. Pleased to meet you, Vale." Kaito bowed at me and Elijah. We both stood there awkwardly not knowing if we should bow back. Kaito was dressed far less casually than the rest of the group. He had on a pressed, white button-up shirt, black slacks cinched up with a black belt, and polished black business shoes. His coal shaded hair was shaped professionally with a single blonde strip hanging down and curling onto his forehead.

"My name is Felix. Welcome, brother." Felix stepped forward and stuck his hand out. I went to shake it, but he grabbed my forearm. I was confused at first, but I realized what he was doing. I grabbed his forearm in return and exchanged one solid shake. Felix wore a green tank top with similar baggy shorts as the other guy who Skipped behind us. His accent sounded...Irish or Scottish? I couldn't pin it down in the moment.

"Hola, amigos. Soy Esteban." Esteban waved at us while scrolling on his smart phone. Esteban was dressed in plain blue jeans with a graphic t-shirt that had the logo, "A24" in bold lettering on the front.

"I'm Lucien, but everyone just calls me Lu." The smug face behind us finally introduced himself. He then Skipped back over to his friends.

"And I am Morrick. The fearless leader of this little band of Skippers. Did I use that term correctly?" Morrick looked back at his troupe and then back at me.

"Um, it's great to meet all of you. Sorry, this is all a bit overwhelming. I just discovered my ability today." I admitted.

"No kidding! Your Rip is loud—we could hear you a mile away." Lu chastised.

"My...*Rip?*"

"I think they are referring to how we got here, Vale. When you Skip you must create some sort of tear in space. In other words, 'A Rip'." Elijah added his two cents to the conversation. I can't believe I forgot how quick he was on the uptake of information. I smiled back at him and in that moment wanted to kiss him.

"Bingo! He's got it. That's a smart friend you have there, Vale." Morrick complimented. "Does Mr. Elijah share in our ability?"

Everyone turned their gaze to Elijah who turned as red as a ripe tomato. "Uh, no no. I'm just a boring, everyday, high school teenager."

The room erupted into laughter.

"Nothing boring about you, my boy! With a mind as sharp as that! Come. You both are invited to visit my manor." Morrick announced and then vanished without even the faintest whisper. One by one each of the Travelers started to Skip into thin air. A cacophony filled the dilapidated warehouse, causing it to shake and shutter dust from the ceiling.

A zipper.

Popping bubble wrap.

Tiny fireworks.

A whistle.

Sizzling bacon.

Rolling Thunder.

All unique sounds to each Skipper.

"Wait! Where is it?!" I yelled back.

"Just focus on Morrick's Rip. It's very powerful. Focus and you'll know what I mean." Liv said, gave us a two finger salute, and vanished followed by the noise of a rubber band snapping. *Focus on his Rip?*

"The hell is that supposed to mean?"

Only the quiet sound of distant seagulls, ocean waves, and faint dripping kept us company.

"Maybe it's like a form of energy that only people like you can sense. What does it feel like when you're about to Skip?" Elijah brainstormed.

"It feels like a doorway or a giant zipper is opening up, and then it just sucks me in. I can always feel a slight pull when I start to focus, and then there is a tingle down my spine."

"Great! That's it then. Focus on that feeling. Close your eyes and go towards the Rip with the strongest pull." Elijah spoke, enthusiastically.

"How do you know all this?" I looked at him, quizzically.

"Intuition. I like piecing information together. Mainly why I want to be a scientist of some kind. I'm just not sure what field I want to study yet." Elijah shrugged.

"Huh, I never knew that about you. I mean, I knew you were interested in science, but I didn't realize how far your ambitions went."

"You never asked."

Ouch. I guess that's true. I've been too wrapped in my own feelings these past few years that I barely noticed the interests of my friends. I was having a crisis of my own still figuring myself out. I rubbed the back of my head out of habit. Tension and discomfort found their home in my chest, making me think I was a bad friend. Just then, he kissed me and laughed. "Hey, it's okay. Get out of your head, will ya?"

"Yeah, sorry." I tittered, awkwardly. "Let's go see where this Morrick guy lives."

I closed my eyes and wrapped my mind around the room. I instantly sensed tugs in every direction, but one in particular nearly dragged me off my feet. I jolted forward, but caught myself.

"Whoa! Vale, you okay?" Elijah touched my shoulder.

"I'm fine. It's just...really strong. Unlike mine or any of the others. Hold onto me, Eli."

I focused again and isolated Morricks' Rip in my mind. I tried not to resist the pull, but the force was too great for me to control. We were thrust onward as if caught in an angry, torrential undertow that pulled us into its depths.

☄ LANGDORF MANOR

As quickly as we left Hawaii, we arrived in the foyer of a grand mansion. There were two red staircases with white marble banisters on either side of the foyer, that led up to a mezzanine and merged into one set and then split again. One side led to the west wing of the house and the other to the east wing. In the center of the top landing was a strange, eerie painting. A lone fountain stood tall and spilled pure, blue water, but the garden around it was dead. The sky was black and the moon was full and blood red. It matched the dark red of the staircase rugs. Around us were pillars and archways made of the same white marble, and the door looked to be made of redwood. Above us hung an enormous, ornate chandelier that was fitted with hanging crystals that glinted and dazzled in the electric light. The floors shared similar white marble as the pillars and banisters. More red rugs accented the floors in various places, leading to each section of the house.

"Whoa...This is..." I said, astonished.

"So cool!" Elijah started taking pictures with his phone, smiling wide. His eyes glinting with excitement.

"You'd never think, with the way Morrick looks, he would live in a place like this."

"I mean, anything is possible. Are you really that surprised?"

Elijah shrugged.

"Eli's got the right idea. You should listen to him more." Liv emerged from one of the archways on the left. "Welcome to Langdorf Manor. Follow me, I'll give you the grand tour."

Liv started showing us the first fl oor. Our first stop was the study, hung with many portraits of past owners of the mansion. Each bore the surname of Langdorf. There were many tall bookshelves filled with every kind of book, new and old. Arranged neatly in a square were brown leather couches facing a large, ornate fireplace with a head piece in the shape of a raven. At the far end of the study was a redwood desk, scattered with papers and books that were heavily tabbed. Behind the desk was a stained-glass window that stretched almost to the ceiling. It depicted a woman sitting near a clear pond with her feet in the water, while several children played and splashed about. The whole room was a writer's dream. It made me wish I had my laptop with me so I could just sit by the fire, reading and writing for hours.

"That's enough of this room. Come this way." Liv gestured and we followed her across the foyer again to the east side of the manor where the dining hall and kitchens were.

The dining hall was quaint compared to how tall and long the study was. There was a decorative rug stretching the length of a polished redwood table. The chairs were also made of the same wood and had pure white cushions that felt like sitting on a cloud when I tried one out. Above the table was a half size version of the chandelier we saw near the entrance. The table was set for ten people, but I only counted eight from Morrick's group.

"There are two extra settings on the table. Are there two more people we haven't met?" I asked aloud. Liv giggled at my question.

"Nope, you counted right. There are eight of us and two of you. Morrick was hoping you both would stay for dinner. That is to say, you are welcome to stay for dinner if it pleases you. His words, not mine. I'm not that polite." Liv stuck her tongue out at us as she backed toward another door.

She beckoned us toward the kitchen where the scents of spices and sugar wafted through the air. Elijah turned back toward the dining room for a moment to snap a picture, and I took the room in full frame. Set in the celtic-knotted brasswork of the chandelier were small candelabras holding lit black wax candles, which made the whole room feel old and Gothic.

"Gorgeous." Elijah whispered to himself. He looked down at his phone to check the picture. He caught my eyes, "What?"

"Nothing. Just admiring you." I whispered. Elijah blushed even more and put his phone away. I liked that feeling. Elijah was usually the confident one that caught *me* off guard, but I was a quick study.

"Come on, guys. Let's not lag behind. We have a lot more to see." Liv stood next to the kitchen door and put her hand against it. "Now, just to warn you, what you see next may seem strange, but trust me when I say that it's really cool." She swung the swinging door open and we stepped in. The first thing I noticed was that there were no chefs nor kitchen staff. Food was being prepared by objects that should naturally be inanimate.

"Holy..."

"...Shit!" Elijah finished my sentiment.

The kitchen utensils and stations were moving on their own and preparing everything according to an open recipe book on a stand in the corner. We looked at Liv. I guess she could read our expressions, because she pointed to the ceiling. Written and glowing on the ceiling were strange carvings and markings that I'd never seen. They radiated a sickly yellow color.

"What the hell is that?!" I shrieked.

"Morrick says it's part of his studies. He calls it, 'Spatial Runick Manipulation', I think." Liv explained, sounding disinterested.

"Whoa. This is insane. It's like magic!" Elijah shouted and was about to take a picture, but suddenly there was a swift cracking sound like a whip being snapped. Liv appeared behind Elijah and snagged his phone. "Hey! What the hell?!" Elijah turned and grabbed at her. She jumped back and put her hand out.

"Chill out, Normy. Morrick doesn't like people taking pictures of his work. He says it's still very secret until he publishes or whatever. Here's your phone. Taking pics of the house is fine, just nothing Morrick deems 'private'." Liv sheepishly handed Elijah's phone back and he snatched it aggressively.

"Could have told us that before you committed an S&S." Elijah inspected his phone for damage.

"An S&S?" Liv raised her eyebrow and crossed her arms.

"What? A Skip and Snatch. Kind of like Breaking and Entering. I figure Skippers should have terms t oo." Elijah shrugged and placed his phone in his pocket.

I patted him on the back. "He enjoys naming things." I looked to Liv.

She looked at both of us and uncrossed her arms. "Charming. Anyway, on with the tour!" Liv spoke half-enthusiastically. I lightly shoved Elijah as we left the kitchen and gave him a sharp look.

"Ah, what was that for?"

"Chill out Mr. S&S." I reprimanded him.

"She called me 'Normy'. That hurt." Elijah put his hand to his chest and smirked coyly.

"Oh I'm sure! Since when are you all sensitive?" I whispered to him.

"Hey Vale, I have feelings."

I gave him another light shove and he grinned guiltily. I waited for Liv to be around the corner when I pulled Elijah aside and kissed him on the lips. "I'm not sure what divine intervention caused all this to happen, but I am just glad I'm here with you." I spoke softly.

Elijah smiled back at me, brushed back my hair, and sighed. "Me too. You should know, I always liked you, Vale. I know I talk about my sexual endeavors a lot, but the truth is that I never had a connection with any of them." He admitted while having his hands on my hips and my hands linked behind his head.

"So you had zero suspicion that I was gay?" I asked.

"Almost none. There were moments, but I was too nervous to test it out. I liked our friendship and instead of doing anything to risk that I just left it alone, but now..."

"Now everything has changed." I finished and we both scoffed at the enormous understatement.

"Hey love birds! You two coming?" Liv called from the foyer.

We lowered our arms and chuckled. "What do you think? Should we stay for dinner?" I nodded at the table.

"Well, let's finish the tour and play it by ear, okay?" Elijah suggested and gave me a quick peck on the nose. My heart fluttered as I grasped his left hand. We met back up with Liv who waited with arms crossed while checking her dark blue nail polish for chips.

Liv spotted us, looking down at our linking hands, and there was a tiny twinkle in her eyes. "Right. Onward!" She dramatically gestured to the right set of stairs and up onto the second floor. She took us first to the east wing of the house showing us the rooms of Eliza, Lucien, Kaito, and herself. The others in their group didn't have rooms with Morrick, and Elijah took notice as we stopped in the hallway talking to Eliza. She had changed into ripped jeans with a black shirt that had a Radiohead logo on the front. Her room was covered in things like animal furs, teeth, horns, and other memorabilia from Australia as well as many band posters, a record player, and a large shelf full of records and CD's.

"Dang! You must really like music." I commented as both Elijah and I sifted through her collection.

"Oh yeah, I used to collect them when I was just a girl, but when a fire took everything I had to start over and this is the result of several years in the making. Liv's always borrowing my music." Eliza said, cheerfully.

"Well you have great taste, 'Liza." Liv said, picking earwax out of her ear. "That's the only compliment you get for the rest of the month."

"Love you too, Liv."

"Any special editions?" Elijah asked.

"Oh yeah, I have plenty, but only for the really good albums." Eliza winked. She continued sharing her trinkets and the tales behind them. Her life seemed so fascinating. Then again, all eight of them seemed that way.

"So why only four rooms? What about Ember, Felix, and Esteban?" Elijah asked, finally getting a word in edgewise from Eliza's excited storytelling about her multiple, terrifying encounters with Kangaroos and other wildlife in Australia.

"Oh, well Morrick asked them, but they declined. They seem to be happy with their own arrangements." Liv interjected.

"But there aren't enough rooms anyway, right?" I rubbed the back of my head and Liv looked at me like I was an adorable toddler asking why the sky was blue.

"Things aren't always what they seem. You'd be smart to remember that going forward." Her silver eyes glimmered at me and she clapped her hands together making her rings clink. "Anyway, I haven't shown you the best part of the house! C'mon!"

Liv waved her arm and Eliza followed her back the way we came. Lu also emerged from his room, nodded at us and Skipped away. Kaito's room was at the end to the left and was the only one still closed. At the very end was a redwood, ornate door that I could only guess was Morrick's room. As curious as I was, Liv and the others would start to wonder where we were if we wandered off. Elijah pulled at my shirt and I followed him back around the corner, toward the west wing.

We reached the next hallway and poked our heads into the left door first. Inside was a wide and tall gym fitted with all the bells and whistles of workout equipment, plus a full court that could be adjusted for a number of sports.. Felix and Lu were playing a game of one-on-one basketball when suddenly Felix Skipped and reappeared in front of the basket ten feet off the ground and slam dunked the ball.

"Aye! That's literally traveling! You're playin' dirty, bro." Lu complained. Felix seemed to find Lu's annoyed behavior hilarious, as he stopped and waved at Elijah and me watching from the doorway.

"Vale! Check this out!" Elijah was already across the

hallway looking in another doorway. This room was absolutely staggering to behold. It was a rec room with billiards and a Foosball table, but it also had a three-lane bowling alley on the right side of the room. In the back of the room was a computer lounge with every gaming console imaginable, and high end computers with a sound booth in the corner for recording. A door next to it had a sign that read, "Video Recording Room". On the left side of the room was a snack bar with all my favorite chips and candy, a popcorn machine, soda machine, and a DJ booth next to that. All over the ceiling and walls were soundproofing panels and LED lights to give the room a multicolored, electric feel. Lastly, hanging from the ceiling near the DJ booth was a projector that pointed at a pull-down screen.

Elijah was already way ahead of me and joined Ember and Esteban in a game of pool. Esteban offered him some popcorn as Ember gave him a pool cue. Eliza and Liv had already started a round of bowling and Kaito was in the DJ booth playing some 90's trance music. I was so busy watching everyone else that I didn't notice Kaito leave the booth and come up to my left side. He waved at my coyly and I waved back. He wore all black sweats now with a hat stitched with the "Bose" logo.

"You like what you see so far?" Kaito asked in a thick Japanese accent. I nodded and glanced back at the others.

"So far? You mean there's more to see?" I jerked my head back to Kaito.

"Just one more place, but in my opinion it's the best part of the house." Kaito started walking out of the rec room. Instinctively, I follow. Opening a glass door at the end of the hall, he announces, "Welcome to Langdorf Manor's greenhouse." Leading me inside, the room opens up into a canopy of lush green leaves and vines. My sense of smell is overpowered by a flood of lavender, roses, peonies, lily-of-the-valley, and many other flora I can't recognize. Even the scents of citrus and fruit fill my nostrils. An array of every color and practically every type of edible or harmless plants covered every inch of the planters. It filled the bulbous greenhouse all the way up to the metal catwalks. Kaito guided me through the two levels of the well-kept greenhouse and explained different species of flora to me. It felt like we spent hours there, and I certainly could.

"I would love to just sit here and write. This place is so inspiring." I glowed.

"You're a writer?" Kaito asked.

"Sort of. I like writing, but only journals and poems so far. Of course I left my laptop at home."

"Well, you can come back anytime you want. I'm sure Morrick would love to have you." Kaito offered and patted my shoulder. There was a moment of silence and Kaito started again. "He found me too. In Japan, I mean. I just got fired from my job at a big software company for leaking confidential, but damning, information about a few dozen CEO's. They never took legal action, but worse. Much worse. They tried to have me killed." I listened to Kaito tell me his story, as my heart filling with empathy. I turned toward him. "The world doesn't take kindly to whistle blowers," He Continued. "I was bloody and beaten when I managed to escape my captors' clutches. It was raining and I managed to lose them by running down a small alleyway. They must have circled back, because they almost found me again. That's when it happened." Kaito Paused.

"You Skipped." I guessed, and he nodded.

"I was transported to my childhood home, but no one lives there now. Even so, I still felt safe. I hid out there for a few days.

That's when Morrick found me and brought me here. That was over a year ago." Kaito finished and we found a bench to rest on. The only sounds that filled the room were trickling water and the buzzing of insects somewhere among the vegetation.

"When I first Skipped today it took me and Elijah to Dolores Park in San Francisco. We were attacked by some homophobic idiots from my school, who happened to be at the same beach as us. It was supposed to be a peaceful end to our summer get-away, but...well, here we are." I shared.

"San Francisco must be where you feel most safe and where you can truly be yourself." Kaito responded, gazing up at the dimming sky through the glass ceiling.

"So Morrick is like an adopter? Fathers people like us? Does he know where this power comes from and why it suddenly activates?" I had a lot of questions and after Kaito opened up to me I felt this was the perfect time to get some answers.

"He's more like a mentor but yes, I suppose you could think of him like a father figure to us. Although some of the others still have their families, some of us are orphaned or barely adults. Morrick believes that this ability is sentient in some way, meaning it isn't genetic but that it finds you and infuses with you."

"Like a divine gift from God?" I asked.

"Maybe, but he believes science and alchemy can explain it. You've seen the carvings around the manor I assume? Those are some of the things he is experimenting with. He's an incredible genius that no one seems to know about. Not yet, anyway." Kaito finished and Liv appeared around the corner.

"Oh there you are! Kaito, time for dinner. Vale, as I mentioned before, you and Elijah are welcome to join us."

Kaito gestured to her and she disappeared back around the

corner with a sly grin.

"Thanks for showing me this. It's truly amazing." I said.

"Of course. I was the last new person. It is nice to finally show someone newer this place." Kaito smiled, twiddling his thumbs, and looked down at his lap.

"I guess we should join the others." I slapped my legs and stood up, turning to leave the greenhouse.

"If I might be so bold, what you and Elijah have looks very special. I wish I had the courage you both do." Kaito stated, plainly from his seat.

"Oh, um...listen. I appreciate that, but this is all still new for us. We only kissed and found out I had this power today! So, I mean, thanks? But I'm hardly a role model." I chuckled. Kaito stood, bowed, and gave me an understanding nod. He lifted his hand pointing me toward the exit. As we took our leave, I heard a small, sad sigh come from Kaito. In that moment, I wondered what other scars he was hiding and how deep they must go.

10 ALCHEMY

I made my way back toward the foyer and down the large staircase. I spotted Elijah waiting for me at the bottom, his eyebrows furrowed as he looked at his phone. I sensed a pulse of urgency from his stance.

"Everything okay?" I asked.

"I think so. It's just that I have no signal here. There's no way of knowing where we really are." Elijah slid his phone back into his pocket and glanced toward the front entrance.

"There's nothing but forest out there, for miles." Elijah said, a slight tremble in his tone.

Ember appeared suddenly, wearing a different outfit than before. Her clothes were more elegant and traced with gold and silver. She wore different bangles, and a necklace set with a glittering ruby that laid flat on her chest. "Morrick told me that this mansion is somewhere in the Maryland Black Hills, and something about it being full of energy." Ember explained with a wave of her hand. It was a relief to know that we were still in the United States, but to Skip from Hawaii to here? I still felt stunned at this ability. "I see Liv already gave you the grand tour. So, what's the verdict? How are you liking our enchanting safe haven?"

"Oh, uh...Ember, right? I think it's breathtaking. I don't even know what to say. There's just so much I'm still processing." I admitted. I took a deep breath, attempting to temper my anxiety and excitement.

"I completely understand. When I first came here, it was a lot for me to accept. What I was...the existence of magic...although, Morrick insists on it being science, we have yet to understand. He often uses the word "Alchemy", but I still don't completely understand how it works, and if I'm being honest, it kind of freaks me out." Ember leaned against the banister, playing with her bangles as she breathed her words in a blasé tone.

"Yeah, it's...wait, do you smell that?" Elijah sniffed the air, grabbed my wrist, and pulled me to the dining room. The table was filled with courses of soups, salads, meats, and beverages of all kinds. It was like Thanksgiving, Independence Day, and Christmas all wrapped into one grand feast. We all sat down and before we could serve ourselves anything, Morrick walked into the room. He wore less baggy clothes now. Instead, he sported a modern suit with fresh white gloves emblazoned with a golden "ML" on the back. His slicked back gray hair had a shine to it and he wore a simple white, masquerade mask. I could tell he was European and the parts of his face I could make out were wrinkled and littered with age spots. His eyes were a milky white, but his awareness was sharp. *Was he blind?* I wondered.

"Thank you all for joining me for this special occasion. Tonight we welcome a new Child of the Seam to our family." Morrick stood next to his chair at the end of the table and began his speech. "And to your friend as well, thank you for coming along. I understand we are complete strangers, and all of this must be a bit grandiose, but as you can clearly see now we mean you no harm. Vale, is it?" Morrick nodded his head in my direction.

"Yes sir." I answered and straightened up in my chair.

"Tell us, how old are you?" Morrick asked.

"We're both seventeen. Thank you for having us, sir. I have so many questions to ask you and—" I trailed off and Morrick smiled, putting his hand up.

"All in due time, lad. Let us enjoy our meal first, and then we can discuss whatever you wish in my study. I too have some questions that need answering." Morrick sat in his chair. He snapped a finger and something on the table lit up dimly. Just then, a bottle of wine lifted from the table, uncorked itself, and poured some of its contents into Morrick's glass. Underneath the glass water jugs glowed another yellow symbol. An invisible force lifted the jugs up and tilted them, pouring water into our glasses. "What do you and your guest wish to drink, Vale?" Morrick asked sincerely.

"Umm, rootbeer?" I stated. Morrick wiggled his fingers and snapped again. The bottom of our glasses glowed as well, and instantly our water turned dark brown and began fizzing. Elijah and I looked at each other and then at our glasses again. "Go ahead. Try it." The room was silent. Everyone eagerly stared at us, save for Lu and Eliza who looked impatient.

I shrugged at Elijah who was still dumbfounded and shook his head at me. I grabbed my glass and took a big, daring gulp. The flavor was sweeter and richer than any root beer I had before. The carbonation burned the back of my throat and made me tear up.

"That's incredible! How...?" I asked. None of this should be possible at all and sitting next to me was a man who not only could Skip, but could use some other sort of power as well. Does this mean magic is real like Ember said?

"Alchemy, lad. We'll talk later. Eat and be merry!" Morrick announced, and the others spared no time filling their plates.

I leaned over to Elijah and whispered. "Isn't this amazing? Could you ever imagine anything this fantastic would happen to us, Eli?"

"I don't know, Vale. This doesn't seem right. I just have a bad feeling. Can we go home soon?" Elijah grasped my wrist tightly and looked at me with a gaze that made my heart hurt. He looked terrified.

"Okay. Let me talk to Morrick first, and then we can go. Will you be alright until then?" I asked, and he nodded. I glanced down at his hip and remembered that he still had his gun on him. If anything, I knew he could handle himself. I only hoped it wouldn't come to that.

We both ate and chatted, getting to know the Travelers a bit more. Their stories were similar, they all came about their abilities through a moment of extreme stress or bodily harm coupled with the need to escape. No one went into much detail, but I saw a sadness in each of their eyes when they recalled their pasts, as well as a joy when they spoke of the new family they found here at Langdorf Manor. By the time it got to be Morrick's turn, I'd all but forgotten what the others had shared. He stole my attention and my short term memory failed me. Morrick spoke of a war he was in and how he was nearly blown to pieces on the battlefield. He Skipped, back then, to his home where he felt safe. He never specified which war he was in, but I didn't think it polite to press further.

As quickly as the dinner began, it ended. Morrick waved his hands and snapped both his fingers. In a moment, all the dishes were lifting off the table and floating through the swinging door, into the kitchen where I imagine other alchemical tools began cleaning. Morrick stood up.

"Once again, thank you all for coming. This was a delightful evening. I will see our guests off after we have spoken privately. Vale, I will meet you in my study. It is the red door at the end of the right corridor on the second floor. I shall leave the door unlocked." Morrick then vanished within his Rip and a gust of otherworldly wind swayed the chandelier.

"The dude sure does love an exit." Lu muttered out loud. He stood up from his chair and walked over to Elijah and I. "C'mon, my room is on the way to Morrick's. I can make sure you make it." I got up from the table and Elijah was about to follow when Lu put out his arm, blocking him. "Uh, you probably should wait here for Vale. Morrick likes to talk to the newbies alone. You understand, right bro?"

Elijah glared at Lu, who kept his eyes on him with a blank stare.

"Sure thing, '*Bro*'." Elijah mocked, settling back into his seat. The others already left by foot or Skipped away. As Lucien led me up the stairs I looked back at Elijah and smiled. My gaze was matched with worry stretched across his face. I sighed and continued on my way to speak with Morrick. I yearned for answers that, only several hours ago, I was completely unaware I needed.

11 SPACE AND TIME

"**K**eep going. The door should be open." Lu said as he strode into his room.

"Uh, Lu?"

"What's up, little man?" He asked, just as he was about to shut his door.

"I was curious how you came to find Morrick, specifically I mean?"

"Hm. You got it mixed up; it's the other way around. Besides, that's a story for another time. Go on. He's a very busy man." Lu shut his door and locked it from the other side. I was left in silence. This was the first time since I arrived at the manor that I could not hear voices or any other sounds but those of the house settling. The smell reminded me of a well cared-for museum, some parts old and some parts new. The bright, crimson door was rightfully the centerpiece of the hallway with the fixtures and hinges being made of a dark, polished black metal. I took a deep breath and strode to the door, turning the gold knob, and let myself in with one, brave motion.

I made sure to close the door behind me, turning on my heel, and taking in the gorgeous master bedroom. It was complete with a king style royal bed frame with a clear canopy, an adjacent study similar, but smaller than, the library downstairs.

The master bathroom shined with white porcelain and black marble. Lastly, there were elevator doors to the far left of the room, and to the right was a window with red curtains fitted with gold drawstrings. The curtains were drawn back and tied to metal support poles, revealing a clear view overlooking the whole greenhouse from above. Beyond that, to the right, I could make out part of the back acres of the house. There, in the fading twilight, stood a generously sized hedge maze.

Morrick isn't here so perhaps I should have a look around, I thought. The study is what drew me in. I began scanning each shelf, tracing my fingers along the old, yet pristine, spines. Morrick had an amazing collection. From Dante's *Inferno* to *The Odyssey*, from the works of H.P. Lovecraft to the *Necronomicon*. He had writings that were considered dangerous or taboo in the publishing world. Some of the more common literature I read previously, because of school assignments or from my own curiosity. Other books I only heard of, but they weren't listed in any library annex since they were either banned or too rare to find.

What Morrick said in the dining room stuck with me. He was able to make items float, and could change ordinary water into root beer through Alchemy. I spotted a book on that topic. The ware and tear of the book revealed its old age and constant use. *The Fundamentals of Alchemy* by Nicholas Flamel was the title, etched in gold letters on the front of a blue cover. *Where have I heard that name before?* I tried to recall. I began flipping through it when the elevator doors opened.

A tiny bell beckoned me as the metal shutters slid away from one another. I closed the book and quickly stashed it in my bag. I'd only borrow it for a week or so. He'd barely notice. Looking around first to see if someone else had entered the room, I found that I was still alone. I cautiously moved toward the elevator uncertain of where this fancy metal box would take me. I didn't remember seeing any elevator access on any other part of the manor. Where did it lead?

I released a breath I wasn't fully aware that I was holding in, and walked onto the lift. It was a simple, chrome lift with only one button above a key slot on the outside, and two buttons on the inside. As I stepped in I could see there were LED lights on the ceiling. The elevator looked newer than the rest of the house. My stomach knotted as the doors closed and I descended into the bowels of the mansion. The low hum of electricity and gears guiding me down was almost comforting. The elevator halted with a soft bump and the doors opened to a pitch-black room. I didn't move for a few seconds. It was silent and cold, metallic air caressed my skin.

"Hello?" I projected.

My voice reverberated off what sounded like metal walls. I kept my torso back while cautiously stepping out with my right leg in front in case I needed to jump back into the elevator. Just as I stepped off out, more LED lights flickered with a bright luminescence. They lit up a short, chrome corridor, similar to the paneling in the elevator. I was alone. Still, I felt as though I was being watched.

I moved toward the end of the hall where there was a massive circular door. It looked like a vault entrance inside of a bank. Next to that was an electronic screen that read, "Tap to Begin". Curiosity lead my quivering finger to tap the screen, and the words vanished.

"Retinal Scan Required." A robotic, feminine voice said, and the camera below the screen activated. I could see my face displayed on the device.

"Uuuhh…" I stammered.

Morrick's voice crackled over the intercom. "Vale, don't worry about that thing. I can let you in from my side. Sorry about the theatrics, but I figured guiding you in would be much easier, so I could get started on some work."

Metal gears thunked and clacked as the vault-like door slid open, rolling left into the wall. Behind the door was an enormous room. The walls were not chrome, but pure earth, rock, and stone. Raw gems were scattered across the walls and ceiling. The floor was covered in thick, metal panels save for the center of the room that had a few steps leading up to a circular, glass contraption. To the left of the contraption were supercomputers, generators, and a command center complete with all the blinking buttons a curious kid could ask for. Clicking away on the keyboard in the center console was Morrick. He changed out of his nice suit and mask back into his loose clothes that covered most of his body and head.

I took in the sights and wandered over to one of the computer screens. Displayed on the screen were foreign symbols and mathematical formulas. They were all interconnected to form a large circle with several smaller circles surrounding the center. I raised my hand to touch the LCD screen when Morrick appeared to my right, startling me.

"If you please, don't touch anything. These are very delicate calculations." He said and reached past me to check the screen for himself. I moved away from the console and stood in front of the large glass chamber.

"What is all this?" I asked.

"This…is my laboratory, dear boy. This is where I not only study the alchemical and natural sciences, but that of our shared ability." Morrick answered matter-of-factly while facing me.

"It's incredible. What about the big glass room?" I pointed up the stairs to the center of the subterranean chamber.

"Ah yes, that *is* something truly special. You see, I've been studying our ability to, Skip, as you would call it. The spatial energy we are able to manipulate is unprecedented in anything science has ever witnessed; well, short of a black hole forming." Morrick's movements and tone sounded like that of a college professor. "I assume you've learned about the life phases of a star by now in school, yes?" He waited. I nodded. "Very good. This 'Gravity Well' as I like to call it, or GW for short, has an astounding pull."

I listened intently to what Morrick was saying, but stuck my hand up in a shy motion. "That's the 'Rip' you were talking about earlier? We can Skip through space-time, right?"

"Time. Yes! Time! Exactly. You are *almost* correct, Vale. We can go through Space with relative ease, but Time is another matter. As powerful as my GW has grown I still can't go forward or back even a minute. So, this glass chamber is for multiple Travelers to stand inside of and, if I can figure out the right set of formulas, together we might open a portal through time." Morrick finished his thoughts and waited patiently for me to respond.

"What does this mean for me?" I asked, feeling a thousand times more overwhelmed than I did prior to following Liv down that alleyway.

"Of course. My apologies, young one." Morrick spoke softly and took a step closer. "You have questions about your own ability. I just get so caught up in sharing my pride and joy with new Travelers I often forget how you must be feeling."

"That's fine, sir, but yes. How did this happen to me? *Why* did it happen? Don't get me wrong, I am grateful for it, but I'd be lying if I said I'm not scared." My throat was dry and suddenly I felt a deep exhaustion begin to set in.

"You, no doubt, listened to the others' stories of how they came about their abilities? Do you see a similarity with how you discovered yours?" Morrick asked, but I could tell he already knew the answer.

"A moment of desperation to escape..." I breathed.

"Precisely. How? I believe certain people have an energy locked inside them that only manifests when they are pushed to their limit. As for the criteria of that energy, I am uncertain. By all accounts, it is random. All of you, myself included, live in vastly different walks of life and have differing personalities." Morrick touched his forehead in speculation.

"But why?" I asked, almost lost in his words.

"Curious that you ask that. Are you religious?"

"I-um...well, I suppose I'm Christian. My heart wants to say this was a gift from God, that I was meant to accept it, and use it for good, but my mind..." I paused.

"Go on." Morrick gestured, calmly.

"My mind wants to take this power and just run away. I don't know. Before all this I was just accepting myself for other reasons, and I was afraid to bring it up to my parents. Now, *god*, I'm so overwhelmed and tired." I leaned back against one of the consoles and slid down to sit. I held my face in my hands and rubbed my temples. I felt a hand rest on my shoulder. Morrick crouched down, supporting himself with his cane in one hand and comforting me with the other. Mysterious as this man was, he appeared earnest and thoughtful.

"Vale. Listen to me. Shame must only come from doing harm. You have not done any harm. You are discovering who you are, as many others have before you. When courage enables you to reveal the truth to those you love, it may hurt them. So often the truth does. In those moments remember, you have a community here with me and the Travelers. You are never alone. As long as you know that, try not to fret too much about the *why*." Morrick's voice was softer than his normal rasp.

I sighed and picked myself back up off the ground. "Thanks Morrick. That means a lot. I'll try."

"Anytime, dear boy. As for the exhaustion you are undoubtedly feeling, try ingesting electrolytes. In my studies involving this ability I find that it can...heavily wear down the body and dehydrate us." Morrick turned away from me, touching his face. There was a thick silence, before I broke it.

"Oh, that makes sense, but I have to get going. Elijah and I need to get back to California. Thank you for dinner, by the way. It was delicious!" I said and started back toward the elevator.

"One more thing, Vale. That boy you brought with you, I don't normally allow outsiders, that is to say 'non-Skippers', in my manor. It is obvious you both care for each other. In the future though, I would only ask that you come alone if that is no trouble?" Morrick stared at me and his tone was serious. It almost sounded like a demand the way he said it.

"Uh, sure. I'll talk to him about it. I'm sure he'll understand."

"Excellent. Safe travels." I could see Morrick's face form a smile underneath his bandana just as the elevator doors dinged and closed. I sighed again as the lift took me back to Morrick's room. My mind was a little more at ease, but I had a lot to mull over and sleep definitely sounded nice right about now. Making my way down the hall again, I patted my pockets and checked my bag for all my belongings. Everything was still there, albeit sprinkled with sand and water, but safe.

"There he is! Ready to head back?" Elijah was sitting at the bottom of the stairs, patiently waiting for me. I couldn't help but smile back at him.

I nodded and sighed.

"Everything alright, Vale? Did you get the answers you needed?" He asked.

"Sort of. Nothing as concrete as I hoped, but I'm trying to make sense of it all." I expressed honestly and Elijah grabbed my shoulders.

"Hey, life hardly ever makes sense. Don't strain your brain too hard trying to solve a universe of problems. Sometimes you just gotta take it as it comes at you." Elijah smirked and kissed me on the forehead.

Just then, Liv appeared from thin air on the steps behind us, making Elijah and me both jump at the sound of her Rip. "Sheesh, skittish are we?" She teased.

"I'm never going to get used to that." Elijah complained.

"What's up, Liv?" I caught my breath, smiling at how easily-frightened we were.

"I almost forgot to give you this. You chased me only to get 'trapped' so I figured you deserve a prize. Not to mention, I may have seen you gawking at it back in Hawaii." Liv pulled out her other hand from behind her back. She held up the leather bracelet that caught my eye back in the Hawaiian surf shop. It had the Celtic knots mixed with tribal markings I admired. The more I looked at it the more I felt it symbolized how I felt in that moment. There was a connection to something ancient.

"Here." Liv grabbed my left wrist and strapped the bracelet on. "There. Suits you fetchingly. Anyways, are you heading out?"

"Oh, yeah. We gotta get back." I peeled my gaze from the bracelet long enough to answer her. "And thanks." I smiled at Liv and lifted my wrist, that now bore a bracelet, to eye level.

"Alright, see you again soon, Vale? Eli." Liv posed the question more to me, but gave Elijah a quick wink.

"We have school, but as soon as I can find time I'll come see you all again." I shrugged, glancing at Elijah nervously, as I could feel his disapproving glare. Liv nodded, gave a two finger salute, and vanished.

I turned to Elijah and held my hand out. "Ready?"

"Yep." He said shortly, grabbing my hand. I hesitated for a moment looking at him. "What?" He scoffed.

"Sorry." I muttered and closed my eyes to focus. My Rip opened, in an instant the thunder clapped, and we were gone.

12 BARE BEARS

We were met with the sound of crashing waves and lonely seagulls drifting through the iridescent glow of early dusk. We were back where we began. Part of me felt a little relieved, but that might just be the exhaustion. I nearly stumbled when we exited my Rip, but Elijah caught me.

"Whoa! You alright?"

"Y-yeah. Just really tired. Morrick said that Skipping saps our energy and dehydrates us so we should go buy a sports drink or something. I don't want to turn into a raisin." I laughed, but laughter was not returned. "Are you okay?" I could tell by his annoyed expression and his plain tone that he had something on his mind.

"I don't think you should go back, Vale." He sighed.

"What? Why? Didn't you have a good time? You saw how kind they were to us." I debated. "And that amazing alchemy! It's like nothing I've ever seen before."

"Yes, that's all great, but it all seemed *too* perfect. They seemed too prepared for your arrival." Elijah pushed back.

"But they are the only ones like me, Eli. What am I supposed to do? Not talk to them ever again? I can't do that. You should know how important it is to find your own kin." I retorted.

"No. That's not what I mean." He said, sheepishly rubbing his neck. "I just don't trust that place. At least, not enough for you to go alone and with all of them. Maybe I should go with you, I just—"

"You can't." I interrupted. "Morrick doesn't normally welcome 'outsiders', his words, into his manor. Tonight was a one-time thing." I hated admitting that to Elijah, but it was only fair that I told him. It would make things worse if I kept it from him and I can't start keeping secrets again. Not anymore.

"You see what I mean?! That doesn't strike you as sketchy?"

"I get it, Eli. Really I do." I allowed silence to wash over us like the distant waves washing over the rocks and sand.

I glanced around and saw a kid playing on his own. He looked a little sad, but then another young girl approached him and handed him a perfect looking sand dollar. The boy instantly lit up and whooped with excitement.

"How about this? I won't go back to Langdorf Manor unless they seek me out first. For now let's focus on school, our families, and us." I hesitated on the last word and blushed when I said it. *Us.* That felt thrilling to say out loud.

"Fine." Elijah sighed and smirked. "That's fair, but Vale I'm telling you, please be careful. Not all of them are who they say they are." The sternness in his voice was something I hadn't felt before. This was something new and it only made me feel safer with him. Safer, and turned on? Jesus...who am I kidding? I've wanted to tear his clothes off ever since we first kissed this morning, but we've been a little preoccupied since then. I can't believe it hasn't even been a full day yet. I felt a headache settling in and I rubbed my temples before returning my attention to Elijah.

"Hey" I grabbed Elijah's wrist and pulled him to me. "When

am I ever *not* careful?" I looked into his eyes, set ablaze by the last rays of daylight. My gaze moved down his face, caressing his soft, supple lips and lining the frame of his dark stubbled jaw and upper lip. Elijah didn't respond, but returned my gaze, placed his hand on my left cheek, and pulled me in for a passionate kiss. I breathed him in as our lips pressed together. We stood there for what felt like an hour, but must have only been a minute, just holding each other and moving our mouths in sync. Everyone and everything else faded away into the background. We were the only two people in the world and my spirit soared. I wrapped my arms around him, never wanting this feeling to end, and our hearts intertwined and danced in rhythm.

Elijah pulled away and I still had my eyes closed, lost in the moment. "Let's go somewhere private." He whispered in my ear and I knew exactly what he had in mind, but we couldn't "do the deed" in the car. Someone was bound to see us. A hotel room, on the other hand, would work. Only problem is we are both underage and couldn't rent a room. Of course we would be careful not to leave a trace of our presence. We would only need it to freshen up and sleep, then we'd be on our way. Our parents expected us home by tomorrow afternoon, or at least before it got dark. Elijah told his dad and I told my parents we would be staying with his cousin Greg who lived in the sleepy coastal town. That was the understanding we set. We were determined to make the absolute most of the time alone we had left. I'd never met Greg and I don't think I will now.

"I know just the place. Grab on." I stuck my hand out and Elijah grabbed it enthusiastically, making a loud slap in the process. With a thunderous thrum and crash, we were gone again. We appeared in front of a twenty-four hour convenience store. We wasted no time grabbing the sports drinks and snacks that we wanted. Once we paid and were out of sight from prying eyes, we vanished again. I Skipped us to a ritzy hotel that I had been to once in Morro Bay.

We appeared in room 302. Dark gray wallpaper, gray silk sheets and pillows, and the sleekest black metal furniture decorated the room. The bathroom was huge with a large round tub fitted with jets, with gray-tiled counters and flooring in a large glass shower. The layout made it feel like a real apartment with a full kitchen setup, living room, and the bedroom as well as the bathroom separated by their own walls.

"Whoa! This is boujee!" Elijah exclaimed, throwing his bag down and jumping onto the king size bed.

"You like it? Just another one of my family outing memories." I explained, setting my bag on one of the chairs. Glancing around, I noted that the door was locked, but not latched shut. "One sec." In a few swift motions I paced over to the door and threw the latch across the bolt. Elijah was already messing around on his phone when I came back into his view.

This would be a good time to shower. I thought. I had some fresh clothes in my bag and I could just use the hotel supplies to wash myself. "I'm gonna get cleaned up." I stated.

"Oh?" Elijah peeked up from his phone, setting it down on the side table. "I should too." He jumped up from the bed and scooted by me into the bathroom. I looked at him, my face flushing hot. "What? No need to waste water taking separate showers." Elijah smiled, winked, and started to strip. First his shirt, then his shoes, and finally his board shorts with no underwear beneath. He started up the shower and it didn't take very long for it to get hot. "Are you just gonna keep staring or are you gonna join me, dork?"

I took that as my invitation to strip. I was completely naked in front of Elijah for the first time in our lives, and my body immediately reacted. I pushed down on my crotch to hide my excitement as I entered the shower. Elijah pulled the door closed behind me and the steam started to fog up the glass.

"You don't have to hide from me, Vale. You have nothing to be ashamed of. You're gorgeous." Elijah chuckled and moved my hands to my sides. He kissed my neck. Electricity surged through my entire being, right down to my feet. Elijah let the warm water run over his body. He pulled me in closer and I closed my eyes. He gently rubbed my back as he continued kissing my neck. He had a little pudge around his belly and chest, and was built sturdy and strong. The dark hair covering his body sent my mind into a spiral.

Seeing him like this, bare and vulnerable, made me feel better about the way I looked. As he mentioned to me that morning, he also had stretch marks in multiple places and in the gay community I supposed we would both be considered bears, or cubs because we're younger. Elijah stopped kissing me to wet down his whole body under the shower head and I nervously moved in closer. I caressed his arms and he hugged me gently to him, soaking me in the process. Our bodies fully touched as he kissed me under the hot water and I let my hands wander. He did the same. We intimately washed each other and, once we rinsed, we dried each other off.

We both stayed naked as we made out, moving toward the bed. Elijah laid down first. I recalled that I had slipped the box of condoms into my bag last night on a whim. I slid over to the chair my bag occupied, found the box, and ripped a single condom free from the strip. I wore a coy smile, holding it up as I approached the bed again.

"Oh ho! So you *knew* we would have sex, did ya?" Elijah raised an eyebrow and propped himself up on his elbows.

"Not really, I don't know why, but I—" I stammered.

"Get over here, mister!" Elijah grabbed my wrist and pulled me onto the bed. We made out playfully, the intensity rising with the fires of our passion.

Faces flushed red.

Moans.

Sweat.

Heavy breaths.

Fireworks.

Sighs.

"I think I love you, Eli."

He paused, grinning at me, and covered in sweat. "I think I love you too...Vale. Is it too soon to say that?"

"I don't think so. We've known each other practically our whole lives."

"Yeah, we really have, huh?" Elijah turned onto his side, placing his hand on my chest, and gave me a peck on the nose. It never occurred to me what my first time would be like. I never imagined it would be with my best friend, but here we were, in a hotel room together, completely naked. I was in heaven and I couldn't wait to do it again with him.

We cleaned ourselves up with a spare towel and then laid back down on the bed together, not bothering to put any clothes back on. Elijah wrapped me in his arms and legs then kissed me on the forehead. *Was it too soon to be saying those words?* I second guessed myself. We *have* known each other for most of our lives, but only today admitted our feelings for one another. At that moment, it didn't feel rushed at all. If anything it felt as if it was long overdue and I believe that was the answer to my question.

"Soooo, today was pretty wild...right?" I said.

"That's putting it mildly, but yes. I would have never imagined doing half the things we did today. Even...*this*." Elijah admitted, giving off a tired sigh. I played with the hair on his chest as I stared into his eyes. My mind drifted back to Elijah's handgun in his bag.

"I've been meaning to ask you...why did your Dad get you a gun? You've never mentioned it and I was pretty shocked when I saw you had one." I asked, but he didn't answer right away. He breathed steadily, staring up at the ceiling. Just by looking, I could tell there was pain in his eyes and he was remembering something horrible.

"It was around the time I came out. So, about two years ago. Ironically, it was one of the main reasons I ended up coming out. I was newly embracing the fact that I didn't just like girls, but I liked boys too. I had just turned fifteen, you remember the party." Elijah paused for my reaction.

"Of course! It was really fun, I even remember noticing you in a different light. That might have been the first time I was physically attracted to you." My realization caused him to smile and plant another forehead kiss on me.

"That's sweet, Vale. You may not recall, but you wanted to stay over, but I was pretty adamant about being alone that night. It was because I was meeting up with someone from the Rainbow Tunnels app." Elijah continued and I listened intently without saying a word. "Well, two someone's actually. They were a guy and girl couple who wanted to have a threesome..." Elijah took a deep breath, continuing to look up at the ceiling again. His eyes welled with tears. "They said they were underage, like me and that the girls' parents were out of town.

So, I met them at her place thinking it was just going to be a crazy, fun experience, but it, uh...it wasn't." He stopped talking as his voice began to shake and tears streamed down his face. He covered his eyes with his hands and sobbed gently.

I was grief stricken when I realized what it was Elijah was trying to say. My eyes started to tear up as I held him closer and cried with him. He pressed his face into my chest and his whole body shook with each sob. I rubbed his back and shushed in his ear to comfort him. After a few minutes, Elijah regained his composure.

"Thank you." He sniffed, wiping his cheeks that were now drenched.

"I had no idea, Elijah. I am so sorry that happened to you, but just know you're safe now. I won't give you a speech about being more careful, because I'm sure your Dad already gave you that talk. Besides, look at what we did today. I'm hardly the poster child for being careful." I joked to lighten the mood and Elijah laughed, between sniffing and wiping his eyes free of tears.

"Right. Makes sense. That's why my Dad gave me a gun. So, nothing like that would ever happen again." Elijah's voice was serious and it gave me unease to think that he would ever have to use the gun on anyone.

"Thanks for sharing that with me, Eli. I'll keep you safe from now on, I promise."

"We'll keep each other safe."

"Deal." I nuzzled his nose with mine. Turning my back toward him, he cuddled me and slowly we both started to drift to sleep.

We jolted upright just as the door to our room made a loud clang as its bolt was caught on the latch. "How the hell? Is someone in there?" A gruff sounding man shouted through the crack in the door. Elijah put his finger to his lips, I nodded. We gently crawled off the bed, gathered our clothes from the bathroom, and our bags from the chairs. "Hey! I hear you in there! Open this door, you squatters!" The man shouted again. I stuck my hand out to Elijah as we both stood holding our clothes with one arm and our bags on our backs. I visualized the car and Skipped us away.

We dropped out of my Rip giggling, hearts pounding, and breathing heavily behind the car. With a quick scan there were no other people in the beach parking lot, and the sun's light was just beginning to illuminate the sky. "That was hella close!" I sighed and choked down some air.

"Yeah, but worth it." Elijah winked and slapped my butt.

"Hey!" I squawked and shoved his arm. He snickered and started to put his clothes back on. Within a few minutes we were dressed, sitting in the car.

"What a day..." I breathed out heavily. It's crazy to think so much could change in just one day. Neither of us had any clue these events would transpire and nothing would ever be the same.

"You can say that again." Elijah echoed. "Wait, what time is it?"

I glanced at the clock on the car dash. It read: five-thirty AM. "Dang it's so early. I wish we could have slept in longer." I groaned and shoved my head into Elijah's shoulder. He hummed lightly as if he was thinking something over. "What are you scheming?" I looked at him accusingly.

"I'm wounded you would think that, Vale! I am an upstanding citizen and scheming is below me." Elijah exaggerated his voice, assuming a British dialect. "But…"

"But what, trouble maker?"

"First, were you wanting to go home right now or did you want to find something else to do?" He asked, earnestly.

"Honestly…" I yawned. "I think I'm ready to go back, but can we hang at your place for a while?"

"Sure! That should be fine, but how cool would it be if we didn't have to 'drive' home?" He asked and I knew immediately what he was suggesting.

"You want me to Skip the car?!"

13 TWO WORLDS

"You can at least try." Elijah shrugged. I looked at him, pushing worry to the forefront of my thoughts hoping he would be able to see it on my face. At the same time, I wanted to impress him further, I wanted to test my limits. Gripping the steering wheel tighter I looked out to the beach, bathed in the silver glow of fog. Fishing boats were setting out to sea for the day and the quiet lull of seagulls echoed above us.

I closed my eyes, as I did many times yesterday, and focused on the front of Elijah's house. I could hear the chirping of birds, smell the fresh cut grass, feel the warm valley air on my face. My focus enveloped my whole body, Elijah, and eventually the car. It was as if I was stretching a rubber bag over us. The tension was becoming almost unbearable and an explosive headache began in my frontal lobe and gripped my whole brain.

Thunderous surges erupted around us, louder than any Skip I experienced so far. The car shook and rattled violently. I could hear Elijah's voice yelling in panic, but he sounded muffled and distant. I was jolted back to reality by a metallic THUD. My eyes snapped open to Elijah clutching the safety handle above his window.

"You okay?" I winced, grabbing my head, pain pulsating throughout every cortex.

"You did it..." Elijah said, shakily, pointing out the windshield. We were sitting in the driveway of his home, staring at the garage door. We both immediately unbuckled ourselves and stepped out to assess the damage. We searched the whole exterior of the car and there didn't seem to be a scratch on it. That was lucky. My parents would have killed me if I wrecked the car. Then revive me just to ground me for the rest of my new life.

I looked at Elijah, smiling wide, and he glanced at me, but his smile quickly melted away. "Vale...you're bleeding." He gestured to his nose. I touched under my nose and my fingers were bathed in crimson. My vision dimmed and I suddenly felt heavier than the car I just transported. Elijah managed to catch me before I hit the ground and I felt him guide me to the front door.

Darkness.

Tingling started at my fingertips and trailed up my arms. I grabbed for something and felt soft fabric in my fists. Upon opening my eyes I saw that I was lying on Elijah's bed with the afternoon sun lighting his room. Band posters covered the walls. Near his window was an automated rising desk with an expensive computer setup neatly organized on top. It reminded me of a command station from all the *Star Trek* episodes Elijah made Lauren and me watch in middle school. I propped myself upright and saw that I was wearing a new pair of boxers.

I swung my legs over the edge of the bed. My headache was almost completely gone, but a tinge of pain still pulsated at the back of my skull. A tapping came from the bedroom door, followed by the knob turning. Elijah came walking through holding two cups of ice water and a chocolate bar.

"Oh good, you're awake!" Elijah exclaimed, nearly dropping

the glasses before setting them on the side table. "I don't know what happened, but you just passed out. So I brought you up to my room. Thankfully, my Dad wasn't awake when we came in. I think he slept through his alarm cause I saw him leave in a hurry this morning. Weird though, it's Sunday. His car shop is usually closed today. I don't know, maybe he has a special request from a client or something. That happens sometimes..." Elijah trailed on, but I just sat there on his bed, mostly naked, and listened to every word that came out of his beautiful face. His expressions were priceless. I could tell he was anxious in his way. He always talked on and on whenever he was nervous or worried. *Did he really carry me all the way to his bed and change me?* I thought, admiring his thick arms once again.

"Eli...Eli. It's fine. I'm fine. Skipping the whole car was... *alot*. Perhaps I should start smaller, like a bike or three people instead of two." I calmed him as he stared at me with those fiery mirrors emblazoned in his skull.

"Three people? You're planning on telling Lauren?"

"Well, I was thinking about it. I feel like we can trust her, but I suppose we don't have to tell her right away?" I shrugged through my thoughts trying to glean some insight into Elijah's feelings about the matter.

"You're right. She should know, but the timing needs to be right. Let's sit with this for a while. Okay? Just you and me." He said that last part as a statement, but the look in his eyes made it feel more like a question.

"You and me." I responded.

"Oh right! Here." Elijah quickly grabbed one of the glasses of water and handed it to me then started opening the chocolate bar. "I figured you needed to hydrate after what you said about

Skipping before and what it does to your body. The chocolate always seems to help me perk back up after an exhausting day, so here." Elijah snapped off a little square of chocolate and put it up to my lips. I hesitated at first, blushed, and then opened my mouth letting him slide the piece onto my tongue.

"Thanks." I muttered, mouth now full of sweetness. Elijah took a piece for himself and we both just sat there for a moment eating chocolate and sipping at our waters. It was so quiet in his house. Ever since his Mom left all those years ago, it had just been him and his Dad. I remember being little and coming over for sleepovers, birthdays, and Thanksgiving. His Mom was always the best host. My Mom seemed to be best friends with her. Everything looked happy on the outside and it felt like that happiness could go on forever, but it wasn't meant to be. One night, in the early hours of the morning, Eli's mom packed some bags and left in a rideshare. None of us ever saw her again. Whenever I asked where she went I was either met with, "Who cares?" or "To find the life she always wanted, but never had." No other details were offered and I never pressed further.

"Alright." Elijah slapped his hands on his thighs which shook in his shorts. Those shorts drove me crazy, as they showed off his hairy legs really well. "Let's get you and your Mom's car home. I'll drive you and then walk back to my place."

"But you don't have a license, remember?" I raised one eyebrow at him in protest.

"Vale, you live down the street. You're literally in the same neighborhood. C'mon. Get dressed. I'll be fine. I set out some of my fresh clothes for you by the way. Let me know if they fit." Elijah grabbed the empty water glasses and the chocolate wrapper then left the room.

Laid out on his office chair was a white tee that said, "Science f&*#ing rules!" on the front and a pair of plain black shorts along with some fresh white socks and my own shoes Elijah must have retrieved from my backpack. I quickly dressed and Elijah entered the room again just as I finished tying my shoes.

"You look great! They seem to fit you well." Elijah beamed at me, making me blush yet again. I took a moment as I stood to look around his room again. His room had all sorts of fun light up trinkets and gizmos pertaining to sci-fi, video games, or photography. I admired Elijah's eclectic interests in not only science and logic, but creativity and art. He always seemed to float between those two worlds perfectly while most of us struggle to be competent in one or the other.

"I think I'm ready. I just remembered I have some silly starter assignments I need to complete before tomorrow so it's probably good I'm going home now." I walked toward Elijah to leave, but he stopped me. "What?" I looked up at him submissively.

"Forgetting something?" His eyes darted to the floor near his bed where my backpack sat.

"Oh right, thanks." I went to go grab my backpack, but Elijah caught waist band and pulled me back for a deep kiss. I melted in his arms and we continued. I could feel a heat bubbling up inside me and the kissing became heavier until he was shoving me back onto his bed. Clothes were obviously a nuisance as they ended up on the floor We were once again entangled with each other, the thralls of passion taking over our every movement.

It was uncomfortably hot outside and by the time we arrived back at my house, sweat was beading from both our foreheads. Elijah safely parked the car in the driveway, where another car was also parked—my dad's expensive electric vehicle that he just had to have ever since he got a promotion. He washed that car meticulously every Sunday. At times it felt like he cared about that car and his work more then his own son, but what do I know? I was just an ungrateful teen with an attitude every time I dared to open my mouth. And like clock work, there was my Dad, scrubbing the inside of his tire rims with a toothbrush.

"We're here! See? Safe and sound."

"I never doubted you for a moment." I lied, but Elijah immediately saw through me.

"Yeah, okay smart-ass." He retorted. We got out of the car, Elijah clicked the fob to lock it, and tossed me the keys. I caught them with ease as I rounded the front to hug him. Just before I could reach Elijah my Dad popped up from the other side of his electric eyesore.

"Welcome back you two! Did you have fun at the beach?" My Dad spoke as if nothing was wrong. Not a single strand of remorse, regret, or sadness in his voice. He truly was completely oblivious. That, or he really didn't care about anyone's feelings, but his own.

"Yeah, it was a great time, Mr. D! Thanks for letting us use the other car." Elijah chimed in for us as I just stood there, behind a pair of sunglasses, glaring at my Dad.

"Of course! See Vale! I can be a nice guy, right?" Dad joked, but it felt more like he wanted his own ego buffered. What was with the older folks and wanting constant validation after they've hurt someone? Maybe apologize instead? Or go to therapy? Now *that* was a joke. My dad, in therapy? Never in a million years. He's much too prideful for that.

"Sure, Dad. Thanks." I said, barely trying to hide my disdain.

"No problem, buddy. I'm gonna finish up here. Elijah, always a pleasure." Dad's round cherry cheeks may fool his clients, coworkers, and my Mom, but I saw who he really was. I saw through the manicured lies and cheerful facade. He was selfish. He thought as long as he did the bare minimum of being a parent and raising a child, then anytime I commented on his parenting style he could just call me "ungrateful, disrespectful, or snide".

Whatever.

He'd never change. It would be in my best interest to just avoid him until I graduate and go off to college. Lauren, Elijah, and I all had this plan to get into the same college in Colorado, to experience life in a different state with four seasons. I could experience a true white Christmas with people who accept me completely. That'd be a dream come true.

Elijah nodded to my Dad and walked me up to the porch where he could no longer see us. Elijah pulled me in for a tight hug and snuck a kiss on the cheek before letting go.

"See you tomorrow. We're walking to school together?" Elijah asked, his face looking like a desperate puppy.

"Of course! See you tomorrow." I said and blew him a quick kiss. I sighed heavily as he left my sight, and I went inside.

My mother peaked around the corner just as I entered, her golden hair swirling with lush curls that dangled just below her earlobes. She was dressed in her Sunday best and the familiar scent of roses wafted from her presence.

"Well good morning! Or should I say afternoon? Your Father and I missed you at church today. You just got back?" My mom approached me, placing a well-manicured hand on my arm.

"Yep. Car is in one piece too." I said, handing her the keys. She gave me a look that only meant one thing—she was disappointed in me. "What, Mom?" I said, after an awkward silence.

"Oh nothing. It looks like you had a good time, but I'm just glad you're home." She sighed.

Home. Right. If only it still felt that way.

"As long as you are safe, but Vale, you know the rule: call us with updates. We didn't hear from you the entire time. We just want to know that you're okay." Mom reminded me. I rubbed my arms anxiously then looked at her, nodding my head. "Okay then. Ya hungry? We got In-N-Out. I figured you would be home later so I got you your favorite order. Good thing you're back too, it's still warm." My mom announced and tapped my arm twice.

"Yes! Thanks Mom! I'll be down in a second. Let me just drop my stuff in my room." I said excitedly which made my Mom giggle.

"No problem, sweetheart. Hurry or it'll get cold."

I waved, acknowledging her comment as she walked away and I sprinted up the stairs. As grateful as I was for Elijah taking care of me when I came to, the chocolate bar and water was not going to be enough. My stomach growled ferociously and I wasted no time running back down stairs.

When I got down to the dining room Dad was nowhere to be found, but instead he was in his office, working and my Mom was chatting on her cell phone with someone from her elderly care hospital she managed. As much as I know mine and my parents' views on queer people don't align, I still do have a great relationship with both of them, and I am always impressed with the careers they have made for themselves. My dad is a multimedia and entertainment wiz who was essentially a major freelancer in the Central Valley for every kind of celebration or party that exists. My mom, on the other hand, is a registered nurse and an administrator. Growing up, on days that I was off from school, I would sometimes go to work with my Mom and hang out in her office coloring or doing homework while she made her rounds or filled out paperwork.

As I got older, I would help my Dad out with gigs that involved setting up sound equipment or capturing video of a ceremony. He could then go home and spend hours on his computer editing and creating more playlists of music or forming montages for clients. I was grateful to have parents who kept up with the current music of the day, and didn't just live in the past. It was refreshing to go from hearing worship music one day to hearing USA Top Twenty the next. Today being Sunday was obviously a worship music day and as the band The Glorious Unseen played over the house speakers, I munched down on my double-double burger. So I guess, if I'm being honest, it wasn't all bad.

I managed to scarf down my burger and fries in record time. No sooner had I reached my bedroom again, Elijah was calling my phone. "Hey you." I answered, shutting my door for privacy.

"Oh good, you're still alive!" He jested.

Wow! I'm not *that* fragile, you know? Plus, my Mom got me food so I feel much better now." I explained, as I paced back and forth in my room.

"Great! You should take it easy though and no you-know-whatting."

"I figured after a bloody nose and feeling like my head was about to pop that might be a sign to chill out." I said and threw myself backwards onto my bed. I stretched and yawned, before relaxing back into maximum comfort. "I'm still thinking about last night...and earlier."

"Me too. It was so much fun and I..." Elijah paused.

"You...what? Say it, Eli."

"I never thought in a million years I would call my best friend my boyfriend. It's like something pulled directly out of a gay film."

"Oh, so now we are officially *boyfriends?*" I joked, but prayed it was true.

"I mean, aren't we?" Elijah asked, sounding uncertain which was unlike him.

"Absolutely!" I didn't hesitate. "Why so unsure all of a sudden?"

"Well, what if our parents find out? More importantly, your parents, Vale. They don't even know that you're gay." Elijah's voice changed to a whisper as he talked about this subject. The possibility, or rather the fact, that my parents would eventually find out I was gay was terrifying to say the least, and I couldn't imagine how they would respond if they knew I was already dating a boy. I cringed at the mere vision in my head.

"We'll just have to keep it private for now. Is that okay? We can slowly start telling friends, but I don't want my parents to know yet." I said, a storm of anxiety brewing in my chest.

"I'm okay with that, Vale. Just like your ability, this will be our little secret. However long you need, it's your coming out journey." Elijah's sincerity brought tears to my eyes and I sniffed loudly enough for him to hear me. "You okay, handsome?"

"Yeah, thank you. I love you, Eli."

"I love you too. Keep resting. I'll see you tomorrow."

"Absolutely." I sniffed again and wiped my tears away. "See you then."

The next day I felt a hundred times more rested and with my new-found energy I was ready to take on my Senior year. After getting ready for the day and meeting up with Elijah, we arrived at Fresno High School. The campus' black iron fences, pillars and parapets of squared concrete buildings, and well groomed grass still held a layer of morning dew. It welcomed us into its pristine, dystopian maw. We headed toward the library as usual, and we made our way inside for our week-day routine. As Elijah and I entered, there looked to be someone already sitting at our typical spot.

"Good Morning, Lauren!" Elijah exclaimed a little too loudly. Lauren looked up from her phone with her glaring green eyes and shushed him. Lauren wore fresh braids in her long, black hair with gold colored rings and pendants layered meticulously in an appealing pattern. Her dark complexion had a glow to it this morning as if she was at a spa all weekend.

"Hey Lauren, how was your weekend?" I whispered and sat in the chair next to her around a wooden coffee table.

"Vale! It was great!" Lauren said and hugged me tightly. "We had so much fun! My dad and brother were like the same person when it came to how uncontrolled they were. Mom and I just trailed behind them mostly and did some shopping. Then later on, we got facials together. It was needed for our final year of high school, right?" Lauren laughed to herself and Elijah, sitting to my left now, shushed her back. Lauren gave another dagger-like glare, before shifting back into a smile toward me. "What did you boys do all weekend? Hopefully stayed out of trouble, or did Elijah make you break into an old house again to go 'ghost hunting'?" We hadn't gone ghost hunting in a long time, but it was just one of many adventures we three had when we were a bit younger. Lauren was always the reasonable one that didn't want to get into trouble, I was the shy one that just wanted to be included, and Elijah was the wild child that acted like a true leader. That all feels like ages ago now. It's amazing what a single weekend can do to change the course of an entire life.

"Listen, that was a mutual decision. Vale was all for it, weren't you?" Elijah asked, thinking he already knew the answer.

"Oh yeah, as much as a kid wants to go to the dentist." I teased and he bumped my shoulder with his. "But in all seriousness, we...have something to tell you, but it can't leave this circle."

"Oh, okay? Everything good with you guys? Did someone get hurt or something?" Lauren said, as she scooted closer to us.

"Well..." before I could start verbalizing my thoughts Elijah grabbed my hand and entangled his fingers in mine. I looked down at our hands in plain sight of Lauren's view then back to Lauren whose mouth fell open and curved into a huge smile.

"We're kind of a thing now." Elijah said and Lauren squealed in delight, a cacophony of shushes following her.

14 OFF CAMPUS

After the initial shock had set in, Lauren had all the questions. I told her my side and how long I had been secretly hiding that I was gay. I even told her how I thought about using Rainbow Tunnels, but I always got scared and ended up deleting it. This was news to Elijah as well.

"Wow...so you mean, I'm your first?" Elijah asked, as we walked across the quad to our first period class.

"Yeah, I suppose you are." I blushed.

"Alright, you two! Behave yourselves. I'll see you in class." Lauren winked and made her way toward the classroom. She still wore a bright smile until the moment she left our sight.

"Ssshhhh! You want everyone to hear?" I blurted out at Elijah.

Elijah laughed, but immediately stopped when he saw the smile drop from my face. Across the quad, were the same three guys that attacked us at the beach. They stopped in their tracks when they saw us, gesturing and whispering to each other. They seemed cautious, but confused. Good. I preferred that. Hopefully that would be the end of it and we could get through the school day without any problems. The three, tall, muscle-bound bigots lazily walked into the same building we were going toward and Brian, the biggest among them, gave us a smug smirk and a nod.

"Tch! Forget them. They may have cornered us in that fight, but as far as I'm concerned, we won. I can only imagine how dumb-founded they must have been. Their tiny brains can hardly comprehend the existence of queer people let alone someone who can Skip." Elijah ranted and it made me feel better about the whole ordeal. The truth is that I still felt guilty that he got hurt in the first place. The cut on his forehead was still noticeable as well as a faded bruise on his cheek.

"Agreed, but it's probably best we try to avoid them for the rest of the school year."

"No promises. Especially if they come for us." Elijah cracked his knuckles and neck at the sight of them.

We shared our final thoughts on the matter and entered our Trig class. I didn't like math all that much so I was glad to get through it first thing in the morning. In fact, I wasn't good at math to begin with and the only reason I passed every math class before this one was, because Elijah and Lauren tutored me. They both were whizzes in logical subjects and sometimes would let me copy their homework. Plus, we would have study-gaming sessions to prepare for tests.

The first period end-bell rang through the halls as did the squeaking of dozens of sneakers. Second period was weight lifting P.E. which I was alone in since Elijah had a college-level engineering course to go to. I had to remember to breathe when I saw the same three guys from the beach prepping the dead lift station. I walked in and made a beeline to the water dispenser to fill up my water bottle. As I had my back turned, I tried to ignore the gazes burning holes in my gym shirt when I felt a tap on my shoulder. My heart jumped into my throat and got stuck when I saw that the three were standing, imposingly in front of me.

"Hey, guys! H-how's it goin'?" I tried to smile as a cold sweat started to bead on my temples.

"That's all you gotta say?" Brian demanded. I hardly ever interacted with them through the years aside from his tormenting, so it seemed odd they would be obsessed with me after ignoring me the whole first week of school. I thought the bullying was over, but perhaps the events at the beach made me a target yet again.

"What do you mean?" I barely got my question out when Brian was on me, clutching my shirt in his fist, and slamming me against one of the mirrored walls. Surprisingly, it didn't crack, but he caused me to drop my water bottle which spilled all over the floor. The commotion got the attention of the other students who were preparing to work-out or just entering. "Ah! What the hell is your problem?" I grunted.

"How the hell did you do it, *fag*?" Brian spat.

"Hey, Bry. Ease up, people are watching." One of his lackeys warned, but Brian ignored him in his rage.

"I don't know what the hell you are talking about!" I glared back.

"That's bullshit! People don't just vanish into thin air!" He yelled.

"Brian!" An adult voice came from the doorway to the weight room. Brian looked back and released me from the wall. I shoved his shoulder with mine as I scooped up my almost-empty water bottle and placed myself on the other side of the room. "Principal's office. Now." Our gym teacher, a medium height, stacked woman who looked as though she could be an MMA fighter, demanded Brian to leave. Brian's face was beet red and the realization of defeat washed over his face. I could swear I saw tears welling up in his eyes, but it could have been the lighting. Brian's friends started to follow him when our teacher stopped them. "Just him. You two stay and clean up this water and then you are staying after class to help put away all the workout equipment." The two boys clicked their mouths and hissed their teeth passively in defeat as they walked over to the mop closet.

"Thanks." I said.

"No problem. Are you ok?" Ms. Tremble, as we would call her, asked sincerely. We called her that because of how she made all the men around her nervous wrecks.

"Yeah. Nothing bruised or dislocated. Guess that means I'm good," I joked and Ms. Tremble gave a rare smile.

"Good. Class, start stretching and getting warmed up while I escort Brian to make sure he makes it to the Principal. Nobody lifts any weights until I get back. Understand?" Ms. Tremble ordered and everyone in the room confirmed.

Being the nosy writer that I was and someone who believed in justice, I knew I had to get a chance to hear Brian's conversation with the Principal. I waited until the other two bullies retrieved the mop and bucket to slide into the broom closet and closed the door. I needed to make this Skip as quiet as possible, but I didn't exactly know how. *What if I focus on slowly peeling open my Rip?* I thought. It was worth a shot.

I focused on the outside of the Principals office, the scent of paperwork fresh from a printer, old wood, and dust. With my mind I visualized a zipper slowly opening and revealing the image in front of me. As I stepped through, little pops, like tiny firecrackers going off, sounded and I vanished. For some reason I was still standing in near darkness, but when I looked up I could see through slits in a door. It took me a few seconds to realize that I was standing in the Principal's coat cabinet. I covered my breathing with my hand, watching Brian, the Principal, and a third man who I recognized as the school counselor.

"What is your obsession with these kids, Brian? This is the fourth time, on record, that you have been acting out violently or aggressively toward other students. Why is that?" Principal Myers asked. Brian was looking down at the desk in front of him, silent as a turtle and recoiling into his shell.

"Brian. It has come to my attention that, these boys that you keep abusing, you call them the hard 'F' slur. Is that right?" Mr. O'Laney, the school counselor, asked, his gentle demeanor bringing a calmness over the room. Brian gently nodded, tears starting to show in his eyes. "Forgive me for bringing this up, Brian, but this is getting serious now. I thought we talked about this. There is nothing wrong with you and it is okay to be who you are and love who you want. I guarantee you, no one cares, but this externalized self-hatred hurts more than just you. You understand?"

What? What the hell was he saying? Was Brian gay this whole time? I suppose that made a lot of sense. I could see tears begin to flow on Brian's cheeks as he silently sobbed.

"You don't know what he's like. You don't have to live with him." Brian spoke through wet sobs.

"Your father? No, I suppose we don't and I can't imagine how hard it is for you." Mr. O'Laney sympathized and gave a look to the Principal who nodded. "Brian, listen. This aggression toward your peers needs to stop and you know that no one here will judge you. If things at home or school get overwhelming you know my door is always open."

"This is your final warning, Brian. You understand? No more

bullying. You need to talk through these issues and you are not in a place that is unwilling to help you." Principal Myers sternly dictated. Brian nodded, wiping his tears on his arm. "Also, apologize to Vale Dagwood since he seems to be your most recent victim."

I thought I'd done enough snooping for now. I got my fill of gossip to last me the rest of the school year. I focused once more and Skipped back to the broom closet in the weight room as quietly as possible. I always wondered about the reactions of people if they could hear the sound of me Skipping. They must be pretty freaked out, but thankfully I would never be there to find out first hand. That's sort of the point, I guess.

Just as I came out of the closet, Ms. Tremble came in through the front entrance. A few moments later, Brian walked in with a frown on his face. His eyes darted toward me and immediately away, as he let out a visible sigh. Class continued as usual and finally the bell for lunch rang. I was still covered in sweat as the warm sunlight hit my reddened skin. Elijah, Lauren, and I either sat together on the grass and ate or went off-campus to grab a bite to eat. It depended on our mood for the day. Upperclassmen were allowed to leave school during lunch. This was one of those days that I definitely felt like going off campus.

"Where are you guys off to?" Lauren asked as Elijah and I were walking toward the edge of campus after meeting up in the quad.

"Thinking of getting some sandwiches." Elijah said.

"Oh great! I'll go with you guys."

"No!" I said abruptly. "I mean, you don't need to go with us. We'd be happy to get you one and meet you back here."

"Okay, Vale. Dang, thanks sis." Lauren winked. "Pastrami on rye, no mustard. Got it?"

"Got it. Be right back." I said and pulled Elijah along with me off campus, into the parking lot, and out of sight.

"What are you doing? Why'd you make her wait on campus?"

"Because she doesn't know about my ability and I kind of want to keep it that way." I whispered.

"Why would that matter if we are walking down the street for a couple of...ooooohh. You were thinking of Skipping...to where exactly?"

"You'll see." I smiled and held out my hand. Elijah grabbed hold and we Skipped away.

We were met with the smell of coffee and the sight of foggy, damp streets lined with cobblestone and quaint, old buildings. There were a few bystanders walking by, but most were indoors at this hour. Street lamps were our only light source on the thinly populated roads. *I forgot to take into account that it would night here. Would anything still be open?* I thought and how serendipitous, right across from where Elijah and I appeared, there was a cafe-deli shop.

"Where did you take us?"

I cleared my throat and stood in the center of the road with my arms spread out. "Welcome to Sicily." I said in a fake Italian accent.

15 PRANZO E MAGIA

We entered the small cafe and were greeted by curious stares and whispers in Italian. A warm palette of tans and browns surrounded us in the form of wood paneled walls and dark wood furniture. The other customers could probably tell immediately that we weren't from there. The barista at the front counter waved us over with a gentle smile, but the bags under his eyes told a different story.

"Cosa posso portarti?" The barista asked. Neither of us knew Italian and looked at each other sheepishly. The barista rolled his eyes, "What would you like?" He said in English and his pleasant demeanor dropped.

"Oh, two tuna sandwiches and pastrami on rye?" I asked.

"e caffè?" The barista asked, scribbling on a notepad. That question I understood easily enough.

"Two, medium caramel macchiatos, please." I requested.

"Sit where you like. It will be out in a moment." The barista gestured to the sitting area and then turned on his heel to face the bar behind him.

Elijah spotted a small table in a secluded corner of the cafe, next to one of the large, front-facing windows. We sat down. Looking out at the dimly lit streets, I could see the town was sitting on a cliff side overlooking a beach, the ocean, and beyond. I felt Elijah touch my hand, bringing my attention back to him. There were few vehicles out at this time of night, but a Vespa carrying a man in a tux and a lavishly dressed lady in pink sped by. I could hear her laughter over the buzz of the Vespa echoing into the evening air.

"Why Sicily?" Elijah asked.

"Why not? Sicily seems like one of the best places to get Grade-A sandwiches and coffee, right?"

"Okay, but how are you even able to bring us here? I thought you had to have been somewhere or seen it to Skip to that location?" Elijah leaned in to whisper, so no one else could hear us. Slow jazz played over the shop speakers, but I doubted it would be enough to mask our voices.

"My parents. They have videos of their honeymoon here and they showed them to me as a kid. I remembered recently and thought it would be fun to bring you. In fact, they came to this very cafe and sat in this very spot back then." I adjusted my posture, looking toward the barista who was still preparing our food, then leaned toward the table.

"Aw, that's actually really sweet! And you thought to bring me here? Vale, you're something else." Elijah's cheeks glowed pink and he beamed at me as he placed his hand on mine.

"Don't mention it." I shrugged confidently and interlaced our fingers. "The real question is, how are we going to pay for the food? Last I checked, we don't have any euros."

"Hell if I know. It's not like we are regulars here. Dine and dash?" Elijah suggested. I didn't see any other way. As much as the thought of stealing made me nervous, he had a point.

"Sure, but let me see something." I reached into my messenger bag and pulled out the alchemy book I borrowed from Morrick and flipped to the table of contents.

"Where'd you get that? Looks old as shit."

"Shush. I'm looking for something that will help us out." I was searching for an alchemy symbol for invisibility. This would be the first time I cracked open the book since being in Langdorf Manor, but if what Elijah and I saw there taught me anything it's that the power of alchemy was something of wonder and mystery. "Here we go. Rune of Shrouding."

Just as I found the right page, the barista walked over with all three of our sandwiches, wrapped, and our coffee in tan paper cups topped with black plastic lids. "That'll be twenty euros, please." The barista stated. I needed to get rid of him or cause him to look the other way. I desperately looked at Elijah for an answer.

"Oh, my mistake. I completely forgot, we need a third caramel macchiato." Elijah said with a smile. The barista gave us a side eye and sped back to the bar to make the third coffee. "I'd say you have five minutes tops. Hurry up with whatever your plan is." Elijah's smile melted away instantly and his voice was hushed, yet frantic. I nodded and continued to read.

According to the page, the Rune of Shrouding was a symbol shaped with an X and a V overlapping each other. The instructions were to write the symbol on a scrap of paper and to place it on the recipient's chest, but for longer effects the recipient should eat it. After which, the caster or recipient need only, with intent, snap their fingers.

With intent?

What was that supposed to mean? Rapidly, I flipped to the index in the back and looked for Intent. By definition, intent meant to do something with purpose, but the way the book defined it was believing in a rune's purpose fervently and without doubt.

Belief.

That's all it took? What's scientific about t hat? It was apparent that there was a lot I didn't know about the world around me, and there was a lot I didn't know about Morrick Langdorf. Perhaps Elijah was right. I needed to be careful.

"Hey! Vale, you ready? We're running out of time." Elijah waved his hand in front of my face. I reached into my bag again and ripped out a blank page from a notebook, tore it in half, and drew duplicate symbols of the Rune of Shrouding. I slid one to Elijah and started putting everything in my bag, including the sandwiches. The coffees we would have to carry by hand.

"Put this paper under your shirt, on your chest and snap your fingers with the belief that it will make you invisible." I explained without hesitation. He looked at me, dumbfounded and smirking. "It's not a joke. Remember what we saw at Morrick's house. That was real and it came from this book!" I gestured toward my bag and Elijah seemed to understand as his face got serious and became focused. In one motion, he stuffed the paper under his shirt, took a deep breath, and snapped his fingers.

"Did it work? I can still see myself." Elijah asked, but I could only see his clothes and backpack floating in the air. It was like a ghost was wearing his clothes.

"Um, it worked. I can't see you, but everything you're wearing is still visible."

"Oh, that's hilarious!" He laughed and his clothes jiggled in his seat. I smiled and snapped my fingers. "Whoa! I see what you mean."

"Grab the coffee and let's get out of here." Just as I ordered, the disposable coffee cup closest to Elijah began floating as did mine, feeling my hand wrap around it. We moved toward the door and wide eyes shot back at us followed by sharp gasps when the bell above the door rang. I looked back at the barista who was awestruck and tilted a jug of milk absentmindedly, spilling its contents onto the floor. I pushed my other hand on Elijah's backpack and rushed through the door with him, leaving the gawking patrons and barista to ponder what unreal event they witnessed.

We were half way down one of the paved street ramps that descended the cliff and toward the beach when I stopped. "Wait, Eli. I think the coast is clear. Go ahead and take the paper off your chest."

Elijah was laughing as he reappeared in front of me. I removed the symbol from my chest as well as we continued to catch our breath. It worked. It actually worked! I wish I had known about alchemy a long time ago. It would have made ditching class and hiding from my parents a lot easier.

"That was crazy!" Elijah exclaimed. "Morrick just *gave* that book to you?"

"Not exactly…I sort of borrowed it from his personal library, but maybe he won't mind?" I questioned my own reasoning. No matter how curious I was, something in my gut told me I should not have stolen from someone like Morrick.

"Vale, c'mon! Really? We know jack shit about that guy and his…followers? Cult members? I don't know what to call them!"

"Travelers." I interjected.

"Whatever! But then you go and steal something from him? He sounded pretty adamant about me, an 'outsider', not taking pictures of his work or returning to his fancy house. What makes you think he will be okay with you taking a book of alchemy from him?" Elijah laid into me with as stern a voice he could muster. I flinched and recoiled into my shoulders as his voice bounced off the cobblestone underneath the buzzing light of a lamp post. "Look," He sighed. "You need to be more careful."

"More careful? What do you mean? We just stole food by going invisible in the middle of a cafe in Sicily through means of Skipping and magic. I think we are *way* beyond careful." I fired back.

"Yeah, fair point. Shoot! What time is it in California?"

"Oh, um, almost one in the afternoon." I said, checking my phone and noticing a few missed calls and texts from Lauren. "Oops, we missed lunch. Lauren's gonna be pissed."

"We'll make up an excuse: 'the line was super long and their register was malfunctioning.' That should work." Elijah, being seasoned at lying, spat it out with zero effort. *And he was lecturing me about being careful. That's rich.* I thought.

"You ready?"

"Huh? Oh, right. Let's go." I held out my free hand and thought of a secluded area behind our school where no one would see us appear. Instantly, we left Sicily behind us and arrived safely back behind the main building of Fresno High School. I reached into my bag and handed Elijah his sandwich and Lauren's since he had an art class with her next. It was quiet and it didn't look like anyone was outside which meant we were already late for our next period. "We should get to class. I'll see you when school lets out, at the parking lot." I said plainly and started to walk away when I felt a hand grab my forearm.

"Hey, hold up, Handsome." Elijah said and I relaxed, letting him pull me to him. I still felt frustrated with him for lecturing me, and for pushing me to steal for the first time in my life...

aside from the alchemy book. It didn't feel good, and I wore my emotions on my face, which is how Elijah could always tell when I was in a bad mood. "Thank you for lunch. I'm sorry for what I said back there. I'm only worried for your safety."

"I get it." I sighed and smirked. "You're welcome."

Elijah kissed me and I returned the gesture, hugging him afterward. We didn't say anything else after that. We went our separate ways to class and would not meet up again until the bell rang for the final time of the school day.

I rounded the corner, smiling and blushing to myself as Elijah's kiss was still fresh on my lips. I must have not been watching where I was going, because next I knew I collided with another human who resembled a brick wall in stature and mentality.

"Oh crap! I'm sorry...oh. It's you, Brian." I stepped back a few more paces in defense.

"Hey Vale. We need to talk. I know about your secret and I think you know about mine." Brian's face was serious, but with a tinge of pain behind his eyes. It felt like desperation meeting melancholy, and they danced together with each word he spoke.

"I don't have time for this. I have to get to class." I attempted to push past him, but he stepped in my path.

"Look, I'm sorry for the things I said about you. I don't know why I treat people the way I do, but..." Brian paused, his eyes red and dry from crying. "I don't want to be that person anymore. I want to be confident like you and Elijah."

"Congrats, you're gay or bi or pan or whatever. I accept your apology. Can I go to class now?" I dismissed him. Brian once again stepped in my path.

"See, but that's just it. I sincerely am sorry and yes, I believe

I am attracted to guys, but that's not the thing that is still troubling me." Brian said, suspicion oozing from his tone and demeanor. I believed Brian when he said he was sorry, but I knew exactly what was coming next and I was prepared to dodge the question.

"What would that be?"

"You, Vale Dagwood, are a teleporter. I don't know how or why, but I can't deny what I saw at the beach that day and I am almost sure you were hiding in the principal's coat closet this morning listening in on our private conversation. A similar sound as the day at the beach startled me, the Principal, and the Counselor. Nothing was there, but I knew it had to be you." Brian pointed his index finger at me and looked as though he had cornered a small animal in a cage.

I laughed hysterically and really tried to sell it. I teared up, clutching my stomach. "Are you serious, man? 'Teleporting' isn't real. I don't know what fantasy world you live in, but Eli and I managed to get away that day and just ran for the pier. We wondered why you didn't chase after us, but we were just grateful to get out of that scuffle." I passed by him, successfully this time, and patted his shoulder. "I forgive you, really. Let's just forget what happened and move on." I left Brian standing in disbelief in the middle of the hallway and wiped the sweat from my brow when I was out of sight.

16 AN EDGE

few weeks went by without much notice. Elijah and I would go to school and then Skip around before going home to finish homework, or...that's what our parents thought we were doing. We even used the Rune of Shrouding to pull pranks on some of our other classmates and family members. The only catch was we had to be naked while using it. Otherwise, they would see our clothes floating in mid-air, which would be a scary sight for them, but we didn't want anything to be traced back to us. So we swallowed our fear, taped paper with the rune drawn on our chests, stripped in the locker room, and plotted. It was also fun to use for...other activities. It was like sleeping with a ghost. Totally fitting considering it was well into October.

The Friday before Halloween week came quickly, and it was the day of the first senior trip of the year. All the seniors got to miss out on classes and go to Yosemite National Park to camp for the whole day and night. From what I heard over the years, it started with a three mile hike into the park. Then we would set up camp and there would be autumn-themed games, like bobbing for apples, searching for and decorating pine cones, and there was always hot apple cider and plenty of food to consume. Last year, everyone heard that the previous seniors waited for the teachers and chaperones to fall asleep so they could spike the apple cider with hard liquor and go on a midnight hike. No one got hurt, but when some of them were exhausted and throwing up after staying up all night, the adults instantly knew what was up. Those who participated were banned from the rest of the senior trips that year.

Now, as a high school senior, I sat near the back of a school bus sputtering toward Yosemite. The eighties-style synthwave music of The Midnight played in my ears as I read more mysterious pages out of Morrick's alchemy book. I was closely studying a symbol that looked like a Y overlapping a triangle and made it look as if the triangle had wings. It was called the Rune of Wind and it gave the wielder the ability to float or even fly. I reached into my messenger bag for a notebook and a pencil. I began practicing drawing it when a familiar face peeked over the seat in front of me, his chin resting on his arms.

"I'm bored. Whatcha doing?" Elijah asked, leaning over to look at the book. He tilted his head to read the header. "Rune of Wind, huh? Sounds...terrifying."

"What? You've never wanted to fly?"

"No and before you ask, I have never flown in a plane before and not sure I ever want to." Elijah shivered as he confided his acrophobia with me.

"I would have never thought. So when you nearly fell off Niagara Falls—"

"I practically pissed myself, but I tried to play it cool to impress you." He admitted.

I reached for his arm and rubbed it lightly with my thumb. Lauren sat down roughly next to me, bundled in her UCB hoodie while she reached into her bag and pulled out a protein bar. She was the first of us to already get accepted by a college and come next autumn, Lauren would be on her way to attend University of Colorado: Boulder. "What are you two up to back here?" Lauren eyed us suspiciously, peeking her head up next to Elijah.

I dropped my pencil in the middle of the alchemy book and my notebook with it to save my spot. I attempted to hide it from her gaze as I slid it back into my bag. "Right." I laughed. "As if we'd make out in the back of the school bus with all our other classmates nearby."

"I mean, it could be hot." Elijah jested and I kicked the back of his seat while all of us snickered quietly.

"But in all seriousness, did I actually see you doing home-work on a senior trip, Vale?" Lauren asked, moving to sit next to me. She leaned against the opposite window to me and propped her feet up on my lap.

"What? Oh that! Just a bit of extra-curricular stuff I'm doing. Super boring, you wouldn't like it." I waved off her suspicion as best I could and she seemed to move on since she didn't bring it up the rest of the bus ride.

After a while of sitting in the back of the bus, and the winding roads swaying the massive vehicle side to side, I started to get a little queasy. Ironically enough, Skipping didn't affect me in that way, but put me in the back seat of a long drive and my stomach begins doing cartwheels. It was one of my poorer choices to sit in the back, but there was more privacy so I guess beggars couldn't be choosers. I slid down the window next to me and leaned my face into the wind, closing my eyes, and focusing on clearing my mind.

Finally, the bus shuddered to a squealing halt in the parking lot of Yosemite National Park. My face must have been pale, because Elijah wore a concerned frown. "You gonna be okay?"

He said, patting me on the shoulder.

"Yeah..." I sighed. "Just need to stand on solid ground and walk around a little." I stood up with my book bag across my torso and followed Lauren out as Elijah slid behind me, his hand gently rubbing my back.

Just as we exited the bus, the chaperones were already unloading our hiking packs and supplies. Elijah and I collaborated earlier before we had to meet at the school, managing to pack both our gear in and on one pack. I spotted a black pack with bright green cords and made a beeline for it only for Elijah to grab it from me and start to strap it to his back.

"I can carry it."

"Thanks." I smiled. "Just let me know if you want to switch at any time."

I took a moment to take in the scenery. The crisp fall air brushed across my face and filled me with a seasonal electricity. The trees started to change color, their leaves and needles capturing the sunlight in a fiery autumnal display. I breathed in deep and let a warm rush wash over me. Autumn inspired me more than any other season and this was the perfect trip to take to harken in the spooky times. Elijah nodded at me and pointed over to some bathrooms that students were crowding by after claiming their items. So, we headed over to join them. Followed by Lauren who donned a purple and blue hiking pack.

"Alright class! Is everyone here?" A fit, middle aged man with dark brown hair that was graying on the sideburns spoke aloud to everyone in my class. It was Mr. O'Laney, the school counselor. He double-checked with a woman holding a clipboard who I recognized as one of the history teachers. "Okay, great. Everyone is present. So, we are going to start heading onto the trail in five minutes. If anyone needs to use the restroom please do it now. Otherwise, there will be an out-house at the campsite. It's about a three mile hike in and we will be stopping at the two mile mark for a lunch break and to get some cliff pictures if you want. Once we get to the campsite—"

I tuned out Mr. O'Laney's voice when I felt something strange. We were standing in the back of the crowd, but I could swear that someone was watching us. I heard a rustle in some bushes past the bathrooms and turned my head to look toward them. Elijah grabbed my hand and rubbed it with his thumb.

"What's wrong, Vale?" He whispered.

"I'm not sure...It could be nothing." I shook off the feeling and pointed my attention back to Mr. O'Laney.

After a quick stop in the bathroom, we were on our way hiking through Yosemite. The path was clear and smooth with a few inclines every several yards or so. After a couple of miles, we came to a cliff that overlooked the entire park. The edge of the cliff lined a wide distance and all of nature was spread out before us. Left of us climbed a mountain wall about forty feet and curved at the top. Right of us was the only path down into the valley. The whole class stopped here and began drinking water, unwrapping prepped meals, and taking pictures near the cliff's edge.

I picked a spot on the cliff where I could safely look out, eat my lunch, and privately pour over the alchemy book some more. Elijah had gone with Lauren to explore some far-off part of the cliff near the tall mountain slate. As I munched down on my lunch of a homemade chicken wrap and studied the rune and its rules closely, Elijah broke my concentration with a yell in my direction. I glanced over at him and his face looked pale white, and frantic as he gestured for me to follow him.

Setting the remnants of my meal down on my bag and taking

the alchemy book with me, I rushed over. "What's going on? Why do you look so panicked?" I attempted to get answers out of him, but mainly what I got were grunts and fragments of sentences followed by heavy breathing. It wasn't until I rounded the corner that I heard the echoing screams of Lauren coming from over the cliff side.

"Part of the cliff gave out and Lauren fell. I can't reach her!" Elijah finally managed to form a complete sentence.

"Please help me! ELI! VALE!" Lauren held onto a thick plant root and a thin slit in the rock for dear life as she screamed for us to help her. Tears streamed down her terrified face.

"Lauren, hold on! Shit! Think. Think, Vale." I wracked my brain in my adrenaline-fueled state. I felt the alchemy book in my hand and remembered the Rune of Wind at that moment. I had never tested it, but it was a chance I had to take. If it worked then Lauren would be safe, but if not...No; I can't even give that space in my mind. This *would* work.

Without wasting another second, I pulled the piece of paper with the rune drawn on it out of my notebook, crumpled it, tossed it into my mouth, chewed, and swallowed hard.

"Oh God! I'm slipping!" Lauren screamed again and as I looked back over the cliff side she seemed to fall in slow motion. My eyes darted to the bottom of the valley beneath her. My whole body tingled, instantly I Skipped down to the valley floor. I managed to barely get out the word, "Fly" as I pushed off the ground with all my strength. Holding my arms out, I soared into the air darting directly into Lauren's trajectory. I felt her body hit my arms and I clutched onto her, holding her close with all my might until we soared over the cliff side. Gently, we landed back near Elijah, who was still in shock and awe. I set Lauren down on the ground. She had fainted, but just as her body touched the rock she awoke in a panic.

"Whoa! Whoa! Lauren! You're okay. You're safe." I started to comfort her and hug her close.

"How did...but I fell! I remember that. And Vale, you...you vanished from the cliff edge. It felt like someone caught me and was carrying me. What happened?" Lauren was in absolute shock, but seemed to be grateful to be alive nevertheless.

Looking to Elijah for an answer, I locked eyes with him. I think he knew what I wanted to ask, because he just nodded at me. I sighed and helped Lauren back to her feet.

"Lauren, this might be really strange to hear, but I can teleport, erm, Skip as we like to call it. That's part of how I saved you." As soon as I spoke, Lauren's eyes were serious and I thought for sure she was going to smack me.

"This isn't a joke, Vale. I almost died!" She yelled at me.

"I'm not joking. Watch." I fixed my gaze on a tree behind Elijah and pictured myself behind it. I stepped through my Rip and then I was behind the tree.

"Where'd he go?" Lauren yelped. I stepped out from behind the tree and walked back to the spot I was standing before.

"I told you. Not a joke."

17 NOT SO INCONSPICUOUS

A half hour passed since I saved Lauren plummeting to her death. Thirty minutes of quiet panic since I flew into the air to catch my friend, but it felt like an eternity. We sat in a triangle, hidden behind a large rock, away from the gawking eyes of our peers and chaperones. Elijah gave Lauren her water bottle and a snack to calm her nerves. I explained things more thoroughly as she took deep breaths. Her face went from being flushed to color returning to her cheeks. The beach, the mansion, the alchemy, I told her all of it. Elijah was sitting next to Lauren, his arm around her for comfort. After I was finished speaking Lauren didn't say anything. She was quiet for what felt like forever. When it looked like she was about to respond, we were interrupted.

"Is anyone over here?" A woman's voice rang out. It was one of our other chaperones. She rounded the corner of the large boulder. "Hey, kids. C'mon, lunch ended five minutes ago. Everyone is waiting."

All three of us reacted as if we were caught doing something wrong. We quickly dusted ourselves off and grabbed our things. I remembered my stuff was still by the spot where I was eating before Elijah called for help. The cross-armed adult waited for us to pass her so she could herd us back. I spotted my things on the way and scooped them up, stashing the alchemy book back in my bag.

"We'll talk later tonight." Lauren whispered to me, grabbing my hand and giving it a light squeeze followed by a smile. "Thank you."

My heart jumped in my chest for joy and my eyes welled up with pools of tears. That was the second time this year I saved one of my best friends from falling to their death. I didn't know what would happen if I lost Lauren or Elijah. I'm not sure I could bear it and the sheer fact that Lauren was still willing to continue with the camping trip as normal shows how strong-willed she was. If all this hadn't scared her off, nothing would.

It was hard to talk about normal topics for the rest of the day. Elijah led most of the conversations, thankfully. I was too deep in thought and constantly dipping in and out of daydreams. At one point, I was walking by myself and I noticed Brian and another boy from the school choir walking side by side. The two were chortling and smiling together. Brian looked especially happy. I had never seen him like this in the four years that we'd been classmates. I only ever saw him smile when he was tormenting or intimidating someone, but this was a nice change. After what I witnessed in the Principal's office, I admit I was still mad at him, but I understood how he became who he was. I decided to forgive him during our conversation at school and now it looked like he might have a legitimate chance at happiness. *Good for him.* I thought. It was strange to think, but Brian and I were now in the same boat. Neither of us had come out to our parents and we were afraid of what would happen if or when we did. That doesn't mean I wanted to be friends with him, but I understand him.

The sun began to dip further to the west and behind the peaks of the surrounding mountains. A gentle breeze flowed through the valley and cooled the sweat coating my body. It was nice to get exercise like this after all that Skipping around. Skipping made things easy, but it also made me lazy and I didn't want that. Then again, Skipping exerted a different kind of energy and caused a different kind of stress that I wasn't used to. I passed out when I successfully Skipped Me, Elijah, and my Mom's car over a month ago. Not to mention the nosebleed. It was probably nothing. Just stress from a muscle I was not used to using. That's all.

I pulled myself out of my thoughts when we arrived at the campsite. It was then that I realized what my body must have been telling me for hours now, but I easily ignored it thanks to the adrenaline that coursed through my veins. My bladder gurgled uncomfortably and I rushed for the out house. *Maybe dried apricots weren't such a good idea for a hiking snack?* I thought. Thank God for baby wipes, because they certainly made it so I wasn't completely uncomfortable for the rest of the trip. As I washed my hands, I breathed out sweet relief and went out to join my friends and classmates.

Everyone was already well underway with setting up their tents and the chaperones prepared the grills to feed the whole class with burgers and hot dogs. I watched as Lauren swiftly pulled something out of her bag and made a beeline to the adult in charge of grilling. She handed him a pack of what I assumed to be veggie patties. That was new. She normally didn't shy away from meat, but perhaps that was yet another change in the current trend of changes. I guess some other students had the same idea, because by time the grill was fired up there were several packs of veggie dogs and patties sitting on the park table ready to be cooked to a smoky perfection.

While the food was being prepared for the masses of hungry teenage bellies, mine included, groups of people played different games. There was a forest scavenger hunt, a small archery range, horse shoes, and a game of flag football in motion. Some, such as myself and Elijah, took to lounging in camping chairs near our tents. I had my laptop out, still fully charged, and was typing away on an empty document. I wanted to notate everything I had learned about alchemy and my ability thus far. I made sure to lock the document in a hidden, password-protected folder so no prying eyes or snoops could read my secrets. As for Lauren, she was more athletic than Elijah and I. She was busy indulging in all the activities the camp grounds had to offer. I think it helped her clear her head too. I could imagine she had a lot to think about, which only made my heart race and incited further anxiety.

I guess I wasn't able to hide my feelings very well, because Elijah poked my arm, soda in hand, to get my attention. "Vale. She'll be fine."

"Huh? What?" I looked up from my laptop, confused as to what Elijah was saying, my mind still heavily focused on the alchemical runes and what I was able to do hours prior.

"Lauren. She'll be alright. You did great and I, for one, am beyond proud of you." Elijah said, relaxed and sported a gray tank top with a grizzly bear printed on the front and black sweatpants.

"You sure you're going to be warm enough in that? It's bound to get much colder tonight." I responded, glancing over at him from head to toe.

"Ah, I'll be fine." He waved me off. "Besides, I have you to keep me warm." Elijah winked and I squirmed, suddenly grounded back in reality. I closed my laptop and stashed it in the tent with my other belongings.

"I'm going for some hot cider and maybe some chips to snack on. Do you want anything?"

"For my boyfriend to enjoy himself." Elijah raised his eyebrow at me.

"Yeah, yeah. I know. I'll get right on that." I chuckled, shaking off his remarks as I headed for the snack t able. I know he was trying to be supportive and caring, but it irked me. Sometimes I needed to stew in my thoughts in order to fully process my emotions. Especially now since this trip was a good opportunity to do that, but he was right on one thing: I do need to enjoy myself. Get outside of my head for once and take in my surroundings. Even when Skipping around the world I was deep in my own head. It was a hard habit to break.

I approached the snack table and grabbed a red solo cup then ladled some still steaming cider from a pot into my cup. As I took a sip, Brian came up on the other side of the table, grabbing a paper plate and piling on chips with a few spoons full of salsa.

"Hey Brian, having a good time?" I asked, sincerely.

"Vale! Yeah, I'm having a blast! How about yourself?" This new enthusiastic tone coming from Brian was something I still needed to get used to.

"Well enough. I saw you talking with what's-his-name from the choir. You two seem to hit off."

"Oh, you mean Glen?" Brian scratched the back of his head and looked in the direction of another group of students. Glen was sitting among them, grinning and joking loudly. Brian's cheeks turned pink as he turned back to me. "You could say that."

"I'm happy for you. That's great." I lifted my cider to him

and started to turn away when he stopped me.

"Do any 'Skipping' lately?"

My blood ran cold and my whole brain sparked with panic. How the hell did Brian know that term? If he truly was using it in the way I think he was using it then it meant he overheard a conversation I had or worse, he saw me save Lauren. It was bad enough I was forced into telling Lauren my secret, but now the one person who tormented me and many other students for years, the one person I was just being able to forgive, knew both my secrets.

I took another sip of cider in hopes that the warm spices would soothe my nerves and my twisting stomach. I turned on my heel to face him again, wearing a fake grin. "You mean, like through fields of flowers? C'mon, Brian. Don't buy into those gay stereotypes."

"Nope. Not this time. You know exactly what I mean. I saw what happened on that cliff side. I went to go find you to chat, actually, but when I saw your things just sitting there I figured you and Eli went off to go smooch or whatever." Brian moved around the table and stood a few feet in front of me. "So, I went looking for you. That's when I heard the yelling. You wouldn't have known I was there, because I was behind that big boulder near you three. Just as I was about to interrupt, that's when I saw you do it." Brian wore a self-righteous smile across his face as if he was a hungry mountain lion finally cornering its prey after a long hunt.

"You saw me...do what, exactly?"

"I. Saw. You. Skip." Brian leaned in and whispered, his lips landing hard on the letter P. "That's what you guys call it right? Not teleporting? Too obvious I suppose." Confidently, and without missing a beat, Brian grabbed a large chip from his plate, scooped some salsa, and munched down on it, slow and loud as if saying, "Checkmate."

"Brian, I—"

"Vale, please stop. Don't deny it. I won't tell anyone, I promise you that. Even Glen. Your secret is safe with me, but damn! That is so *cool!*" Brian exclaimed and I gestured him to be quieter. He realized how loud he was being and instantly quieted down, looking around cautiously to make sure no one heard him.

I paused for a moment, sizing up the dopey jock with deep blue eyes that could make a snowman melt. "Fine." I sighed. "You're right, but like you said, you can't tell a single solitary soul. The only people that know are Eli, Lauren, and now you, apparently. I still need to talk with Lauren though so don't go spouting your mouth off."

"Dang, Vale. Since when did you get so bossy? Aye Aye, Sir! Lips zipped!" Brian mimicked a sailor's salute and mocked me before turning to go back to his group of friends only to quickly turn right back to me. "Oh! Can you travel anywhere?"

"I mean, sort of, but it's a little more complicated than that."

"Can we go somewhere tonight? We can wait until everyone falls asleep. We'll talk about it then." Brian started to rush away again, before yelling back one last time. "Think about it!"

I felt utterly defeated. My shoulders dropped and I rolled my eyes as I rotated back toward mine and Elijah's tent. As I slumped back into my chair and angrily sipped at my fragrant seasonal beverage, Elijah took notice.

"What's eating you suddenly?"

"Brian knows." I outright admitted.

"He knows...what?"

"Elijah. He knows." I glared at him waiting for the light bulb to go off above his head.

"Oooooh...Well, *fuck.*" There it was.

19 CHANGES

The rest of the day was an anxiety-driven, frustration-infused, blur. A class full of students sat around a campfire that was carefully curated by the adults. Elijah, me, and Lauren all sat together roasting marshmallows. The smoke from the fire wafted and swirled with cinders rising up to join the twinkling stars above. I stared upward and wondered what it would be like to step into that vast ocean and transform into one of those stars. Would I be missed? Would people wish upon me? Would all my problems just melt away?

Elijah jumped up in front of us and startled me back to reality as he aggressively taught us the "proper" way to roast a marshmallow. He was insistent that we hold the marshmallow above the flames and slowly turn it for two to three minutes until golden brown. Lauren, on the other hand, believed the best way was to stick it directly into the fire until it resembled a charred meteor. They made me the deciding vote, and after much deliberation I decided to do it my own way. I toasted it on the top flames until it caught fire and I quickly blew it out. Half was golden brown and the other was a bit charred. Perfect fifty-fifty ratio. Lauren and Elijah groaned and glared at each other with their mouths full of s'more.

By the time everyone was in their tents and falling asleep I was still a nervous wreck and the only thing that gave me an ounce of solace was reading over more of the alchemy book in the privacy of mine and Elijah's tent. Lauren had her own tent that she pitched right next to ours, but she was still sitting out near the fire talking to Elijah and other classmates until close to ten at night.

The light from my small, crank lantern illuminated the entirety of the tent and the pages of the book in front of me. I skimmed through basic runes about levitating objects or assigning objects with a specific purpose. There weren't as many extraordinary runes in the book as the ones I had already tested. That is until I got near the back of the book. The top of the page read, "Rune of Transfer" that looked more complicated than any other rune I saw so far, and it seemed to have many different uses. Its main use was described as transferring substances, a mass of objects, people, or energy into another directed location.

Directly below that was listed a counter symbol that seemed to be self explanatory in its name. The "Rune of Reversal" could reverse the effects of any alchemical effect, no matter how complicated, but it can only do so once per caster, per twenty four hours. There was a side note in the margins in red ink that read, "Alchemy can only solve problems of an alchemical nature or goals that are simple to achieve. Natural occurrences or those caused by mechanical means cannot be remedied."

As I mulled the meaning of these words over in my mind I was knocked back down to earth as the entrance to our tent unzipped. I instinctively closed the book and slid it under my pillow. Elijah poked his head into the tent and looked down at me.

"Hey cutie." He whispered. "Everyone is in their sleeping bags now. Even the teachers and parents. Lauren is just grabbing a flashlight and is going to meet us behind the outhouse to walk a little ways from the campsite so we can talk privately."

I nodded at him, releasing some of the stress I felt throughout the day as I relaxed my shoulders. I quickly threw on my hoodie and my shoes, then grabbed my lantern on the way out. I made sure to turn off my lantern before exiting the tent so as to not be seen. Elijah was still standing near the tent, watching me come out. He looked at my face as if searching for something in my expression.

"What?"

Elijah said nothing, but instead grabbed the sleeve of my sweater and pulled me in for a tight, warm hug. He was wearing his hoodie too and as my face rested on his chest I felt safe. I hugged him tighter and we swayed gently. I kissed the small of his neck and Elijah matched his face with mine, kissing me sweetly. I sighed in relief, as I breathed in his scent.

"Thank you."

"Pst! Hey!" A sharp whisper approached from across the campsite. Elijah and I looked over at who it was, but I already knew. Brian stepped as softly as he could across the dirt, being extra careful as he passed by some of the chaperones' tents. Both of us put our fingers up to our lips to signal him to be silent. Brian mouthed, "Oh! Sorry!" as he continued to tiptoe toward us.

As Brian reached us we gestured to him to follow us without saying a word. All three of us moved across the campsite, picking up pace as we distanced ourselves from the tents until we were behind the outhouse. Lauren was standing with her lit flashlight in one hand and her other hand was shoved into her hoodie pocket to keep warm.

"Hey...you three?" She said, furrowing a brow at Brian.

"He knows and he wants to come along. Let's start walking so we can talk. My anxiety about this conversation is already to the moon and back." I said flatly, walking in front of Lauren and continuing down the trail into the forest.

"Wait up, Vale!" Lauren whispered sharply. "Give us some space guys." She spoke back to Elijah and Brian who trailed behind. "I'm not mad at you or think you are some sort of freak, if that's what you believe. In fact, I think you are incredible. I know you said your ability to 'Skip' just came to you one day, but I wish we knew how."

"Thanks, Lauren. I really needed to hear that." I sighed. "Me too. Maybe it was dormant and it awoke in a moment of need. Maybe I was blessed by God or the universe or whatever. Who knows? All I know is that no one *else* can know."

"And Brian?" Lauren accused.

"He figured it out and he saw me save you today. I'd like to see you explain that away."

"So your original tormentor who was present for the triggering of your power and terrorized you originally for perceiving you as gay, you guys are now...what? Friends?" Lauren's tone was that of a protective older sister, condescension included.

"We're...friendly, but I wouldn't call us friends just yet. I forgave him. I'll let him tell you why that is. Not my story to tell."

"Oh alright." Lauren finished and we walked for a moment in silence, looking up at the stars twinkling in between the tree branches. "Can we go somewhere?" Though it was dark, I could see her face light up.

"Where did you have in mind?" I asked, stopping in the middle of the trail.

"England? We could watch the sunrise over there."

"Did someone say we're going to England? Hell yeah! Count me in!" Brian enthused as he and Elijah approached us on the trail.

"I guess it's decided then. What were you two talking about back there?" I asked.

"Oh ya know, boys." Elijah smirked and Brian glowed bright red enough to make out his face in the dim light of our lanterns.

"Oh?" Lauren said, glanced at me and then looked back at Brian. "Oh! Gotcha. Welcome to the club, Brian."

"And which club is that?"

"The Gay Club, the Friendship Club, the don't-tell-anyone-Vale's-secrets-or-I'll-hobble-you Club...take your pick!" Lauren glared at Brian, slapping her flashlight in her hand as if it were a metal pipe.

"Take it easy! Vale and I are cool now. I admit, I was a major ass—"

"You think?" Lauren interrupted.

"And I'm working on my issues. I can't be myself at home, but I'm trying to be better at that while at school. Oh and by the way, the other guys that were with me at the Beach and in the weight room at school, I don't hang out with them any more...or at least they won't even acknowledge me any more." Brian's voice got low and his head dipped down. I could feel sadness coiling around him light a straight jacket. He sniffed loudly and stood up straight. "But it's fine. Things will get better eventually. That's why I'm here with you guys now. I'm trying to make new friends. I want to be a better me." Brian's bright smile glowed in the scarce light.

"You sort of blackmailed me into a friendship, but that's fine. This is fine." I half-jested.

"Heh, yeah. Sorry about that. It started out with just making amends, but also there was this itching feeling that you were hiding something *big* and I just *had* to know what it was!" Brian spoke enthusiastically as if he were a young Sherlock Holmes, having cracked his first case.

I looked over at Elijah for confirmation.

"Good enough for me," He shrugged.

"Not me. I'm not so easily convinced. I'll be watching you, B." Lauren threatened and pointed two fingers from her eyes to Brian.

"I thoroughly count on it, *L*." Brian replied.

"Now that that's done, does anyone have a video of London that I can watch?" I asked.

"What? Why?" Lauren asked, one hand on her hip.

"Elijah and I discovered that I can only Skip to places I have physically been or places that I can thoroughly imagine being in. The imagining part is hard so it helps to have a real life example of what that place looks and sounds like." I explained.

"I think I have just the thing." Lauren pulled out her phone from her sweater pocket and tapped the screen a few times. "My dad does some consulting for international law firms every once in a while since he's pretty well known in his field and has gained a lot of respect over the years, not to mention a few PHD's—"

"Get to the point, L." Brian interrupted. Lauren glared back and continued.

"The *point* is...he sent me a video of himself in London right by Big Ben. Here." Lauren handed her phone to me and I pressed play on the video displayed.

"Hi baby girl! Dad here, obviously. I just wanted to say happy first day of your senior y ear! I can't believe how fast you have grown and I promise that when you graduate we'll go somewhere nice. London, perhaps?" Lauren's dad spoke in the video and the camera angle shifted to look behind him. He was standing near an enormous building, the Elizabeth Tower topped with a familiar clock. "I'll tell you something though, it smells like wet dogs and petrol out here, but I guess that's to be expected in a city. Anyways, I'll see you in a day or two. Love you, sweetie!" The video cut out and I handed the phone back to Lauren. I closed my eyes and started to envision the things I saw and heard in the video. Light rain, honking cars, people's shoes pattering against wet pavement, the chime of Big Ben, it all began stringing together in my mind. A clear picture formed in my head and I could feel a Rip opening in midair.

"Everyone hold onto me, now!" I shouted in a hushed tone.

Immediately, I felt three sets of hands latch onto me and I pushed us through the Rip I created. A crack, a flash, and we were standing at the bottom of the very same clock tower I saw in the video. I quickly glanced around. The streets were mostly abandoned and there was some light forming in the sky.

"Whoa! That was...*insane!*" Brian shouted, his voice bouncing off the bricks and pavement of London, England.

"We're here? We're actually here?" Lauren looked around in bewilderment. "I can't believe this. Imagine—"

"I know, imagine how—" I interjected only for Lauren to interject right back.

"How much money you'll save on travel! You never have to take a car or a plane anywhere again!"

"Oh, well I suppose that's one way of looking at it. Only problem is the more I Skip, the more exhausted I feel. A little over a month ago, I Skipped us and my mom's car, with all our stuff inside from the beach, back to Eli's house. I got a nose bleed and basically passed out. I would be lying if I didn't say that Skipping all four of us didn't give me a slight headache." I explained further, but I may as well have been talking to mannequins, because I got no response out of Lauren or Brian as they were still touching every brick and cobblestone around them.

"Oh sorry, were you saying something, Vale?" Lauren finally snapped out of her shocked state to ask.

I smiled back as I recalled how Elijah and I reacted when we first found out about my ability. Had it really only been over a month? It felt a lot longer. "I was just asking if you wanted me to Skip us up to the tower balcony next to Big Ben to get a better view of the sunrise?"

"Oh my God, yes please! Can you do that?" Lauren's eyes lit up and I thought they were going to burst out of her skull.

"Alright, everyone hold on again." I ordered and they all complied. I looked up to the balcony of Elizabeth Tower, then checked if the coast was clear, and Skipped us up to the landing. Lauren and Brian were in awe again, looking out over the ledge and then disappearing through one of the archways to the main clock room.

I looked out over all of London and could see the sun's rays peeking over the horizon. Elijah stood next to me facing away from the sunrise and looking toward where the other two were wandering around.

"Strange." Elijah said.

"What is?" I looked over at him.

"There's broken glass, busted metal bars, and scratch marks in the atrium."

"Yeah? Maybe someone broke in. I'm sure they deal with vandals all the time." I shrugged.

"I suppose. It's almost like there was a huge fight or something."

"Maybe. How are you doing?" I asked, earnestly and placed my hand on his forearm.

"Me? I'm fine, all things considered. I'm proud of you, ya know." Elijah placed his hand on mine, looking directly at me.

"I know." I sighed. "Truth be told, I have been terrified all day. Not only because of what happened to Lauren, but because I feel overwhelmed with everything I am learning about myself lately. I feel this pressure inside my stomach that is building into my chest and I feel like one day I'll pop and fly away like a loose balloon."

"I know that feeling. I felt it when I first came out to my dad and then your parents found out. It's funny. I had feelings for you even back then, but I shoved them down for the sake of our friendship. Then, when I was assaulted I felt that overwhelming feeling you described. It was hard on my dad too. He didn't know how to talk about it and neither did I, so he paid for my therapy sessions." Elijah revealed. I juggled between blushing and clutching my heart that ached for him.

"Did it help?"

"It did. I couldn't talk to anyone about who I was or my past until then, and it felt good to let it all go."

"Is that why you have such a nonchalant attitude about everything now?" I joked.

"Partially, but I genuinely couldn't give two shits about what negative things people think about me. If they're thinking it then it's none of my business. It's when they start flapping their lips that they can expect to catch these hands." Elijah held up his hands and waved them in a slapping motion. I laughed along with him, playfully grabbing his hoodie strings and tightening his hood around his head. "Hey!" He giggled. That contagious laugh again. A warmth wrapped around me as the sun crested over the horizon, rays of light illuminating us.

We held each other as we looked out toward the sunrise and the city of London waking up for the day, the river Thames glistening and flowing below.

"Wow! Do *not* go in there. It is a *mess*!" Lauren exclaimed as she and Brian wandered back out of the atrium and peered over the balcony at the same sight Elijah and I were enjoying.

"This is incredible. I still can't believe we're in England. Maybe we should explore a bit?" Brian suggested.

"Shouldn't we be getting back to the campsite in California?" I asked.

"Why? Everyone's asleep and a chaperone might do a patrol of the tents, but considering our tents are zipped up then there is no reason to look inside. As long as we get back by sunrise in California they'll have no clue." Brian laid out the plan which made me recall that he was a master of stealth when it came to avoiding adults. As much as I didn't want to admit it, he was trying to be helpful.

"Brian's got a point. Even if we show up and everyone is already awake we can say we were on a morning hike to stretch and wake our muscles." Lauren said, and to my surprise she was agreeing with Brian. I never thought I'd ever see that in a million years, but times change and nothing brings about change more than your friend telling you he has superpowers.

"I have a point? Does this mean—" Brian chirped.

"Ah! Don't push it." Lauren stopped him with one palm held up to his face.

"In that case, sure. Let's explore London! I'd say we have just under ten hours to get back to the campsite anyway." I conceded.

"Are you kidding? That's basically an entire day! C'mon, Vale. Skip us back down to the street and we'll start the day off right with some hot coffee." Lauren ordered, enthralled with a day of fun ahead of us. I was exhausted at first, but the feeling went away when I realized how rare of an opportunity this was. Not only rare, nearly impossible.

As we clasped hands yet again I took a moment to look everyone in the eyes and remember this moment, remember their faces. It was probably the happiest I felt in a long time. Not bitter-sweet happiness or complex melancholy, but pure irrevocable joy. The sun burst behind Elijah's head, casting him in shadow and I focused on the streets below that now began to roar with traffic. Right before I pulled us through my Rip, I heard the crunching of glass and the clatter of hollow metal coming from inside the atrium. My head turned to look and I caught a glimpse of a figure lurking in the shadows, watching us. In a snap, we vanished and reappeared on the sidewalk once more.

19 EXHAUSTED FRUSTRATION

What proceeded was an exciting, caffeine fueled adventure in London. We trekked on foot from shop to shop perusing clothes, books, memorabilia, and most importantly, food. We stopped to take pictures with our phones in front of Buckingham Palace, the Tower of London, and the British Museum. We decided to take a tour of the British Museum which we didn't have to pay for, since I Skipped us in through a side entrance, past security.

The many different artifacts and art that were displayed there would make one's head spin. We came across an exhibit that housed Celtic findings from Scotland and Ireland. Among all the troves of treasures and ancient tapestries were carvings that looked familiar. I stepped closer to the red velvet guard rope that blocked anyone from touching the exhibits. I peered as closely as I could and then it dawned on me. Those were alchemical symbols. Old and carved in faded stone, but I was certain that was what they were. However, they were symbols that weren't anything like I'd seen in Morrick's book. Almost like they were the rudimentary symbols that inspired the alchemy I was reading about.

"Found something you like?" Lauren stepped next to me, examining the stone as well.

"I think so. Do you remember me mentioning to you how I met others like me and their leader being this scientist that studied alchemy?"

"I guess so. Truth is I hardly remember much of what you said after you saved me. My body was still in shock and I don't think I could retain anything at that moment." Lauren admitted.

"Well, alchemy is real. Magic, or science-based magic, is real. Eli and I saw it for ourselves at Morrick's Mansion. You recall me reading a book on the bus, right?" I asked.

"Yes, *that* I do remember and you seemed pretty dismissive about it so I left it alone, but go on."

"That is a book of alchemy I...um, *borrowed* it from Morrick's private library and I've been studying it. These runes on the stone match up in some way with the runes in the book. Ugh, damn. I didn't bring it with me." I explained, frustrated that I chose to leave it behind.

"Where is the book now?" Lauren asked.

"In mine and Elijah's tent, under my pillow, but listen. I wasn't able to save you simply because of my ability to Skip. I was able to save you with a rune that allowed me to fly."

"Whoa. Okay, this is a lot. So, let me get this right, you can teleport—"

"Skip." I corrected her.

"Right. Skip. Not only that, but you found a group of other people who can Skip too and are led by a dude who is some sort of scientist who studies magic?"

"Magick with a 'k'." I clarified. "To be clear."

"What's the difference?"

"Well, one is pertaining to stage performances and the other is referring to real pagan craft." I expanded, but Lauren's face said it all. She was skeptical.

"And none of that sounds shady to you at all?" Lauren asked, her arms crossed as she leaned back.

"Maybe? I mean, they were the only ones like me that I found...or they found me. I don't know, but I had to know more about them and that's how I met Morrick Langdorf." I rubbed the back of my head, cringing as if I was being reprimanded by my parents.

"That's his last name? You're kidding me, right? And you didn't think to question that? He sounds ridiculous."

"You have to understand, Lauren. I was just—"

"No, Vale. *You* have to understand something. What you did, following some random group of strangers and going to a weird dude's mansion, God knows where, was incredibly stupid and dangerous for both you and Eli." Lauren laid into me and who could blame her. She had been protective of me and Elijah since grade school. No one messed with her, and if anyone picked on us it almost always immediately stopped. Lauren made sure of that. Even Brian felt her wrath at one point, but I suppose he didn't learn his lesson, because he kept finding reasons to torment me until recently.

"We *were* cautious though. Elijah had a gun with him." I blurted out. We both looked around to see if anyone heard us. Thankfully, no one else was nearby along with Elijah and Brian viewing a different exhibit.

"Excuse me? Since when does Eli have a gun? What other secrets are you two keeping from me? Or should I go throw myself off another cliff to get you to talk?" Lauren was clearly pissed. I didn't mean to keep things from her. I only wanted to protect her until I found out what this ability was. The fewer people that know the better. I didn't have that option anymore and it seemed no matter who I told they were inevitably going to be in harm's way.

I took a deep breath before responding. "Look. I'm really sorry we didn't tell you all of this. I have been so overwhelmed trying to get answers to things I barely understand myself. Can you blame me for wanting to spare you from the chaos?"

"Oh, Vale…" Lauren put her arms down and her face softened. "I understand, okay? Honestly, I was mad, but there isn't anything we can change about the past. I'm in it now and weirdly enough, so is Brian. Don't shove us aside. We can handle ourselves."

"Yeah, he is a pretty unlikely ally. I think he just wanted to join for free traveling." I shrugged.

"It is a pretty great perk, I'm not gonna lie." Lauren laughed and I joined in. She looked at me for a moment and then pulled me in for a hug. "I've got your back. No matter what. We'll work through all this together."

"I appreciate that, Ren." I said in her ear, using a nickname only I called her in moments when we got heartfelt and sincere. It was like my own little signal to her that I loved her dearly. She was practically my sister. Releasing from our hug, we scanned the exhibit room. "Are you ready to find the guys and head back to the campsite? I think the sun is starting to rise over there now."

Lauren stretched and yawned while nodding. "Oof, I'm gonna sleep so well on the bus. It sucks that you can't fast forward time itself so we could be home already."

"I could Skip us all home, but then the chaperones would panic after four of their students just disappeared."

"Got it. Stick to normal travel once we're there. Good plan, but I am *not* looking forward to that hike back to the bus."

Lauren complained.

I chuckled, patting her on the back as we walked toward another area of the museum looking for Elijah and Brian. Entering an exhibit of crusade artifacts, I found them standing next to each other. At first glance it looked like they were just standing together, but as I got closer it was clear that Brian was too close for comfort and his hands kept touching Elijah's hand, lower back, and arm. The flirtation was obvious and it took everything in me to not rush up and punch him square in the face. What really made my heart sink was that Elijah didn't seem to be doing anything to deter him, but I swallowed my sudden rage as best I could and interrupted their conversation.

"Oh hey Vale. You enjoy the rest of the Muse—" Brian started to talk, but I stopped him.

"Yep. It's cool. Are you guys ready to go back now?" I asked, rigidly.

"Um, I suppose." Elijah said, a look of concern on his face.

"Good." I turned on my heel and strode away toward the main entrance. Lauren paced up next to me as Elijah and Brian followed. We reached the entrance and I immediately led us to a concealed alleyway where I could Skip us without any prying eyes spotting us. "Everyone circle up and grab on."

"Hey, are you okay, hun?" Elijah whispered to me before clasping onto my hand.

"Everything's fine. I'm just tired and want to get back."

Crack.

Snap.

Flash.

Rumble.

We arrived safely on the trail where we started before we departed for London. I shoved Elijah's hand away from me and marched off in the direction of the campsite. I put my hood over my head as I passed the outhouse.

"Where did you kids go off to?" A demanding voice boomed, and one of the chaperones I didn't recognize took big strides to reach me. Probably another parent of a classmate. I didn't care either way.

"Early hike to wake up." I waved him off and headed straight for my tent. I unzipped the front and tore open the cover to reveal two sleeping sacks and two bags. Everything looked exactly as I left it, but as I lifted my pillow sirens went off in my head. The book was gone, along with my notes! In its place was a single scrap of paper that read:

"This doesn't belong to you."

I silently pounded my fist on the ground, crushing the note in my hand. Someone *was* watching me after all. My suspicions were correct and I felt so violated, but who was it? One of the Travelers? Morrick himself? Another classmate or one of the chaperones? I prayed it wasn't the latter, but I wasn't sure the former would be any better.

At that moment, my brain felt like an overloaded generator ready to pop in an electrical display of sparks and fire. I wish I could Skip home and shove my face into my pillow to scream and cry until this feeling was gone, but I was trapped. Trapped with my jealousy, my rage, my fear. All I could do to push it down was pack up the tent, prepare to leave, and shove my earbuds into my ears. I would ignore everyone and everything until I was home. Elijah would get the hint. He would have to if he didn't want me snapping at him.

The three mile hike out of Yosemite was brutal. Lauren and I fell several times from exhaustion, scraping up our hands and knees. Elijah managed to keep himself upright and Brian looked completely unfazed, the *bastard*. By time we reached the bus, the rest of the class was waiting on us for five minutes, and all my water as well as the remainder of my snacks were devoured. After handing our camping gear off to the bus driver to put in the under carriage, I slumped onto the bus caked in sweat and dirt. I made a beeline straight to the back of the bus, but another group of classmates already claimed it. I took the closest open seat that had an available window and immediately closed my eyes as my music continued to buzz in my ears. I felt a warm presence next to me and the bus shuddered to life. Sleep took me into its embrace.

I awoke to someone gently shaking my shoulder. I sat upright, my neck feeling tense from leaning against the cold metal window. I stretched and yawned as my body cracked in several places. My eyes opened to an empty bus and Elijah next to me, his hand on my shoulder.

"Time to go sleepy-head." Elijah said with a sweet smile.

"Ugh, thanks. I can get us home in a hurry. I just want to sleep." I said in a low, raspy voice and threw my bag strap over my shoulder.

Elijah got behind me again as he did when we first arrived at Yosemite and rubbed my back. My anger had subsided and I was too tired to even care, but my dreams were filled with figures in the shadows watching my every move and voices yelling at me from every direction. It was unnerving and I didn't feel rested at all.

Elijah and I said goodbye to Lauren and Brian as we collected our things and walked onto the school campus to a spot where no one would see us. As soon as we were out of sight I yawned a deep yawn again, grabbed Elijah's hands, and pictured our street. Instantly we were whisked away through space and appeared in front of a house about halfway between our homes. I started to let go of his hands, but he gripped tighter and pulled my attention back to him.

"Vale, what was that at the museum? And don't lie to me. We may have only started dating, but we have been friends a lot longer and I know when you're lying." He said, a stern look on his face, but mixed with a tinge of that same worry from earlier.

"I felt jealous of Brian, okay? He was being all flirty with you and touching you so I got a little fired up."

"I see. Well, you should know that he wasn't flirting with me. He was honestly being friendly. Vale, you have to understand. Brian only recently accepted his sexuality, so he is experiencing closeness with other males in a different way for the first time. Sound familiar?" Elijah explained, looking directly into my eyes.

"I guess you're right." I shrugged. "But you should also know that the alchemy book is gone."

Elijah's eyes grew three sizes and his tone was flat. "What? How? Who?"

"I wish I knew, but all I know is that I stashed it under my pillow back at the campsite, and when we returned it was gone. They left this note." I reached into my pocket and handed him the crumpled up paper.

"Hm, 'This doesn't belong to you.'? Great, Vale! What did I tell you? You shouldn't have stolen that book from that dude!" Elijah yelled, his voice ricocheting off the nearby houses.

"Ow, can you not yell? My head is pounding." I clenched my head and bared my teeth when suddenly, a coppery scent filled my nostrils.

"Vale, your nose." He pointed.

I touched my upper lip and drew back bright red droplets. "I gotta get home and lay down, Eli. Can we talk later?"

"Oh we definitely are going to talk later." Elijah threatened. "But yeah, we both could use a shower and some rest. Text me when you're up and about."

I nodded, waved my bloody fingers, and slumped home, pinching my nose.

The day was dipping into dusk earlier than before as I crossed the threshold back into my home. I was greeted by my father whose face, though a little wrinkled, was still youthful and glowed with pride. He filled the archway in-between the entryway and the kitchen with his stocky frame. It was no wonder he dressed up as Santa every year. Thankfully, he stopped doing that a few years ago. I don't know if it was because he thought I was getting too old for Santa or if he simply got tired of playing the part, but I wasn't complaining. If only it were so easy for me to quit playing the part of, "Perfect, Straight, Christian Son" I would be exponentially happier.

"Welcome Home, baby boy!" Dad hugged me tightly. "Did you have fun on your class trip?"

"Hey Dad. Yeah, but I'm so exhausted. Is it okay if I go straight to bed?" I asked, struggling to even stand. I had managed to stop the bleeding from my nose before I entered, but still needed to hide the blood on my hands.

"Oh are you sure you don't want some dinner first? Your Mom is making a really good meal."

"I'm sure. If she could save me some for later when I'm more...alive? That would be great." I said as I shuffled by him to the staircase.

"Alright, Vale-y Bear. Have a good rest." Dad said, sweetly. As much as I wanted to hold a grudge I found it difficult when my Dad was being sweet again. He did have a short temper at times and he had a knack for raising his voice when he was fuming, but ultimately he was generous and nice in his demeanor. I was just never sure how long that niceness would last between angry moments or silent days of him locked away in his multimedia dungeon.

As I reached my bedroom door I heard the floor creek inside and I was almost certain someone was in my room. I closed my eyes and felt a familiar sense. Someone had opened a Rip into my room. I was sure of it. It had a similar gravitational pull as mine. Taking a deep breath, I turned the knob and was half surprised to find a girl with dyed hair, piercings, and punk rock–style clothing sitting on my bed, legs crossed.

"Liv? What are you doing in my room?" I asked, stepping inside and setting my bag down. Liv said nothing, but looked at me, her lips curling above her shimmering canines. She held up the alchemy book with my notes still stuffed between the pages.

"I had a feeling that was you! Why were you following me?" Sudden anger spilled over the wall of exhaustion weighing me down. I attempted to snatch the book from her hands, but she Skipped away before I could reach it. Her Rip was so quiet. *How did she do that?* I thought. She reappeared by the window, leaning against the wall as she opened the book and began scanning its contents.

"Didn't you get my note or don't Americans know how to read? I can never tell."

"I asked you a question and let's not forget that you are

trespassing in *my* room. So either answer or get out." I demanded, clenching my fists at my sides.

"Tsk, Tsk, Tsk..." Liv clicked her tongue. "So savage. You're not going to offer me a cup of tea or anything?" She paused, sarcasm dripping from her every word. I kept my glare on her. "Very well. Morrick knows you took the book. He doesn't care, so here." Liv tossed the book on the bed. I slowly reached for it, keeping my eyes on her then opening the book to make sure everything was still there as it was before. "He actually hoped you would find it. Dr. Langdorf could sense your curiosity from kilometers away. 'His eagerness and willingness to learn is something we could use more of around here, don't you think?' His words, not mine." Liv gave her best impression of Morrick as she explained her real intentions.

"Then why steal the book anyway? Why follow me and my friends?"

"That's why! You told others! That girl you saved and that big dope. And not just about your ability, which I couldn't care less who you tell about that since it's your life, but you told them about Alchemy, Morrick, and us. That puts *our* lives in jeopardy and we can't have that." Liv got cold and her eyes became more serious than I've seen them before. It was like staring into an approaching blizzard as sharp flurries of ice whiz by attempting to slice into my exposed flesh.

"First off, that girl and that big dope have names." I argued. "Lauren and Brian, they're my friends and they wouldn't tell anyone. They can keep a secret, trust me." I tried to reassure her, but Liv didn't seem to be buying it. How could I blame her? Calling Brian my friend was a stretch, but she didn't need to know that.

"Oh, you mean the whole gay thing? Just a bunch of fairies

and their fruit fly hanging out and keeping each other's secrets? Is that it? Is that why I should trust you?" Liv's words cut deep. I didn't recognize her as the person who I met back in the Hawaiian market. What happened to the fun, rebellious girl who gave Elijah and I a tour of Langdorf Manor?

"Huh. Wow. Thanks for that. I thought—"

"Thought what?" Liv cut me off. "That we were friends?" She mocked and Skipped to be directly in front of me. I didn't realize why until I felt the cold, sharp steel against my throat. I stood as still as a monolith. It took every nerve in my body to not shake with fear and rage. "Listen here, asshole. I may play nice in front of the others and to appease Morrick, but we aren't friends. You're just Morrick's latest pet. Got that? So keep your *fucking* mouth shut about him and the Travelers."

I swallowed hard and looked down at her, meeting her gaze. "Or what?"

"Or my blade will get a little thirsty and who am I to deny it the blood it wants?" Liv threatened. As soon as she finished her sentence she was gone. I gasped, not realizing I was tensely holding my breath, and relaxed my whole body with a relieved exhalation. I caught myself on my bed and could still feel the pressure from her blade on my neck. I punched my bed as I started to shake down from the adrenaline. Curling up on my sheets, tears welled up in my eyes and as they slid down my face, exhaustion overcame me. I slipped into a deep sleep.

My dreams were wilder than ever:

Flashes of Langdorf Manor...

A fountain of blood...

Roaring flames...

I called out for Elijah, but all I got back were screams from the endless void. That's when I saw Liv. She stood facing away from me. I called out, but she did not react. I tugged on her shoulder and was horrified. Liv's hair was grungy and caked with dirt. Her face had deep cuts and gouges in it, but she wore a menacing grin. Her eyes were pitch black and inky tears crawled down her cheeks. In her right hand, she clutched the same knife she had threatened me with. She lunged at me. I screamed as I defensively lifted my arms to my face.

I slowly opened my eyes and my arms were still raised, but I was awake. I could feel my heart pounding in my chest and cold sweat layered my chest and neck. My room was completely dark save for the static standby lights on my computer and other electronics. Rolling onto my side, I checked my phone for the time. It was almost midnight. I wondered if Elijah would be awake or if he passed out like I did. I texted him just to be safe. We needed to talk about Liv's little visit. But first, perhaps I should shower.

As I slipped on my shoes and a jacket, my phone buzzed. Elijah *was* awake and he wanted to meet at the nearby park. I confirmed with a quick text, and made my way downstairs. I made a beeline for the kitchen to grab a water bottle and a granola bar. When I turned to look in the living room, Dad was snoring away on the couch with the glow of the TV illuminating his limp body. I didn't bother turning it off because, knowing him, the moment I did he'd wake up and say, "I was watching that!". Plus, it made it easier for me to slip out of the house.

I slipped the granola bar in my pocket, sipping at the water as I walked to the park. I refused to even think about Skipping at that moment. My head was still pulsating and my dreams didn't exactly help me feel well-rested. The Travelers could track me through my Rips too. That was another reason, no Skipping meant no tracking. However, now they knew where I lived so, did it even matter?

As I stepped onto the park lawn I noticed I was the first one here. The playground was lit up by a few LED light poles and I reminisced about my time at this park with Elijah growing up. Our neighborhood was fairly new when we were kids and by the time I was six they had finished putting the playground in the park. The many after-school adventures, weekend barbecues, and birthday parties we had there flooded back to me. Seeing it now, underneath the white light surrounded by darkness, had me wishing the light would transport me back to simpler times. I know I should be grateful for my gift, but why couldn't I have gotten the ability to rewind time like in that one video game. Then again, I'm not sure messing with time is ever the answer. It only ever makes things worse, according to all the stories about time travel. I wondered if Morrick took them into account, before building his "time machine".

I stuck the water bottle into my jacket pocket and went straight for the swing set, sitting myself on the closest swing. I grabbed onto the cold metal chains wrapped in cracking safety plastic and began to gently kick my legs. Elijah strode out of the darkness as I swayed back and forth.

"Hey. How're you feeling?" He asked, joining me on the adjacent swing.

"Better than before, but I still have a headache and my dreams didn't help."

"Yeah, I can only imagine what kind of dreams you must be having after everything that's happened." Elijah said earnestly, as he began to kick his legs and go into a full swinging motion. "I took a quick power nap, but I had a hard time relaxing until I knew you were rested. I ended up playing video games for a few hours."

"Liv paid me a visit." I meant to build up to it, but my mouth had other plans.

Elijah planted his feet in the dirt and wood chips bringing him and his swing to a full stop.

"She did? How'd she even find you?"

"People like her, like me, we're able to track each other's Rips when we Skip. I'm not very good at that yet, but she is and she was in my room when I got there."

"Okay. So what did she want?" He leaned in closer.

"You were right. They can't be trusted. Well, at least Liv can't. She was the one who stole the alchemy book. Apparently, Morrick knew all along that I took it, but he wanted me to have it. She gave it back to me, but was angry that we told Lauren and Brian about the Travelers and Morrick," I explained and touched my neck where Liv pressed her knife. "She threatened me at knife point, Eli. I was so exhausted by the time she left that I ended up crying myself to sleep." Recalling that moment made my heart sink and made my throat dry, but my eyes produced no tears. They were numb. I wouldn't let the likes of Liv cause me to hurt like that ever again. I stopped my swing and took another sip from my water bottle.

"Jesus! Are you serious?" Elijah stood up from his seat and began pacing. I reached into my pocket and opened the wrapping to my granola bar. "What the hell is her problem? I wish she would try that with me. Oh, if I were there you better believe she would have hit the ground." Elijah spouted angrily as he paced back and forth from the swing set to the jungle gym. I started munching on my snack which stopped Elijah in his tracks. He judged me with his eyes.

"What? I'm hungry." I said, my mouth full of granola. "Want some water?" I pulled out the bottle from my jacket again and lifted it toward him. He grabbed it without saying a word and took a big gulp.

"You know what? Fuck 'em. They don't want us talking about them or their freaky scientist leader? Fine, but we do whatever the hell we want with your ability." Elijah grabbed onto my shoulders and made me stand up. "If Liv wants to track us then let's really give her something to track."

"What're you planning?" I chuckled.

"This. Starting tomorrow, after school, we grab Lauren and Brian and we go wherever we want to go. We are gonna have so much fun that it will make that psycho furious with jealousy." Elijah plotted, keeping his eyes on mine. I couldn't help but smile. I knew this was just his way of taking my mind off things so I could relax. I appreciated him for it, even if it was a tad passive aggressive.

We hugged for a long time. I put my ear up to his chest, listening to his heart, and feeling his body heat. "I wish you could sleep next to me tonight." I sighed.

"I can." He responded, rubbing my back.

"How? My Mom usually opens my bedroom door and wakes me up."

"Easy. Set an alarm so we wake up before your parents. Plus, I know you have a lock on your door. Use it." Elijah winked and wore a grin that made me melt back into his arms.

As I scarfed down the rest of my snack, we made our way back to my house, passing my still-snoring father, and safely locking ourselves in my bedroom. We both began taking off our shoes, and the moment my second shoe hit the floor, Elijah grabbed my face and started making out with me. His breath was minty and his lips tasted like vanilla. I smiled inside, at the thought that he probably planned to be back here with me tonight all along. I wanted that too. I wanted him.

As clothes flew to the floor, we indulged each other. It was only the fourth time we had sex, and we were much quieter this time for obvious reasons, but everything about it was sweeter. It was as if we learned to lean into the warmth of it all, and to savor every touch. Elijah was right, he did help me relax. We finished in unison, kissed gently, and cuddled underneath my blankets as sleep stole us away.

We were startled awake by a knocking on my bedroom door and someone struggling to turn the knob. Through glossy eyes, my vision darted to Elijah. "Get under the bed." I whispered sharply.

"Oh shit!" Elijah rolled as swiftly and quietly as he could off the side of the bed and crawled his naked body underneath.

"Vale! Are you awake? Why is your door locked? You know the rule, young man." Mom called out through the door.

"Sorry Mom! I must have locked it by accident when I went to bed." I hopped out of bed as fast as possible, still completely naked, but managed to grab a towel hanging on a hook on my bedroom door and wrapped it around my waist. I twisted the lock back and cracked open the door to my Mother glaring back at me, already completely dressed and ready for her day. "What's up?" I said awkwardly.

"*What's up* is it's time for church. Hurry and get ready. We have to leave in ten minutes."

"I'm actually not feeling all that well. I think I'm still tired from the trip. Can I please stay home today?" I begged through the space in the door frame.

"Alright. That's fine, sweetie, but make sure to watch the sermon online later." She ordered and sauntered back down the hall. "Oh by the way," She popped up again just as I was closing my bedroom door. "The car is on the fritz. Did anything happen on back when you and Elijah went to the beach?"

"No?" I lied.

"Huh. Okay. Well your father is taking it to the mechanic for me this week anyway. Hopefully they'll figure out what's wrong. Anyways, sleep well, honey." Mom said sweetly and just as I was closing the door again she popped up a third time. "Oh! Speaking of Eli..."

"W-what about him?" I said, attempting to block more of her view of the inside of my room.

"Let him know we would love to have him and Lauren over for game night sometime. You never have friends over anymore, Vale." Mom complained and I felt like my eyes were going to burst out of my skull. *Maybe they won't come over, because ever since Eli came out, you and Dad had a fit and won't let us have overnights anymore?* I thought.

"Cool! I'll let them know. Have a good day, Mom. Love you." I said rapidly, coming out of my bedroom, closing the door behind me, and kissing her on the cheek. I slipped into the bathroom and closed the door as she echoed back my words. I waited a few seconds for her footsteps to recede down the hall and descend the stairs, before slipping back across the hall into my room where a naked Elijah still hid under my bed.

"Coast is clear, Eli."

"Okay, that was insane. I guess we forgot to set the alarm." Elijah said, already gathering his clothes from the floor.

"You think?" I scoffed. "Let's hurry up and get dressed so I can Skip you home."

"Or you can grab your things and just shower at my place. My Dad doesn't usually check on me and he's already left for his Sunday errands by now." He suggested as he started to unwrap my towel from my waist.

"Elijah, you are a bundle of horniness and risky business." I swatted his hand away, grinning at his ridiculous demeanor.

"Thanks for the compliment, handsome." Elijah flirted and continued to stare at me as if waiting for me to be convinced. "We can use the master shower."

"Alright, let's go." I relented. Before I could second guess it, we were showering in the master bathroom of Elijah's house, indulging in each other for a fifth time.

27 DISTANCE

The rest of the day was a big blur. Maybe it was exhaustion or maybe it was almost getting caught by my mom. My mind still went back to my conversation with Liv. Was I still welcome at the Manor? Liv wasn't the one in charge, right? And no way would Morrick order her to threaten me...would he? I knew Morrick was secretive of his work, but that seemed like a stretch. I didn't know what to believe. I barely knew the Travelers. These trailing thoughts carried onto the next day when school was back in session. I hated Mondays.

"Are you still with us, Vale?" Lauren asked, with Elijah and Brian looking back at me, worry spread across their faces. The four of us were sitting at one of the cafeteria tables during a short break between second and third period.

"Sorry. I must be really tired from the weekend. I think I should take a break from Skipping for a bit. It's starting to affect me." I rubbed my eyes.

"And the nosebleeds can't be good either." Elijah added.

"Nosebleeds? Shouldn't you go to the hospital then?" Lauren suggested.

"And tell them what? 'Excuse me Doctor, but I've been teleporting too much and my brain might be bleeding.' Something like that?" I chastised.

"Jeez, my bad, Vale. You don't have to be a dick." Lauren defended.

"No, of course not. I'm only bleeding from my nose every time I Skip too much, I just got threatened at knife point last night—"

"Wait, what?" Lauren interrupted, but I kept going.

"And I'm keeping two of the biggest secrets in my entire life from my parents." I look at Elijah who matches my glance. " Make that three."

"Look, Vale, I'm sorry I didn't mean to—"

"No, you didn't, but don't worry about it. I gotta...get to class." I got up before Lauren could finish her thoughts, and stormed off from the three of them. I was a little surprised when Elijah didn't run after me. I guess he knew when I needed my space. Another bad thing to add on top of all this, I think my grades were slipping. I clearly haven't been focused this whole semester and if I didn't do something it might come back to bite me.

I continued my day in solitude and silence. None of the group talked to me, nor did they get near me. They gave me my space. I was grateful, but I also had a war brewing inside me. I didn't want to punish my friends for simply caring or misspeaking. It wasn't fair to them when none of this is their fault. This all was becoming too much and I had a gut-wrenching feeling that the worst had yet to come. Even when school ended for the day I was left alone on my walk home. I was tempted to Skip, because of the convenience, but held back as it could hurt me worse than before.

When I arrived home, I was still alone. I decided to relax with some video games in my room for the rest of the day and night.

My mom called me down for dinner, but I convinced her to let me eat in my room. I really didn't feel like socializing at all. Holding myself captive with my thoughts, or lack thereof, sounded perfect. Video games offered the perfect escape. I couldn't even get myself to write. That would require me to reflect on my thoughts and emotions which I had no desire to let go of.

It was beginning to get late and my eyelids felt heavy. I only received one text from Elijah, but I didn't respond. He was checking on me and reminding me that Lauren was sorry about what she said today. The thing is, I wasn't mad at Lauren. Maybe I was mad at that moment in the cafeteria, but that anger quickly dissipated. I was confused and overcome by everything. I wanted things to be okay again. I wanted my parents to know it all and immediately be alright with everything, but I knew that was never going to happen.

There was a rumble and crack to the right of me. I was sitting on my bed, Playstation controller in my hand. I looked over, and to my surprise, it was Ember. She was dressed more casually then I when I last saw her, and wore a calm smile on her lips. Her eyes glowed a deep emerald in the low lamp light of my room.

"Hey there, Vale."

"Ember? What are you doing here? How'd you even find me?" I knew the answer as soon as I asked it. Liv told her, but it made no sense why Ember was here. We barely spoke when Elijah and I were at the manor last. I knew next to nothing about her. I glanced at her hands and saw she was holding a small plastic container.

"I spoke with Liv and she told me what transpired between you two. She would never apologize. Too prideful, you see. I know you must be upset—"

"Upset? Upset! Wow…You think?" I abruptly stood to my feet, hitting the pause button on my controller, and lobbed it onto my bed. "She broke into my room, put a knife to my throat, and called me and Eli a pretty homophobic slur! Upset? No, I'm fucking *pissed*." I yelled as quietly as I could to not alert my parents. Ember did not even wince or shy away. She was perfectly calm.

"You have every right to be. Liv can be a handful, but you must understand. She is coming from a place of deep pain. You know she is one of the four that live with Morrick, right?" Ember sat on the window seat behind her, putting the plastic container on her lap. "Well that is, because she was kicked out of her family's house."

"Tch, I can see why. She seems like a serious trouble maker." I scoffed.

"Don't judge a book by its cover, Vale. That is not the reason. She was a good child to her parents. Exceptional grades, an avid church attender, and she was going to college for advanced bio mechanics. She wanted to be a scientist that helped to cure lifelong ailments, birth defects, and diseases. Then her parents found out she was dating a girl." Ember spoke with compassion and empathy, but I sensed a tinge of pain in her words.

"So Liv is…"

"Like you. She still has a hard time coming to terms with it, but we're working through it together. Her ability manifested itself when she was all alone, and she was the first that Morrick found. He introduced her to his work and she became enthralled with it immediately. That's how Morrick tells the story, anyway. I came along much later and we have been quite fond of each other since." Ember's dark hair covered most of her face as she gazed at the floor, blushing brightly.

"You mean you and Liv—"

"Are a couple? Yes. Although, I still live at home in India with my family. They have no idea that I'm pansexual, and I may never tell them. These days it is better for a woman to be perceived as a loner, than it is for them to be seen as queer. At least that's how it is in my country. You're lucky you live in a place that is ready to accept you." Ember said, earnestly.

"Well it's not all rainbows and pride parades over here. My parents don't know either, and I don't think they would accept it. We're a Christian household." I explained and Ember gave me a look of understanding.

"Hm, why is it that heterosexual religious people preach love, but practice ignorance and hatred? All because some wealthy pastor or robed priest stands on a stage and says so? It's ridiculous," Ember admitted, and this was the first time I had seen her express any amount of annoyance.

"You could say that again!" I laughed. There was a moment of quiet between us when we just stared at each other, thankful for our mutual experiences.

"Ah, right. Here. I made you some homemade naan. I'm sorry for Liv's actions toward you. We all really want you to visit the Manor again. We have so much to teach you and I'm sure you could teach us a few things as well." Ember handed me the container and it was still warm.

"Thank you. I appreciate the gesture." I looked around my room, searching for something when my eyes landed on the alchemy book sitting on my desk. "Does Morrick's place have a guest room?"

"Oh yes! Things are always changing and expanding there. I'm sure there is more than one." What did she mean? Is

Morrick able to use alchemy on the whole house? This I had to see.

"Okay. I'll come stay with you all for a few days. Starting tonight. Let me just get my things." I decided, reaching under my bed for a duffle bag and placing it on the foot.

"Oh, so suddenly?" Ember asked.

"Why not? No time like the present. Plus, I have a lot of questions and I need some space from *all this*." I gestured my hand at everything around me, but what I meant was my life here in Fresno. I needed to get away from my parents, school, this town, my friends, and even Elijah. I needed a chance to breathe and figure this out on my own. I didn't care if Elijah would be mad at me for going back to the Manor. These were my people and my only connection to knowledge about my ability. Not to mention the insane magical science of Alchemy. It's as if I stepped out of my boring, mundane life as a teenager into a fantastical YA novel full of wonder and adventure. Now if only a dragon would show up, it would be perfect.

It didn't take me long to gather my belongings and Ember politely waited for me. I made sure to pack the alchemy book and my laptop. I picked up my phone from my side table, but then set it back down. I didn't need my phone. I wanted to disconnect completely. Who cared about the ramifications? I would only be gone a few days and then I'd be back. With my duffle bag zipped up and thrown over my shoulder, I glanced back at my room. I breathed in the warm solitude of my bedroom. My eyes traced the movie posters on my walls and the outline of all my furniture.

"You ready?" Ember asked.

"I think so. Oh wait, one more thing." I remembered that I should at least set up an alibi so that my parents don't freak out and order a search party for me. I quickly grabbed my phone again and texted my mom and dad saying that I was going to be staying at Lauren's house in the guest room for a few days working on projects and getting a head start on studying for finals. I then texted Lauren and asked her to lie for me if my parents asked about me. I made sure to mention that I was not mad at her and that I couldn't tell her where I was going, but I was safe and needed some time to myself. I didn't wait for a reply from either recipient. Instead I tossed my phone inside my side table drawer and joined Ember again. I nodded, she nodded back, and we clasped hands as we Skipped away through the ether, back to Langdorf Manor.

Ember's Rip opened before us and the foyer of Morrick's mansion began to take shape around us. The Rip sealed and we stood on the polished marble floors once again. It felt bigger, as if new rooms and hallways had generated themselves and were inviting me to explore them. The house had a strange air about it as if it were breathing, alive. I couldn't help but feel my stomach churn and goosebumps form on my arms. I could sense eyes watching me, and every nervous twitch I had.

"Let's get you set up in a guest room first. I'm sure Morrick already knows you are here." Ember started leading me down a hallway on the left side of the main staircase. That definitely wasn't there last time and as I followed her I noticed that there were several new doors. The hallway went on for a few yards and then turned right into another hallway of doors. Each door had a strange symbol on them that resembled a sideways Omega from the Greek alphabet.

"What's that symbol? I think I recognize it." I asked.

"Ah, yes. You should. It is technically the marking for 'Life' if it is pointing down or 'Death' if it is pointing up, but Morrick had the doors emblazoned with the symbol sideways meaning, 'Rest'." Ember explained, happily.

"Because the middle point between Life and Death is Sleep." I said, matter-of-factly.

"Precisely. You catch on quick, Vale." Ember complimented and opened the door in front of us. A beautiful, ornate suite beckoned. The bed was dressed in a plush comforter and silk sheets. The bed frame was fitted with a canopy of black mesh curtains tied to each corner post. The room had its own bathroom, mini kitchen, and office area. Everything was either white as pearl or black as onyx with marble counters and tiling being the main theme. "All the rooms look the same, and match the decor of the rest of the house. Morrick is a genius, but his creativity is lacking at times." Ember spoke honestly as she scanned the room with me.

"This will work." I grinned at the outstanding quarters I'd be residing in for the next few days.

"That's great to hear, Vale. You are family now. You share our ability and we must treat you as such. Again, I am sorry for any trouble Liv caused you."

"Thank you. That means a lot." I sat down on the love seat in front of the bed, setting my duffle bag on the ground. "I just want to know why this is happening to me. I feel so lost and scared. I think I have been actively avoiding those feelings, because I have no idea who or *what* I am anymore." My thoughts came pouring out like a busted water line. Ember said nothing at first, then sat next to me, grabbing my right hand in hers.

"You are you. You are still human, only...moreso. You don't need to be afraid. We've all been there and you'll get through it." Ember's hands were warm and soft with each gentle touch.

She caressed my skin to narrate her point that I was still flesh and bone. I was still Vale.

"Right. I understand. Thank you, Ember."

"Always." Ember smiled and started toward the door.

"Oh, about Morrick..." My mind went back to the last time I was here.

"What about him?"

"He told me he is building a time machine of some kind? Why?"

"Hm..." Ember's face stayed flat and calm. "Who can say? He hasn't bothered to tell us *why* he is building it, only that he must achieve it. But, 'Time Travel'?" She let out a small chuckle. "Skipping, as you call it, can't compare." And with that she made her leave, shutting the door behind her.

I found that odd, because someone as smart as Morrick must have a reason for his hard work, his research, and his sleepless nights. Unless, they were hiding something. It was suspicious and I couldn't get Elijah's warnings out of my head. It was then that I remembered I brought some sharpies with me. I quickly unzipped my duffle bag, flipped through the alchemy book to a page about protection symbols, grasped a sharpie, and began tracing the alchemical mark for protection level three on the back of the door. I pressed the cap back on the sharpie and stepped back to look at the symbol as a whole.

Just in case, I thought.

22 SLÁINTE

Silence smothered my room. The kind of silence where you could hear your own heart beat. I didn't bother unpacking anything in case I needed to leave in a hurry. I left my lavish quarters and walked the hall, tracing my finger against the cold, hard walls. I stumbled upon the foyer again and made my way up a familiar set of stairs. Still no one in sight. *What time was it anyway? I was in Maryland, right?* Before I left it was close to midnight, but I wasn't tired. I felt like a ghost haunting the halls of the manor, the chains of my troubles dragging and clattering behind.

That is, until I heard a rumbling and muffled voices talking through the walls. I reached the door to the entertainment center. The sounds were coming from within. I slowly pushed the door open and spied inside. Sitting on a couch in front of a massive projector screen were Lucien, Esteban, and Felix. The others were nowhere around. Lucien and Felix's eyes darted toward me as the light from the hallway seeped into the darkness. Lucien smirked and waved me in as Felix wore a rough, but emotionless expression. Esteban didn't budge from looking at the screen while he munched on handfuls of popcorn.

I stepped in and gently closed the door behind me. Lucien

had already grabbed me a chair by the time I reached them. "Hey!" I whispered.

"Hey! What brings you here, bud?" Lucien asked, whispering below the volume of the movie.

"Ember brought me. She apologized for Liv."

"Ah, makes sense. I don't know what she did, but it must have been bad if Ember came to see you." Lucien understood immediately. It must not have been the first time Liv acted violently.

"Right, but I needed some time away from my home life. It's...a lot right now."

"I getcha, bro. No worries. Stay here as long as you want." Lucien's attitude towards me felt warmer than before, kinder. Maybe he was always kind and I was just a stranger until now.

"What are you guys watching?"

"Oh, some movie called 'Timeline'. We aren't that far into it."

I gazed up at the movie being projected. A group of scientists were all dressed in medieval attire and standing in a circle inside some sort of glass container. They all screamed and were transported to a different time in a forest somewhere. I let myself relax into the chair and enjoyed the movie with my Comrades-In-Skipping. For those two hours I didn't even think of Elijah, Lauren, or my parents. I learned that Lucien is squeamish with blood, Felix has an infectious laugh, and Esteban is seriously knowledgeable about actors, directors, and writers in the movie industry. This is what I wanted—to learn more and grow closer to those with my same ability. Now I had that chance.

After the credits rolled, we all discussed our thoughts on the movie. All four of us seemed to like it to varying degrees and drew comparisons to the work Morrick was doing, "down in his dungeon" as Felix put it. That's when Lucien invited me to go hiking with them in the morning. We were surrounded by forest with plenty of trails and mountain peaks, so it made sense. Felix seemed delighted when I agreed to join them, but I could hardly tell since he didn't say much. Esteban, on the other hand, had no interest in hiking, but was giving me an earful of what movies he wanted to introduce me to. The names were a mix of Spanish cinema and major American titles. His enthusiasm caused me to smile a lot more than I had in the past twenty four hours, and I already felt like part of their family.

We all retired back to our rooms. That night I had a another strange dream. I was in a room with several doors and they all looked exactly the same. Screams and calls for help reached my ears from my loved ones all behind different doors. I followed Elijah's voice through one door, but it transported me into an identical room. Or was it the same room? The screams sounded like Lauren, and I followed them as I did before. The same thing happened, I appeared back in the room of doors. Then my parents called for me, Brian, all the Travelers, and finally Morrick. The result was always the same, but when I opened the door to Morrick's voice something was different. Staring into the darkness beyond that doorway brought me feelings of unease and dread. The darkness seemed to solidify and morph into a thick sludge-like substance that rippled just inside the door, licking the sides of the frame.

Suddenly, something started to emerge from the sludge. First fingers, then a hand, and an a rm. All were pale, skin wrinkled, and decaying. The flesh was practically falling off the bones. The head of this deformed thing started to emerge from the black ooze. Strands of hair were knotted to crumbling skin, and bone was exposed where the scalp should be. My stomach flipped inside me and my heart nearly leapt out of my chest. The figure turned as if looking my way. The figure was me.

"Vaaaaaaaalllllle..."My crumpled doppelganger body limped toward me, speaking with Morrick's voice. I was frozen in fear and could not move. Its eyes glowed a haunting blue and they were void of any life or sentience. It lunged at me. My body hit the floor.

I awoke in a tangled mess of blankets, my shirt and boxers twisted about and soaked in sweat. I was laid out on the floor next to my temporary bed. I couldn't tell what time it was, since the room had no windows. I sighed and lifted myself off the ground, pulling the sheets off of me. I pulled out my laptop, turned it on, and checked the time. It was nearly 6 a.m. I recalled that Lucien and Felix wanted to leave around seven. Even though I knew I would get sweaty again on the hike I had to wake myself up with some hot water and get this nightmare sweat off of me. *What the heck was that dream anyway?* I thought. It felt disturbingly real, but as for its meaning, I couldn't make heads or tails of it. It was probably just stress and lack of decent sleep.

After scrubbing myself clean, I threw on some fresh clothes and strapped on my hiking boots. Just as I pulled my arms through my light jacket and zipped it up there was a knock on my door. I opened it to Felix and Lucien dressed in similar attire to me, but each was carrying a duffle bag. "Hey guys. I just finished getting ready. Should one water bottle be enough for the hike?" I asked, lifting my blue thermos full of water to them. Felix held back a snicker and Lucien wore a coy smile.

"Um, sure Vale. Let's get going. The sun is coming up fast."

Lucien said and started down the hallway. I followed them out and made sure the door to my room was shut tight. I heard a hum of energy rush over the other side of the door. *That must be the protective rune activating.* I thought. Good to know my things wouldn't be touched while I was gone. Especially the Alchemy book. I know Morrick said I could study it, but I still don't trust Liv after the shit she pulled on me. I didn't want her or anyone else touching my belongings or worse, planting a trap for me when I returned. That's when I felt something in the back pocket of my jeans. I pulled it out and instantly was confronted with conflicting emotions. It was the bracelet from Hawaii that Liv gave me on my first visit to the Manor. I knew she wasn't all bad. Ember made that clear, but was it my responsibility to forgive her? Did she deserve a second chance from me? I clicked the bracelet back onto my left wrist as those moral conundrums wrestled in my mind.

As the three of us reached the front doors, there was a large silver bowl sitting atop a waist high marble pillar. It was full of protein bars, granola, and other assorted snacks. I made sure to snatch a few bars before we took our leave. Upon entering the outdoors I beheld the exterior grounds of the enormous manor for the first time. It was just as impressive, if not as ominous, on the outside. Tall white pillars held up the structure all around the perimeter of the house, which led to stone steps. On either side of the stairs were stone statues in the shape of gryphons; the mythical, predatory creatures were rearing up on their hind legs, wings spread out to create an archway toward the entrance, and their jaws agape in a mighty roar. Past the statues was a circular gravel driveway with a massive white fountain in the center. Shimmering like fresh ocean pearls, the structure of the fountain looked immediately familiar, yet different in some ways. A stone statue of a woman stood in the center of the top tier of the fountain, while several stone children stood in a circle on the bottom tier. Water went up to their thighs and water trickled out of spouts in their eyes to make it look like they were crying. The statue of the woman had her hands cupped and raised toward her face, water trickled from her hands and down her body. It was similar to the painting inside the manor, but this sight was not as pleasant. It felt darker, more sinister.

"Are you going to sight-see some more or can we get going?" Felix suddenly spoke with a thick Scottish accent that both startled me and felt threatening.

"Right. Sorry. This way?" I pointed in the direction Lucien was already heading and awkwardly followed.

We reached the edge of the property and went several more yards into the woods until Felix and Lucien stopped. "You ready?" Lucien asked Felix. Felix nodded and stuck out his hand to me.

"Huh? Wait, I thought we were going on a hike." Anxiety began to fill my body and my voice quivered.

"Oh we are. 'Going on a hike' is code." Lucien smirked.

"Code...for what?"

"Just grab hold. We don't have time for this. You came here to learn more about us, right? This is something we regularly have to do." Felix said, more annoyed and rough than before, which I didn't believe was possible.

"At least, tell me what's in the bags." I gestured to Lucien's bag hanging from his right shoulder.

They both collectively sighed, slammed their bags on the ground, and unzipped them. "Black spray paint. Swiss Army knife. Bobby pins. Bolt cutters. Lighter. Flashlight. Rope.

Magnets. Duct tape. Blueprints. Chocolate bars. There. Happy?" They both simultaneously were speaking back and forth as they held up each item to show me.

"What the hell do you need all that for?" I asked, shocked and appalled.

"Time's up. No more questions." Lucien said, slinging his duffle bag back over his shoulder, and grabbing onto me and Felix. Before I could resist, we vanished and reappeared in darkness, the suction from Lu's Rip nearly dragging me off my feet and landing me on my rear. It was cold and the thick smell of polished metal surrounded us. There was a click and a bright light nearly blinded me.

"Ah! Thanks for the warning." I complained, blinking rapidly to regain my sight. Lucien held a flashlight in his hand and pointed it to the ground.

"Shush, quick put this on." Lucien shoved a piece of fabric into my hands. It felt like a ski mask. I wanted to ask about it, but that didn't seem like the best option at the moment. Instead I pulled the mask over my head. I heard a hiss and then the smell of paint. That's when overhead lights flickered on. Glaring fluorescent panels shined down on us and illuminated the whole room. We were inside a bank vault. Tons of private boxes and several pallets of fresh, new dollar bills filled the room. Felix had already covered the cameras and sensors with black paint.

"We're robbing a bank?!" I yelled, and Lucien covered my mouth as they both shushed me again. I tried to get more words out, but they were muffled by Lucien's firm grip.

"Listen. I'm going to uncover your mouth, but you gotta be quiet. I'll explain. We cool?" Lucien looked at me for reassurance and I nodded. He glanced at Felix who also nodded and Lucien released me. "Yes, we are robbing a bank, but we aren't stealing from just anyone's aunt, uncle, or grandma. We are stealing from the billionaires who profit off the unfortunate, and who also call Morrick crazy. This is the bank where all the business people and high profile scientists store their fortunes or most prized possessions." Lucien explained as eloquently as he could in a hushed tone.

"Seriously?" I asked. They both nodded. I thought about it for a moment, glancing around the room until my eyes were pulled back to the stacks of money. My family could be set for life. Mom and dad seemed okay financially as far as they led me to believe, but we could be better than okay. I could afford to live on my own as soon as I graduate. I might not ever have to come out to my parents, or explain any of this to them. It could come from an anonymous "friend" who just wants to see our family flourish. Surely they wouldn't care where it came from once they saw how much it was? "Alright, I'm in, but I get a generous cut for me and my family. Enough to set us up for a long time if not for life." I pointed at them with more assertiveness then I realized I could muster.

"Deal. There are billions of dollars stashed here. Plenty of treasure for everyone." Felix said and Lucien agreed with a huff. With that we started to collect the money first. Lucien spread his hands across the pallets of cash, closed his eyes, and a small shock wave rattled the inside of the vault. Lucien and all the money was gone. All that was left were particles of dust and wood. Felix was already picking locks on the personal safes, and he seemed to be a pro at it. Within ten minutes he had half the room of personal safes open and ready for transferring. Lucien was back as quickly as he left.

"Where'd you drop the money?" I asked.

"Morrick's Vault beneath the Manor." Lucien shrugged.

"Why am I not surprised? Where in the world are we anyway?" I smiled, shaking my head.

"Switzerland." Felix said matter-of-factly.

Lucien gave a tight smile at my realizations, and began emptying the safes Felix had already opened. As we were finishing up a thought came into my head. "Hey, aren't you guys afraid of silent alarms or any trace being left behind? Also, isn't it the middle of the day here? We will definitely be spotted."

They exchanged a look again that only they understood. "Easy. What do you think the magnets are for?" Lucien asked rhetorically. "Stay on my heels." Lucien said and Skipped again. I followed him through his Rip.

We resurfaced inside a grand foyer bathed in early afternoon light. White stone and gold trim covered every surface and shone with decadence. Polished, bullet proof glass ran the length of the sealed teller desks. Strangely, the bank was completely empty, but sunlight poured through the windows of the main hall. Lucien put his finger up to his lips and pointed around the corner. I peeked and just on the other side was a security room. A lone security guard sat surrounded by camera monitors and sensor lights. He was watching something on his phone and didn't seem to notice the vault cameras were blacked out.

Lucien gave a soft whistle that echoed through the bank. The security guard sat up in his chair. Lucien lifted a chocolate bar out of his jacket pocket and waved it in my face before tossing it down the hall making it hit a far office window. The guard stood up and rushed out the doorway and into the hall. As he went in the opposite direction Lucien gestured for us to make our move. As soon as we got into the security room I gently shut the door behind us. Lucien shoved his hands into his duffle bag, bringing out four large magnets with handles. He handed two to me and began pressing his magnets on every computer and monitor. I hesitated a moment, but then followed his lead. Static overtook the monitors, sparks popped from electrical components, and outlets until the whole room went dark, filled with smoke, and the smell of burning plastic invaded my nostrils.

Lucien wasted no time in grabbing me and Skipping us back to the main vault. "That should do it. We were never here. It will be as if ghosts robbed them."

"Braw!" Felix responded in his native tongue.

My adrenaline was at its peak and I was in disbelief of what was happening. All I knew was that I was having the time of my life. Once all the safes were empty and their contents stuffed into duffle bags we gave the room one more look-over with pride in our work. Clunks and clicks of gears shifting shuddered throughout the main vault door. The metal bars that formed a circle began to turn and just as the door started to swing open, we were gone without a single trace.

23 WITHOUT A TRACE

The three of us reappeared in the Maryland forests. Only a half hour had passed since we left, but my body shook with adrenaline and my legs felt like noodles. Lucien and Felix patted me on the back as they walked back toward the manor. "Good job, Scrub. You did great." Lucien complimented, giving me a thumbs up as his defined muscles flexed in the morning shimmer.

"But I still don't understand how the only person there was a security guard." I admitted.

"You don't think we do our research on these places before we hit them? We did plenty of surveillance last week and learned that the bank staff like to take long lunch breaks together. It was almost too easy. That's what happens when people get too comfortable in their safety. They don't see the holes in their defenses." Lucien smiled wide and returned to the manor on foot. I followed slowly, taking in the scent of pine and the chirps of sparrows. The gentle caress of the wind brushed against my sweat-coated arms and the sunlight leaked through the canopy dancing around us in the morning haze. I understood how people get lost in the woods, everything looked eerily similar.

As I approached the fountain in front of the manor, there

stood a tall figure with a cane staring down at the rippling water. "Ah, Vale. Welcome back." Morrick spotted me and gestured to stand with him.

"Hello Dr. Langdorf." I said.

"Oh please, my boy. Just Morrick is fine. You are part of the family now, after all."

"Right. Sorry." I stared down at the water with Morrick and kept quiet.

"I imagine the accommodations are to your liking?" He asked.

"Oh the room? Yes Sir! It's incredible."

"Something wrong, Son?" Morrick asked and I was uncertain what he meant, but perhaps he sensed something in my tone. I did have a lot weighing on my shoulders, but I didn't want to give it any attention. That's why I was here in the first place.

"It's just...my home life and school aren't going well and I imagine it will all still be there when I get back, but I had to get away, to think."

"One can rarely run from their problems. We must face them head on, but taking a moment to reflect on ourselves can be beneficial in those times." Morrick paused and looked down at something in his hand. "Here. I was out here to make a wish in the fountain, but something tells me you need it more than I do." He handed me a shiny, smooth penny.

"Scientists believe in wishing now?" I jested.

"*Intent* is ninety percent the causality in the art of Alchemy, and through that belief it can be quantified. I won't bore you with the complexities, but yes. Wishing is most certainly within the realm of possibilities." Morrick said studiously and gently. I took the penny from his hand and gazed down at it before closing my eyes and flipping it into the fountain. "What did you wish for?"

"Hey, you know the rule."

"Oh yes, I know, but you can't blame an old man's curiosity." Morrick chuckled. I met his goggled eyes and I wondered greatly if he really could see me, but it was nonsense. I saw his eyes before. He was clearly blind.

"Morrick. I need to ask…"

"Yes, my boy? Go on."

"You *are* blind, right? I just wonder how you are able to continue your work. I didn't see any braille in your work space, so…" I left the words hanging in the air as birds chirped and cawed overhead.

Morrick let out a boisterous laugh that made him hold his stomach with his free arm. It trailed off into an almost sickly cough. He whipped out a handkerchief from his jacket pocket and coughed into it. "Oh Vale, you slay me! I do suppose it is my fault for not explaining, but I didn't want to overwhelm you. These goggles are not *just* for show. I infused them with Alchemy. They work perfectly as a pair of natural eyes, if not better. Of course, the moment I take them off the world goes dark. It isn't a permanent solution, but I am working toward one and feel I am very close."

I was so in awe at his explanation that I hardly saw someone shouting at me from the front of the manor. "You right, foul git!" Liv shrieked at me holding an ice pack to her head as Ember and Eliza followed close behind.

"Now, Liv! What is the meaning of this?" Morrick asked authoritatively.

"Not now old man!" Liv barked back at Morrick. "This royal ass put a ward up in his room and it shot me back out of my Rip when I tried to Skip in!" She pointed at me furiously.

"Why were you trying to get into my room anyway? That's exactly why I put it up. I didn't want you touching my shit!" I spat back with all the fury she dished out.

"Well excuse me for trying to leave you this apology letter! Fuck me, right?" Liv shoved a folded up sheet of paper at me. I slowly grabbed it out of her firm grip, unfolded it, and started to read. The apology was sincere enough coming from Liv. She certainly had a lot of pride, but it was the absolute best I was going to get from her.

"Now stop this right now, you two. Vale, you got an apology. Liv, maybe you should have waited to give it to him in person." Ember stepped in to be the voice of reason.

"Exactly. If you'd threatened me the way you did Vale, I'd have done the same. You can't blame him for being cautious." Eliza added. Liv was silent. Her face softened and a calm came over her. Suddenly the tension dissipated.

"That bracelet. You kept it?" Liv said, staring at my wrist. I looked down at it.

"Yeah. It was a thoughtful gift. I wasn't going to simply toss it just because the person who gave it to me was acting like a psycho."

There was an awkward silence that was only filled by wind and wildlife. "Well!" Morrick clapped his hands together. "Who wants some brunch?" He vanished with a zip.

Eliza and Ember both shuffled back toward the manor entrance while Liv and I stood in place. I stuck the letter in my pocket and sighed. "Friends?"

"Yeah, okay." Liv pulled the ice pack from her head and stuck out her hand. I shook it firmly and a rare grin flashed across her face. "God, I need a mimosa, like, yesterday!" Liv said while turning back toward the manor. I gave the fountain one more glance before finally joining my kin inside.

Brunch was more than I imagined. Piles of sausages, bacon, vegetarian omelet casserole, toast, tall stacks of pancakes, coffee, and of course, endless m imosas. Not everyone was seated with us, but I imagine some of them had schedules of their own and things to do. It was rather courteous and generous of Morrick to give freely of his home and allow freedom to come and go as we please. I was only a few sips into my coffee when Liv slid a mimosa in a tall glass in my direction.

"Oh no thanks, I'm not twenty one yet." I declined.

"Aw, don't be dull, newbie. You're among friends. You can let loose, ya know?" Liv pressured.

"I don't know. I honestly don't drink and—"

"And you look like you need a drink. Listen, I may be an asshole, but I know a closet case when I see one. Plus you and your little boyfriend, Elliot—"

"Elijah."

"Whatever. You two were inseparable when I last saw you. Not to mention you can't be adapting well to your sudden ability. Right?" Liv asked, placing the full mimosa glass directly in front of me.

"Liv, leave the poor boy alone." Eliza interjected.

"Hush up, Steve Erwin." Liv spat back.

"Fuck off! Like you're terribly original." Eliza laughed and shoveled a pile of omelet in her mouth.

"Yeah. Okay." I finally said after a moment, grabbing the glass gently in my hand.

"To successfully maneuver through all our bullshit in life no matter when or where we encounter it!" Liv held up her glass, glancing around the table at the others and then to me. Everyone sipped with her and I followed. The freshness of the orange juice hit me first and then the bubbly texture of the champagne danced across my tongue. It wasn't as bitter as I imagined it would be. Much sweeter and flavorful in fact.

Ember stood to her feet then and lifted her glass.

"To Love and Friendship."

Sip.

Lucien went next.

"To new beginnings out there in the world. No offense, Morrick. I am so grateful for everything you do for us, but we have to move on eventually."

"Of course. I have no expectation that any of you will be living here forever, Lu. Children, no matter how old they may be, eventually grow up and must fly the coop." Morrick reassured Lucien and the toasts continued with Eliza.

"To our wonderful host and the bountiful feasts he delivers!" Eliza said with a mouth full of bacon.

"Careful. There will hardly be any bounty left with the way you eat." Liv chided. Eliza cursed at her again and let fly a sausage which barely missed her face.

Felix stood up quietly, staring into his glass. "To my found family where the broken, the lost, the damaged, the scared, the hungry, the confused, and the curious can call home." Felix sipped and sat back down without another word. Everyone, including myself, was taken aback.

"Damn, Felix. That was profound as hell!" Lucien said. "How is Vale supposed to follow that?"

Felix shrugged and I blushed when suddenly everyone's eyes were on me. Slowly, I stood from my chair and raised my glass. I watched the orange liquid jiggle side to side as I thought about my next words carefully.

"To...finding our purpose in life and no longer being afraid of rejection." Everyone sipped and I sipped with them. I nearly collapsed back into my chair in relief when Morrick dabbed his mouth with his napkin and stood to his feet.

"My children, this has been a delightful meal and I leave you with these words. May your thirst for knowledge never die out and may your hearts hammer with magical intent until the day mother earth calls you back to her embrace." Morrick toasted and drank the small amount of mimosa that was left in his glass. As soon as he set his glass down, he vanished. The others didn't seem phased by Morrick always leaving or appearing so suddenly, but I was always surprised by him. His voice rang with wisdom and he moved with a certainty that I wish I possessed.

I finished eating and stood from the t able. "This was an eventful morning, but I think I will go see Morrick in his lab and then take a nap." I announced as I stretched.

"A nap sounds really nice actually. I might do the same." Ember replied. Her eyes rested on Liv who matched her gaze. Liv nodded and both of them excused themselves from the table.

As the others were finishing up I thought about just Skipping to Morrick's lab. I did feel rested and more energized than yesterday so Skipping shouldn't cause me any issues. "Hey...Lu. How do you all make your Skips so quiet? Mine still sounds like tiny firecrackers going off. Which is better than when I first started. It used to sound like a roll of thunder and a clap of lightning." I explained. Whenever I Skipped and people were around, it caused panic and confusion, but I was always gone before they knew what caused it. Of course, that was speculation.

"Ah, that would have been a good question for Morrick, but since he already excused himself I'll give you the TLDR version. I wouldn't worry too much about the sound that comes from you. It gets quieter the more you open a Rip and travel through. If you are worried about others hearing it, well, let's just say 'Normies' can't hear it for some reason. Morrick theorizes that it's because they don't share our ability." Lucian elaborated eloquently, and nonchalantly.

"How can that be true? Eli and two close friends of mine were able to hear my Skips." I contested.

"Were they standing directly next to you or touching you when you Skipped?"

"Hmm..." I thought back. Back to the beach when I first discovered my ability. I thought back to my conversation with Brian at the campsite, back to me saving Lauren from that cliff. "Come to think of it, yes. They all were." I looked at Lucian intently.

"Makes sense. That's the only way they would be able to hear it. Otherwise, even if they were only ten feet away from you, a Normy wouldn't be able to hear you Skip. See it, no doubt, but the sound would not reach them for a reason that Morrick has yet to fully unravel." Lucian took one last bite of pancake and then took his leave. This time he walked around the table, giving me a short salute, before vanishing into an almost silent Rip.

I closed my eyes and focused. Instantly, I could feel the Rip in space opening for me. It was like opening up a zip lock bag now. When I first traveled with Elijah it was like I was attempting to tear through a wall of rubber. Lucian was right, it was getting easier. I stepped through my Rip with ease and barely a crackle was made as I arrived on the other side in Morrick's lab.

"Ah, Vale. Welcome back." Morrick stated without turning to look up from his work displayed on a large glass monitor. "To what do I owe the pleasure?"

"Well, Sir..." I shuffled nervously. "I thought maybe you'd have some further answers. If I'm being honest, I'm feeling stuck."

"Did you notice that Kaito and Esteban were not at brunch?" Morrick remarked. His disregard of my feelings stung a little, but I humored him.

"Uh, I guess I was wondering why they weren't present, but I saw Esteban yesterday. Maybe he's sleeping in? As for Kaito, he seems to enjoy his privacy. I'm sure he'll pop up soon." I shrugged.

"Hm, perhaps you are correct. Anyway, in regards to what you were saying, I would imagine that feeling is normal at such a ripe age. I hardly remember such times. It was so long ago, but please! Sit, sit! Tell me what ails you, my boy." Morrick, still without looking away from the monitor, pointed to a metal stool next to another massive console.

"Where do I even start? I'm sure it is no surprise for me to tell you that I'm gay. Wow, I haven't said it out loud in a while." I sat on the stool and folded my hands in my lap, looking down at all the blinking lights and symbols on the console. "Then there's my ability, which I'm getting better at, but you have to understand that my parents are very conservative, traditional. When Elijah came out as Bi they banned him from staying the night at our house. I can only imagine how they would react if ever I come out to them." I explained, twiddling my thumbs.

"Calm yourself, Vale." Morrick looked in my direction through another glass monitor with nothing projected on it.

"Breathe and get to the point." That felt a little brash, but I understood he was a busy man.

"The point is, how in the hell am I supposed to explain any of this to my parents? What's more, are things just never going to be the same again? Do I hide, or tell the truth? Run, or stand to face reality?" I blurted it all out like word-vomit. I felt as if my heart was full to bursting and my head was throbbing. "And don't even get me started on the fact that magic is basically real! Like, what the fuck is a seventeen year old supposed to do with that? It's just too much!" My eyes were wet and tears streamed down my face. I covered my face with my hands and sobbed. I felt a hand on my shoulder.

"Vale." Morrick's rough voice was gentler than I'd heard before. I looked up at him and his alchemy-infused goggles glistened in the fluorescent lighting. "You will be just fine."

"How could you possibly know that?" I asked, wiping the moisture from my face.

"Because, as you said yourself, you have two choices: hide or face your fears. Just make sure whichever choice you make is one hundred percent the choice you want. It's a waste of time to focus on anything you aren't one hundred percent invested in." Morrick stated plainly and with conviction, before walking back over to his console to continue his work. I took a moment to process his words. It felt almost too simple, too emotionally disconnected, but that's a scientist for you. They always look at the most logical solutions.

"Thanks you, sir. I think that helps." I said, wiping away the last of my tears. I got up from the stool and was about to Skip back to my room for a well needed and alluring nap.

"Oh, Vale. I almost forgot to mention, but an official test run of the time machine will occur in a few weeks. Will you be able to attend the demonstration?" Morrick looked over at me again, motionless, his black goggles boring into me.

"Are you kidding? I wouldn't miss it!"

"You have no idea how much joy that brings me. Thank you, Vale. Ah yes, and Happy Halloween." Morrick said, sincerely.

"You too. Thanks for listening and for the advice." I responded, Morrick nodded, and I took my leave once again through my Rip.

I appeared in the guest room to warmth and a pulsating hum. I turned around to face the door. The symbol I drew was still intact and glowed a comforting blue hue. I wasn't exactly sure how to disarm wards, but I had an idea. I placed my hand on the door and, while focusing on the symbol, I spoke a single word.

"Disable." The ward hummed softly and its glow dimmed until the original markings were all that was left. "Huh, I can't believe that worked. Guess my intuition with this stuff is better than I thought."

I made sure to keep my door locked, but it was more out of habit than an actual precaution. I stripped down to my boxers, turned off the lights, and plopped myself back on the bed. I wormed myself underneath the blankets, breathing slowly, and cleared my mind of all thoughts, allowing slumber to whisk me away.

24 IMPLOSION

A knock on my door shook me awake. Half asleep, I wriggled my way out of my blankets and staggered like a zombie toward the door. I was able to open my eyes slightly as I cracked the door open.

"Hello?" I said, light pouring onto my face from the hallway.

"Oh, Vale. I didn't mean to wake you." Kaito stood a few feet away from the door and bowed as if to apologize.

"Kaito? That's fine. What's up? What time is it?"

"I heard you were staying with us for a few days. I wanted to greet you before you needed to leave again." He said. I continued to yawn and rub my eyes to wake up. "Would you like to join me in the multipurpose room? I have some music I made that I wish to show you."

"Oh, sure. That sounds really cool. Let me just throw on some clothes." I accepted. Kaito nodded as I shut the door and flicked on the lights. The room was unchanged save for the bed sheets being a twisted mess and a stray pillow lying on the floor. I quickly splashed cold water on my face and made myself somewhat presentable before joining Kaito in the hallway.

Kaito smiled as he looked me up and down. "You clean up nicely. Are you ready?"

"Thanks. Of course." I blushed.

Kaito led the way back toward the foyer, upstairs, and to the left where the gym and multipurpose room were located. The door to the hybrid entertainment room was already open, but we seemed to be the only ones occupying the space. That is until I heard rapid clicking coming from the gaming area. We took a peek around the corner and saw Esteban wearing a headset and playing some competitive shooter game on a vibrant, expensive looking PC setup. He took note of us briefly and waved, before going right back to his game.

"He seems to be having fun, but where is everyone else?" I asked.

"Either in their rooms or taking care of things in their own lives. They can't stay here all the time." Kaito explained.

"Do you go to Japan often?"

"Sometimes, but I honestly don't get out much. Only when I have a music gig do I go out and even then, I don't show my face." Kaito motioned to his face as he moved toward the soundproof music booth.

"You mean you wear a mask?"

"Exactly, but come. Have a listen. I've been working on something new I think you will like."

We moved into the sound booth and Kaito locked the door behind us. He hurried to close the curtains that covered the window to the outer room. His presence suddenly changed. Kaito felt...fearful? Frantic? But why the sudden shift?

"Kaito, is everything alright? Why did you lock us in here?" My voice shook as I stayed completely still.

"So we wouldn't be heard or seen talking. As much as I would love to show you my music, that is not why I brought you here." Kaito's face was serious, and now that I got a better look at his eyes, it looked as though he hadn't slept for days.

"Then why did you bring me here, Kaito?" I asked, my nerves quivering.

"I need to warn you about Morrick."

"What about Morrick?"

"Please...just listen." Kaito gestured to a chair in front of the sound console and I complied, taking a seat. "Thank you." Kaito breathed out deeply, peeking out through the curtain to double check that the coast was clear. He grabbed a spare stool from the corner and sat down directly in front of me. He was about a foot away from my face when he started to say his piece.

"Vale, Morrick is not who you think he is. I have watched him carefully for the past several months. When Morrick first found me I was bloody, bruised, and nearly dead. I was grateful for him taking me in, dressing my wounds, and feeding me. I witnessed his unprecedented Traveling ability as well as his Alchemy. It was as if I had entered a true safe haven where I could be myself and do so in the safety of the mansion." Kaito shifted uncomfortably and sounded as if he was on the verge of tears. "I thought everything was going to be perfect from then on, but I was so wrong. He shared his 'inventions' with me telling me the same thing I'm sure he's told you."

"A time machine?" I asked and Kaito echoed my words.

"Not exactly," Anger caught fire in his eyes. "He means to use all of our abilities, like a collective pulse. The machine needs an energy source and we're the batteries. Morrick's place in the machine is the center, and it isn't going to send him through time. In fact, it's not a time machine at all." Kaito's face slowly turned red, and at first I thought it was out of rage, but something felt wrong. The air in the booth felt electric and thick. Kaito straightened up and clutched his core. "Do you feel that?"

"Feel what? Kaito, are you okay?" I stood up from my chair and Kaito followed my motion, struggling to breathe and clutching at his chest.

"Vale...!" Kaito gasped and in a blink he was pulled through an undetectable Rip. A suction, like a star imploding, stole the air from my lungs until a pulse of energy burst outward, shaking everything in the booth and releasing oxygen back into the room. I gulped for air as I frantically unlocked the sound booth door.

"What...the fuck?!" I struggled to say as I stumbled out of the sound booth and onto the ground.

"Que paso? What's wrong, Vale?" I felt a hand on my shoulder. I looked up from the carpet to see Esteban standing over me. I pushed myself to my feet and attempted to form a cohesive sentence.

"Kaito...he just vanished."

"Yeah, that's kind of what we do." Esteban scratched his head.

"No! I mean he was taken! Against his will through a Rip!" I shouted.

"What do you mean? Who would do—" Esteban cut himself off. "Do you feel that? My stomach hurts." And just like what happened to Kaito, Esteban was pulled through a foreign rift. My fight or flight instinct flared, and flight was clearly my reaction as I was out the door, down the stairs, and back in my guest room faster than I've ever physically moved.

What the hell just happened? I thought. Were Kaito and Esteban stolen? Morrick...It had to be him. Who else could use their Skip like that? I didn't know what Kaito was going to tell me, but if what just happened revealed anything, it showed me that Elijah was right to be cautious about Morrick and the manor. I should never have come here. I needed to leave. Get home. Find Elijah. That's all I could think of. That's all that mattered now. I had to get away.

As soon as I reached my room, I roughly threw all my belongings back into my bag and Skipped out of there faster than lightning. My familiar bedroom opened before me and sunlight from midday filled the space. I was back in Fresno. I wasted no time at all sealing my Rip, reaching in my bag for a marker, and drawing the same ward as before on the back of my bedroom door. I slammed my hand on the finished marking and spoke aloud.

"Protect us."

My intent was urgent and strong. I felt a wave of energy flow through me and could hear it wrap around the whole house. I wasn't certain it would work, but if it did then the ward should have sealed the entire house from uninvited guests. The house creaked and settled with the Alchemy. Silence filled the house until someone called out my name.

"Vale?! Is that you? Are you home, honey?" The sound of multiple pairs of rapid footsteps marched up the stairs and trod down the hall to my door. I stepped back and the door flung open. My mom and dad stood in the doorway. The moment I laid my eyes on them everything started to well up, like a dam cracking under immense pressure. I was suddenly overwhelmed with emotion, but I didn't have the strength to tell them any of anything. I bawled instead and ran into their arms. My parents were speechless and only held me tighter as I sobbed into their shoulders.

Once I was able to collect myself and dry my tears, my parents didn't ask any questions. They simply told me to take some time to get settled, and then to come join them for a chat downstairs. *I didn't deserve how patient they were with me.* I thought.

I checked my phone and I had several missed calls, voice messages, and texts all wondering where I was. Apparently, it didn't take long for my lie of staying with Lauren to completely fall apart. They began searching for me after I'd been missing for twenty-four hours. I paused when I came across texts from Elijah. He was asking the same questions everyone else was, except one text where he asked if I had gone "back there". Elijah wasn't stupid, and I think a part of him knew I would have no choice but to return to the manor eventually. In hindsight, that was a huge mistake.

My entire reality was beginning to unravel, and I felt like it was only going to get worse. I breathed deep and braced myself for the talk with my parents. With each step toward the downstairs dining table I thought of what I would tell them. How would I answer their questions? Should I be honest and come clean or should I lie out my ass? Maybe I could spare them some details. Me being gay might be an easier pill to swallow than every insane second I witnessed at Langdorf Manor.

I suddenly realized I was already sitting at the dining room table in front of two pairs of piercing eyes, gazing into me for answers. It took a little over an hour to collect myself. They kindly waited for me to join them, but the expressions on their faces were now anything but kind.

"So Vale...where the *hell* have you been?" Dad ordered.

25 OUT AND AWAY

"The police scoured all over town for you!" My dad barked.

"And you asked Lauren, that sweet girl, to lie for you?!" My mom snapped in unison. I sat still, heart pounding, hands gripping the sides of my chair as my nails dug into the varnish.

"Will you please say something, son?" Dad politely ordered. As a few more seconds went by, he lost his temper; "*God damnit, Vale! Fucking talk!*" My eyes jolted up from the table at both of them. Dad's face was beet red and mom's eyes were glistening with tears, mascara running down her cherry cheeks. It didn't take much for the thin veil of kindness to tear from my parents façade. They weren't known for displaying emotional maturity or boundless understanding.

"I...I needed some time to be on my own. I had some cash stored up, so I took an Amtrak and then a bus to San Francisco. I found a cheap motel that didn't ask for ID. I had just climbed through the window when you heard me in my room." Lying out my ass, it was. I spun my tall tale, and I watched as their faces fared from red to pale as they, no doubt, imagined their little boy out there all alone in the scary city overflowing with gays and hippies.

"I just...what has gotten into you lately, Vale? We only hear from you when you need or want something," Dad started.

"Not to mention, we checked with your school and your grades have been plummeting. On top of that, you skipped several days of school. They wanted to give you a month of detention, but we talked them out of it with a promise that you wouldn't miss a single day for the rest of the year," Mom finished.

"I'm sorry. Things have been pretty...*overwhelming* as of late." I said, looking back down at the table.

"Stop looking down! Look at us!" Dad slammed his fist, on the table which made mom jump. "Explain. Now!" He demanded.

"Well..." I swallowed. "Mom, Dad...I-I'm..." I breathed in deep, closed my eyes, and slowly exhaled. I looked at both of them in the hope they would try to understand. "I'm gay."

The room fell silent.

The only sound was the ticking of the grandfather clock behind me, and the faint cooing of doves outside. Dad slumped back and folded his hands, not saying a word. Mom quietly sobbed with more tears than before, soaking her face.

"It's Elijah, isn't it? He talked you into his lifestyle." Mom said in between sobs.

"What? No! This has nothing to do with him! I figured this out on my own. I've been stressed and lost focus, because this whole time I was trying to build up the courage to tell you both. Every time I thought I was ready to come out, I remembered how both of you treated Eli when he came out, and I retreated." I kept my steady gaze on them as I found the courage I had been searching for. I finally said the words that weighed so heavily on me for so long. The hard part was over.

"You know how we raised you, Vale. You know what the Bible says. This is not a wise choice." Dad chastised.

"Choice? Let me ask you something, did you choose to like women, Dad? Did you choose to fall in love with Mom?" I asked directly.

"That's besides the point. You are straying from God's path, Honey and He doesn't want this path for you." Mom defended.

"Really?! Because I think that is *exactly* the point! The short answer I was looking for was 'No.' You didn't choose to be attracted to who you are attracted to. Also, since we are on the topic of the Bible, do *you* even know what it says?" I leaned into them a fury now coursing through my body.

"Of course we—"

"Wrong!" I interrupted. "You don't! You know how I know that? Because if you really knew your biblical history you would know that the word 'homosexual' wasn't added into scripture until the 1940's. Before that, it originally was referencing pedophilia. So all this time LGBTQ+ people have been attacked by 'righteous' Christians, because of a mistranslation the church itself paid for. A simple google search would have told you this." I spat back, my own righteous anger exploding from me like an erupting volcano.

"Don't you dare talk down to us young man! Your generation thinks you're so damn smart because you grew up with the internet, but you lack the life experience in which we tower over you in comparison." Dad stood up as Mom sobbed into a nearby hand towel.

"Fuck this. Way to be a walking, talking stereotype." I stood up and started to walk away from the table.

"As long as you live under my roof, you will follow my rules. No son of mine is going to be a homo while he lives here! Once you move out, you can live however you want, but until then you obey God's will for you." Dad retorted.

"Do you even hear yourself?" I laughed. "God's will? Or *your* will?" I waited for either of them to answer. Mom couldn't look at me, and Dad resembled a tea pot spewing its steam. "Right. Bye."

"Where the hell do you think you're going?!" Dad bellowed as I ran up the stairs toward my bedroom.

"Vale!" Mom called out as I slammed and locked my door behind me. New tears flowed down and onto my notebooks, clothes, and laptop while I repacked. I packed only the essentials in two bags. I was leaving. Right now.

Fuck them.

Fuck all this bullshit.

Fuck Fresno.

I wished that a massive sinkhole would open up, swallowing Fresno and all its bigoted, ignorant, vanilla ideals with it.

I would live on my own starting tonight and never look back. I would find help to deal with Morrick, but afterwards I wouldn't be returning. I had no home here, and I felt like an idiot for thinking it could ever be different. I was just a lost soul, a corrupted teen, a fag in the eyes of my parents. It was ironic really. The same church that teaches them to love everyone also teaches them to hate those who love differently than them. One giant, cosmic comedy on this stage called life.

I could still hear shouting coming from downstairs. After a few minutes the shouting stopped and I finished packing. As I zipped up my backpack, there was a gentle knock on my door.

"Vale? It's mom. Please open the door."

"Is Dad with you?"

"No. He went for a drive to clear his head."

I sighed and unlocked the door, stepping back toward my bags that sat on the bed. My mother stepped into the room. Immediately she noticed what I was doing. Her eyes were red and dry, but she still looked as though there was a knot in her throat.

"Please don't do this, honey. Don't leave us." She begged.

"You know I have to. I'm not welcome here, not as I am."

"Yes, you are. We love you!" She said, shakily stepping closer.

"You heard dad, and you defended him. Don't worry, I get it. You love each other. You're partners through thick and thin. It's only natural to be who you are. Which is why I need to leave, so I can be who I really am without any of limitations." I said, earnestly. I gazed into my mother's sweet, brown eyes attempting to hold back more tears.

"You're father, he'll come around. We can work through this, just please stay." Mom whimpered and grabbed my hand.

"I can't, mom. I'm sorry." I whimper back.

"Why? Where will you go? What will you do? Are you really going to leave us right before the holidays?" Mom continued to beg, and every guilt trip she could think of came pouring out as she squeezed my hand tighter.

"I'm sorry. It's the only sure way you will be safe." I admitted.

"Safe? What do you mean?" Mom's sobbing seized, and she wiped her raw eyes once more.

"Don't worry about it." It took every fiber of resolve inside me not to tell her everything right then and there, but if she knew about the Travelers, then she would likely be in danger of Morrick too. Though I felt angry and betrayed by them, they were still my parents. A big part of me still loved them.

I grabbed my bags and walked toward the door. Mom stepped in front of me. "No. What did you mean by 'safe'?"

I smiled at her and kissed her softly on the cheek. "I love you, Mom. Tell Dad I still love him too. I hope I can see you again someday." I said and thought of Elijah's bedroom. All my focus honed in on opening a Rip as I stepped backward through the spatial tear.

"Vale, wait!" Mom cried out, her voice echoing into the void as I vanished in front of her eyes. The final, fleeting vision I saw was her shocked expression as my bedroom faded away for what felt like the last time.

26 REVELATIONS

"Jesus! Vale?" Elijah shouted as his room wrapped around me from out of my Rip. I immediately grabbed a marker from my pocket and drew the familiar protection rune on his door, placing my hand on it, and speaking the words once more.

"Protect us from those that mean us harm." The rune glowed blue and hummed as it wrapped around the house. Wood creaked and settled around us.

"Vale, what's going on? What did you just do?" Elijah demanded.

"A lot, Eli. So much has changed." I said, still facing his door. Sadness began to well up inside me as I pictured my mother's face over and over again. My knees were weak and gave way beneath my body weight. I collapsed, hugging my knees to my chest, and weeping uncontrollably into my arms and legs. It all came pouring out, the betrayals, the constant changes, the rejection, fear of the unknown, all of it burst forth like a grenade going off sending white-hot shrapnel into my chest.

I felt Elijah's arms around me. I don't know if it'd been a few seconds or a few minutes, but his body heat was a comfort in that moment. He didn't say anything or ask any questions. He just held me in his arms, pulling my face into his chest as I continued to cry. I wrapped my arms him, clutching his shirt, and buried my face into him.

At some point I fell asleep. I didn't remember doing so, but my body gave in to the sweet allure of rest. I opened my eyes and I was still on the floor in front of Elijah's door, pillow under my head, and a blanket covering my body. My head pulsed as I slowly sat up. My whole body felt stiff and ached from sleeping on the solid wood flooring. My head felt cloudy and it was hard to fight the urge to fall back asleep.

I studied Elijah's room more closely than I had before. It was filled with movie and band posters, stacks of comic books as well as actual novels, a lone acoustic guitar in one of the corners, and RGB lighting lined the frame of the ceiling. The color of the lights were set to a green that draped the walls. Lastly, his computer setup was amazing. A sleek automatic rising desk, two wide OLED monitors, a webcam, a gaming mouse, a gaming keyboard, and a PC tower that would be any high schooler's wet dream. How he or his dad was able to afford any of this was beyond me. Then again, being an only child has its perks as I know all too well.

I retrieved my phone from my pants pocket. Blinking at the glowing screen, there were over thirty missed calls from my parents and dozens of messages. They varied from anger to pleading sadness to confusion. I pulled away from reading or responding, and instead tapped the power button on the screen.

"Oh good, you're awake." Elijah cracked open the door I still sat in front of, and spotted me. I stood up, moving the blanket and pillow out of his path.

"Hi Eli. Thanks for taking care of me." I set the bedding on his mattress and sat down.

"Here. Drink this." He handed me a tall, glass of water and sat next to me.

I did what he said without question, drinking the cool water, feeling it slide down my throat, and beginning to re-hydrate my whole body. I stretched and let out a hearty sigh.

"Feel better?" Elijah asked.

"Somewhat. Listen Eli, first I want to say I'm so sorry for the way I acted a few days ago. I was jealous of the way Brian was being around you, and I thought the worst. And before you ask, yes I went to the manor again."

"Why would you do that? I warned you about those people. They can't be tr—" Elijah started, but I cut him off.

"I know. You were right, okay? I'm sorry, but I don't believe it's the Travelers that are the enemies here. Just Morrick."

"You're sure?"

"Positive. I don't know what exactly he is up to, but Morrick lied. Kaito tried to warn me, but Morrick took him." I explained.

"*Took* him? What do you mean?"

"We were in the sound booth, inside the multipurpose room, when Kaito started feeling strange. I could tell by the look on his face. Suddenly, he vanished inside a Rip." I illustrated what I saw, placing my hand on my core. "This wasn't Kaito's Rip either. I can tell the difference now between someone else's and Morrick's Skipping energy, and it was definitely Morrick. It literally knocked the air out of me when it happened. The same thing happened to Esteban when I tried to tell him about Kaito. I got out of there as fast as I could."

"Kaito and Esteban are in trouble." Elijah stated aloud, but it almost sounded like a question.

"Yes. And, in other news, not to burden you more, I can't

go home. I came out to my parents as gay, and it went about as well as you'd expect. My mom saw me Skip. I can never go back, Eli." Amazingly, I did not feel any sorrow that time. I felt nothing. I had gone numb to the pain, and instead focused on the pending threat of Morrick and the power he possessed.

"Okay, first, you should have led with that. Your priorities are all outta whack right now. Second, what are you going to do? Run away? Live on your own? Constantly evade Morrick? Which leads me to my third and final point, what do you plan to do about him? Or do you even have a plan?" Elijah said matter-of-factly. Understandably, he was the voice of reason here, and I was thankful for that. Lord knows that my mind was completely short circuiting.

"Short answer? I have no idea what I'm going to do. This is all *way* over my head. What am I supposed to do? Stop Morrick? He is so much more powerful and knowledgeable than we know. I'm not a hero. I'm a coward. I didn't ask for any of this." I put my head in my hands, pushing my hair back and resting my hands on my neck.

"No you didn't. Normally, I would be the one to tell you to cut your losses and forget all about them and Morrick, but you saw what happened to Kaito and Esteban. Something very bad is about to go down and we might have a chance to stop it." Elijah rested his hand on my knee and pulled my chin toward his face so that our eyes met.

"We? Eli, I can't let you come with me. I don't even know if I'm ever going back to that place." I stood up and paced from the bed to the window that face the park across the street.

"Of course we're going back. We can't turn a blind eye to whatever this wanna-be mad scientist is doing. The Travelers could be in danger, and they are your friends after all. What kind of boyfriend would I be if I let you go in there alone? Plus…" Elijah climbed to his feet and walked over to his bedside table, opening the drawer, and pulling something out. "We won't be going unarmed." He placed a plastic box with a smaller cardboard box next to it on his pillow.

"If you absolutely insist, have it your way. You are so stubborn, you know that?" I chided.

"If that's not the pot calling the kettle black, I don't know what is!"

"What about Lauren and Brian?" My mind shifted to our friend and my ex-bully who were probably equally as worried about me as Elijah was. Maybe just Lauren.

"We've involved them enough. They will hear from you in due time, but until then we can't put them in harm's way." Elijah said and I couldn't help my thoughts from drifting back to the day we first Skipped to San Francisco, New York City, Hawaii…It was bliss. We started this journey together and it seemed as if we were destined to finish it together.

As I kissed him gently, a ripple ruptured the air thinning the oxygen in the room. A Rip opened before our eyes and a body slumped through it, crumpling to the floor bloody and bruised. We both yelled, startled. At first we could not tell who it was, but upon further inspection I could make out hair highlights, bracelets, and piercings. It was Liv.

"What happened to her? Why does she look like that?" I gasped. Elijah was surprisingly calm.

"Help me lift her onto the bed." Elijah ordered and I followed, picking up her feet. Elijah got her head and arms. As gently as possible, we moved her onto the bed. Liv moaned in pain even in her passed-out state. "Stay with her while I grab some medical supplies."

Elijah left the room and I knelt down next to Liv. I carefully picked up her hand and held it in mine. Her arms and legs had small lacerations all over, as well as a single cut right above her eye which looked worse than it actually was. Head wounds always bled more than any other wound. Bruises covered her arms and legs, and that was only where they were exposed. Who knows how badly she was damaged. What happened? I hoped and prayed that Liv would wake up soon to give us some answers.

It wasn't long before Elijah found his way back into his bedroom, hands full of medical gauze, Neosporin, medical wraps, an ice pack, and a bottle of painkillers. He steadily got to work dressing her visible wounds.

My mind went back to when Elijah and I were ten. We rode our bikes together and we spent all day outside. The neighborhood was our playground. It started to get dark when we were speeding home as fast as our little legs could pedal. My front tire suddenly caught a thin patch of sand on a section of sidewalk and I went sliding sideways across the rough concrete. My left leg and hands were all scraped up and bleeding. I whimpered as I struggled to pick myself up from underneath my bike when Elijah appeared, throwing my arm over his shoulder, and guiding me back to his house. Once there, he cleaned my scratches and bandaged them up with *Dragon Ball Z* bandages.

He now did the same thing for Liv, but with a more practiced, steady hand. Liv slowly started to wake up.

"Huh...What's...going on? Ouch, hey!" Liv sat up on the bed and glared at Elijah. "You?"

"Liv you're fine. You're s afe. Eli is just fixing you up. Do you have any other wounds that we can't see?" I squeezed her hand to reassure her.

"Oh, thank God." Liv sighed and relaxed back into a lying position on the bed. "None that need attention. Just some bruises. Ah!" Liv flinched as she held her side. "Maybe a cracked rib or two, but I'll be fine." She turned her head toward Elijah's door and spotted the active protection rune. "Smart. You must already know about Morrick's deception then?"

"Yes. He stole Kaito out of thin air when he tried to warn me, as well as Esteban when I tried to warn him. I Skipped away as fast as I could and laid down the runes so he couldn't follow." I clarified.

"Kaito...He tried to warn me about his findings. He found some old documents going back almost a thousand years, but I didn't believe him. To me, it sounded like he was losing faith in Morrick and being ungrateful for everything he gave us. I couldn't listen to that slander. So I told him to get his shit together and then I made the worst mistake." Liv went quiet as she stared up at the ceiling. She cover ed her eyes with one hand, but I could hear the trembling regret in her voice as she continued. "It's my fault they were taken. It's my fault this all started when it did. After I told Morrick I went looking for the others, but no one was in their rooms. I Skipped to their usual spots around the world, but I couldn't find anyone. I went back to your guest room, Vale, but you and your things were already gone. I was all alone, but then I felt a pull in my core that I never felt before. It knocked the wind right out of me. Before I realized what had happened, I found myself back in Morrick's lab. Everyone was strapped down onto individual gurneys with an IV drip in their arms." Liv's voice cracked and she became inconsolable as she curled into a ball on Elijah's bed. Elijah backed off and started packing up the medical supplies.

"I think that should do for now. Liv, you should rest. Let's go to the living room, Vale. My dad is out of town at some singles retreat, so we'll be alone." Elijah stood up and led me out of the room.

"Liv, you'll be okay? You're safe here. If you need anything we will be right down the hall."

"Vale, wait." Liv collected herself enough to sit back up. Her eyes held a deep sorrow and terror. "Morrick is more powerful than you know. He isn't some frail old man. He may look it, but it's just a show he puts on. Kaito warned me that the Langdorf family lineage technically ended around the 1400's. Morrick is the last remaining member. Do you get what I'm telling you? Morrick has done this before, lured young people with his Skipping and trapped them in some Alchemical ritual in order to drain them and revitalize himself for another several decades. He has done this dozens of times, and that's what he plans to do with us. We have to help them..." Liv's sorrow turned to rage and panic.

I absorbed her words and shared in her pain. Empathy rippled through my body and I could feel now what Elijah initially felt. We had to help, we had to stop Morrick from ever hurting anyone again.

"Alright Liv, but we're going together. You rest up. I'm sure he won't complete the ritual without us." I comforted her and shut the door to Elijah's bedroom. I recalled Morrick's lab and his enormous steel and glass machine. It had eight points surrounding the center which meant he was missing two key components, Liv and myself.

27 RECKLESS

The Skipper and the Gunman sat together on the living room couch, with hot mugs of chocolate placed on coasters atop the coffee table. Strings of orange lights hung in the front window as Trick-or-Treaters could be heard outside, beginning their All-Hallows Eve plunder. Elijah cleaned and loaded his gun, as I scoured through the book of Alchemy for helpful runes. From our mugs, the sweet aroma of chocolate wafted throughout the room. It was met with the faint odor of metal polish and the gentle tones of *Syd Matters* playing over a portable speaker.

I worked on drawing runes with a permanent marker on blank sheets of paper. Wind, Barrier, Protection, Binding, and Shrouding. Back in Yosemite, I made sure to bookmark the Rune of Reversal. That one was the key to my back up plan. For good measure, I drew up some combustion and water runes as well. I didn't know if we would need to start some fires or put some out.

It had been several hours, and the light from outside had long since vanished beyond the windows. Elijah perked up from watching TV, his gun nestled on his lap. "My bedroom door just opened." He said.

The sounds of a toilet flushing and faucet water rang down

the hall. I peeked up from my Alchemy study long enough to see Liv standing in the hallway rubbing the sleep from her eyes. "What smells good?" She asked.

"Oh, it's hot chocolate. Would you like some? There's some left on the stove." I stood up from the couch. Elijah stayed sitting, his gaze fixed on Liv.

I went over to the kitchen and scooped some sweet, brown liquid into a clean jarrito mug for Liv and rejoined them back in the living room. "Here you are. Did you get enough rest?"

"As much as I could, all things considered." Liv stretched her neck and there was an audible crack as she relaxed, grabbing the mug from me, and taking a sip. "Mmm, thanks. This is great." Liv glanced us over and all our work spread out over the coffee table. "What's all this then?"

"Preparation. If knowledge serves me right, then Morrick's machine won't work unless you and I are there." I reminded her.

"I trusted him. For years I enthusiastically followed him, recruited others, and defended him, but now..." Liv stared out the windows behind us into the dimly lit street. "He has Ember. Vale, we have to save her. We have to save them all."

"And we will, but the three of us need to get on the same page and figure out a plan. The last thing we want to do is go in there guns blazing."

"I have no problem with that idea." Elijah said as he slid his loaded clip into his handgun, letting out a loud *click* as it snapped into place.

"*Clearly.* The goal here is to get everyone safely away from Morrick." I stated.

"Okay? And then what? We all live happily ever after? Morrick just forgets about us?" Liv asked, snark filling her every word.

"Of course not. I'm not an idiot."

"You are if you think anything else has to happen besides *killing* Morrick. As long as he is alive, Morrick will never stop hunting us for his machine. He is faster, cleverer, and more powerful than all of us combined. He probably already knows we're planning something." Liv interjected, roughly setting her mug down on the coffee table.

"Sure, but we are safe here. I put up the protection rune." I reminded Liv and she started laughing. She cringed in pain at her cuts and bruises.

"You honestly believe that wimpy piece of Alchemy will stop him? The only reason he hasn't shown up yet to take us back to the manor is because he knows eventually we will have to come to him. He will let us scheme and plan all we want, but eventually we will have to walk back through those doors. We don't have a choice." Liv had barely touched her hot chocolate, as she paced back to the entryway. She leaned against a tan painted wall, arms crossed, and wore a grim expression.

"Hold on. Sure Morrick has more experience than us, but we have our youth against him. We still have the never ending flexibility and creativity that comes with our age range." Elijah chimed in.

"Why would that even matter? That also makes us naive to think we can beat him." Liv countered.

"Right, but it also makes us reckless. What's something Morrick cherishes more than anything?" Elijah proposed. Liv and I were silent, waiting for him to answer his own question. "Knowledge. All those books, the Alchemy, family history, and clearly he is much older than he originally led us to believe."

"What are you suggesting?" Liv perked up.

"We burn his shit to the ground. Smoke him out. Let's force him to come to us." Elijah said and I had never seen his eyes go as dark as they did in that moment.

"Fuck it. It's as good a plan as any. Vale and I will be the distraction. When Morrick is about to show his crooked mug then, Vale, *you* will stealthily Skip Elijah into Morrick's underground lab for him to gather the others. Then you'll Skip back before he reaches me. Elijah, they may be drowsy from sedatives so make sure to go to the cabinets on the *right* side of the lab. There should be pre-packaged needles of adrenaline behind the glass. If it's locked, break that shit open and get my family the hell out of there." Liv had crossed over to the living room and grabbed a blank piece of a paper with a pen and started to illustrate her plan. She jabbed at the rough sketch with her pointer finger with increasing intensity. "No time like the present though. Better get a move on. Morrick will be able to detect us when we arrive, but the good tidbit is that he won't be able to sense Elijah with us since he doesn't share in our ability. Elijah, *you* are the surprise factor in all this and unfortunately, the plan relies heavily on you."

"Don't worry. I understand. We're going in prepared. Three against one, we've got this." Elijah stood up, tucking his gun in his belt behind his back, and throwing his shirt over it.

"Wait, what about your injuries, Liv? Don't you need to rest some more." I asked, earnestly.

"Hell no. I'll just grab some more painkillers and we can be on our way. I'm not waiting around while Morrick plots even further. We have to strike *now*." Liv said as she moved to the kitchen and ruffled through the medicine cabinet. Having found some stronger painkillers, she took two, and swallowed them dry.

"Alright then." I breathed. "I made some runes for each of you. Here is a Barrier rune for protection. Fire runes, *obviously*. And Binding runes in case we need to hold him in place. I also threw in some Shrouding runes for stealth. They aren't very strong so only use them as a last resort or if I give you a signal." I said as I handed them slips of paper, runic symbols perfectly drawn and labeled on them. "And remember: *Intent* is what drives the energy behind the rune. You have to truly believe that it will work, and it will."

"Vale, what are you planning?" Liv asked, her eyes boring into my mind.

"It's just a back up plan. In the event of a worst case scenario we still have a way to beat Morrick."

"Brilliant." Liv smirked.

We were set. I grabbed a spare, empty backpack Elijah had and stashed the Alchemy book in it. I tucked my share of the runes in my front pockets for quick and easy access, making sure to categorize in my mind which ones were in which pocket. I tightened the straps on the backpack and breathed in deep.

"Ready?" Elijah asked, his hazel eyes glinting in the low lamp light. I stuck out my hand to him.

"With you by my side, always." I smiled at him and he smiled back, yanking me toward him, and kissing me firmly.

"Ummm, do you guys want a moment, or can we dispose of an evil diabolical scientist who is trying to steal our life force and live forever?" Liv said in mock seriousness.

I pulled away from Elijah, grinning wide, and stuck out my hand to Liv. I pictured the fountain in front of the manor clearly in my mind. I could hear the wind rushing through the trees of the forest and the water rippling through the fountain's stone. As always, we vanished and reappeared in front of Langdorf Manor. It was pitch black around the manor grounds, but light poured from the windows and beyond the large doorways. Strangely, one of the doors swung freely with the wind knocking it open and closed. It creaked and banged against the hollow door frame. The manor breathed and groaned at us. It was as if we were staring up at a monstrous beast made of marble, glass, wood, and stone. Its mouth ajar, it invited us into it's seething maw.

29 THE MAW

We stood still in front of the massive, inanimate creature in the pitch black night. A haunting manse that once stood for hope, discovery, and family now felt hollow and devoid of life. Illuminated by the dim sallow glow oozing from the windows, the stone beasts at the entrance looked as if they would come to life at any moment and disembowel us. I gripped the straps of my backpack tightly and took one slow breath. The first steps toward the manor felt heavy and the air swelled around me. Worries of what my life would be like afterward came flooding back. Anxious dread of my own mortality grew with each step. I felt hands on my shoulders. Elijah and Liv stood tall next to me. I didn't recall stopping, but I must have, subconsciously.

"Stick to the plan. Get in. Get the others out and away. Hold Morrick off." Liv reminded us. We both nodded. "Or kill him. Whatever suits you."

"I know exactly where to go and I will work as fast as possible." Elijah reassured me.

"Alright. What do we light up first?" I asked, pulling out a fire rune from my pocket and unfolding it to reveal a sideways V pointed to the left.

"The main library seems pretty flammable. Let's start with

Morrick's precious knowledge." Liv muttered and was already walking toward the open manor door, fire rune in hand.

As we entered, it grew colder than the dark forest and smelled of copper and dust. The entire foyer was in disarray. The chandelier that once hung dominantly from the high ceiling lay shattered, barely flickering with light, the floor below it, cracked and splintered from the impact. The staircase banister was split, broken, and completely torn away in some areas. The walls were scraped and loose wallpaper dangled to the floor. Red streaks stretched sporadically across nearly every surface. Tables and chairs could be seen in the dining area and the library, flipped over or broken.

"Jesus Christ...what happened here?" Elijah broke the silence. I was speechless. The mansion now felt like a murder scene rather than a place of enchantment and wonder.

"Morrick happened. Like I said, I barely managed to get away from him. When I found out who he really was and what he really wanted, I fought back and so did the others. One by one they were incapacitated again and taken. I'm starting to question why I came back here now." Liv's face shifted to an expression of fear and horror. I returned her earlier favor and placed a hand on her shoulder.

"To save our family." I smiled. That seemed to bring her back to the moment, because her face shifted into that of a kid ready to cause some trouble.

Liv crumpled up the fire rune in her hand. "Let's give this asshole a show he will never forget!" She yelled and lobbed the fire rune into the library like a grenade. A sizzling sound could be heard as it flew through the air and landed next to one of the enormous bookshelves. A few seconds went by and nothing was happening.

"Liv—" I said, but was cut off when she put a finger up to me, staring intently at the crumpled ball of paper.

"*Ignite.*" Liv spat between her teeth. Like a phoenix bursting to life from its ashes, the paper ball erupted into a miniature inferno. A shock wave shuddered the windows and doors in the immediate area.

"Whoa!" Elijah and I both shouted in unison. I glanced at him, excitement drawn across his face. I immediately remembered the next part of the plan and reached for Elijah.

"There is no way Morrick didn't hear that. Let's get you to the lab." I said and he grabbed onto my hand. I focused on Morrick's underground lab and I could feel my Rip opening like a zipper behind Elijah. "Please be safe." I looked at him, worriedly.

"Always." Elijah responded, just before I shoved him into my Rip and he vanished. I made sure to close the Rip behind him, and just as I did the front door slammed firmly shut, the air in the foyer was sucked away, extinguishing the flames in the library.

As I watched, Liv fell to her knees, gripping at her throat, her face flushing red. I felt my throat tighten, like the air was stolen from my lungs. It was similar to when Kaito and Esteban were spirited away. I fell to one knee, but managed to hold myself up. My vision began to fade when a shock wave, three times more powerful than what I felt before, shoved me and Liv on our backs. The windows shattered and instinctively I covered my face and stomach from the shards raining down on us.

I gasped and coughed for air once the glass settled onto the floor. I sliced my hand open on a shard as I pushed myself back onto my feet, but I barely noticed as my heart thrummed in my chest. Liv sat up, breathing heavily. I rushed over to her and helped her up.

"Are you okay?" I asked, noticing a few fresh cuts on her arms and face from the glass.

"He's here." Liv shoved my hand off her, and stepped out into the foyer again. Morrick, master of Alchemy and leader of the Travelers, stood atop the staircase looking down at us. I could now tell how different he truly looked. His presence was palpable, and his shadow casting on the wall behind him framed him in an enormous shroud. Pressure increased in the room, and I suddenly felt heavier. Morrick's bandana and trench coat were absent, leaving him in a white button-down shirt with rolled up sleeves, stained with blood, and ripped black slacks. He dawned his signature alchemical goggles which whirred and whined as the lenses adjusted themselves. Morrick's skin was heavily scarred and tattered like old, worn-out leather that was damaged over many decades. His hair was white and balding with purple splotches across his scalp. He showed a sickly yellow, crooked grin and my blood ran cold.

"Vale! Welcome back, my son! It seems you have brought the prodigal daughter back to me as well. Now we can all be together as a family...inside me." Morrick's voice sounded more hoarse than usual and the words he spouted were madder than a hatter on their unbirthday.

"Listen—" Liv started, but I cut her off.

"Listen here, you twisted, used-condom-looking *fuck*!" I bellowed back at Morrick, and for a moment he was taken aback as if no one had ever talked to him in such a manner. I could see Liv in my peripherals, her eyes wide and wearing a tight smile.

"Damn..." Liv said in approval.

"What the bloody hell did you just say to me, boy? Such

insolence!" Morrick spat back and it was then that I noticed he no longer was using a cane. I guess that was a lie too.

"You heard me, you backstabbing piece of moldy shit! You found me, you found all of us, and formed a family. For once we all felt safe and confident in who we were. Whatever happened to 'Shame must come from only causing harm'? Was all of it just soothing lies? We gained strength and comfort from our strangeness together and you spoiled it! I have had a very bad couple of days, and now I find out that you are some wrinkled, sour, pickle from the Revolutionary War who needs *our* abilities so you can siphon them into you and live for another hundred years or so? Is that right? Did I more or less sum it up?" I spat out all my anger, my hatred, my discontent at Morrick in that moment. Mostly, I was trying to stall him for Elijah's sake, but it felt cathartic nevertheless.

Morrick clapped slowly in a condescending manner. "Bravo, young Vale. You got it down to the letter. Well, except for the part about me being a pickle. That was simply rude, childish, name calling. And here I was about to give you my well-prepped, villainous monologue. It seems you've saved me the trouble."

A flash, and...

Not a hint of sound.

A gasp to my left.

Liv was suddenly unconscious and crumpled to the floor. Morrick Skipped to her with a speed my eyes could never hope to follow and, in one motion, slid a syringe into her neck.

"Liv!" I yelled and stepped back.

"Oh don't worry. It's only a sedative. I'm not a brute. They will slip into death peacefully once I turn on my machine." Morrick stated, tossing the empty syringe behind him. It shattered on the ground. I moved my gaze from Liv to him and the temperature in my body began to build.

"Yeah? What about the cuts and bruises on her body? What about this place? It's destroyed." I asked, attempting to stall Morrick further.

"Ah yes, well unfortunately peaceful measures were planned, but could not be taken as poor Kaito had already gotten to the others and there was a bit of a...*scuffle.* Pity really. I gave that boy everything, but he couldn't help his curiosity. He's quite fond of you, Vale. I'm sure you are aware of that. Alas, your heart was set on that mortal. What is his name again?" Morrick stood perfectly still, his hands behind his back, eyes fixed on me. Unwavering, motionless, statuesque.

"Elijah."

"Elijah. Of course. Nice boy as well, but sadly stuck his nose where it didn't belong." Morrick cocked an eyebrow and there was a flash.

At the same moment, I pulled a barrier rune from my pocket and slapped it against my chest, beneath my shirt. "*Expel!*" I shouted and a bright blue aura surrounded my body like an impenetrable layer of skin. Morrick reappeared behind me and tried to stab another syringe into my neck, but the barrier stopped the needle centimeters from my jugular. Morrick yelped in pain as a shock went through his hand causing him to drop the syringe. "Damn! You fancy yourself an Alchemist, do you? Then how will you fare against this, *Little Mage?*"

Morrick reached into thin air through his Rip. A gravitational pull that nearly tore me from the ground released across the area. He yanked out a person who he held firmly by the collar.

"No!" I watched in terror as Elijah emerged through Morrick's Rip. Morrick gripped him tightly and cackled proudly.

"You foolish children really thought I didn't know what you were planning? I allowed Liv to escape so she would bring you back to me. The fact that you brought...*this*...along with you is of no consequence." Morrick eyed Elijah in disgust and then with his other hand pulled a piece of paper out of Elijah's pocket.

"Hey you old perv! Watch where you put those fingers! Damn, how are you so strong?" Elijah bellowed at Morrick as he struggled in mid air to get out of his grip.

"How did you know Eli was here? Liv said you can't sense non-Skippers." I grunted.

"I didn't have to sense him, because your eyes told me everything when I mentioned him. Your expression revealed everything to me." Morrick grinned wide, his teeth an unhealthy yellow. "You know what they say, Vale? Put one's feet to the fire and they will eventually melt." Morrick sneered as he flicked a fire rune near Liv's feet. It set the ground ablaze and the flames danced toward her. "Decide, Little Mage, who you will save. Liv from a slow, ashen death? Or your beloved from a swift decapitation? The choice is yours. Admittedly, I had hoped to save Liv, but my machine will work fine with one less gifted child. She's outlived her usefulness anyway. Either way, you have lost." Morrick mocked.

We were wrong.

I was wrong.

It was foolish to come here and everyone would pay the price for my hubris.

I looked back and forth from Elijah to Liv. Elijah reached behind his back. "Actually, I found something." I scoffed, sweat dripping down the sides of my head.

"Your arrogance knows no bounds, Vale! What could possibly change the outcome now?" Morrick chorted.

"*This.*" Elijah grunted as he shoved the barrel of his gun into Morrick's side and pulled the trigger.

BANG!

A bullet tore into Morrick. It went clean through. Blood poured from the open wound.

"AAAAAHHHH!" Morrick screamed in agonized pain and dropped Elijah from his grip.

I rushed over to the fire that was now trailing up Liv's pants, and released a water rune on the flames. "*Drench!*" I yelled and instantly a pool of water formed underneath Liv, putting out the flames with smoking sizzles.

"Damn you, brats!" Morrick cursed us as he glared through his goggles at Elijah. "*Magnetize!*" He roared and Elijah's gun flew from his hand to M orrick. The scientist vanished and reappeared behind Elijah.

"What the—"

"Behind you!" I yelled, but it was too late. Morrick smacked Elijah across the head with his own gun, sending him unconscious onto the floor.

"So uncivil." Morrick spat out blood, tossing the gun across the room. "It was a noble plan you had for Elijah. The adrenaline, I mean. Brilliant actually, but I moved everything the moment Liv left my sights. I have lived several lifetimes, cured many world-wide ailments, helped humanity for the greater good, and you really think a single bullet will do me in?" Morrick clicked his tongue in disappointment. "No, no, no, Vale. Not tonight. Not ever. *Burn.*" Morrick limped over to me and the light of flames burned brightly from his hands as he held his bullet wounds, cauterizing them shut. He groaned in pain as the smell of burning flesh turned my stomach into knots.

I was frozen with fear. I could not move. It felt similar to the moment I saw Lauren fall off the cliff back in Yosemite, only this was so much worse than that. Morrick didn't need written runes to use magic and *that* shook me to my core. "I'm going to f-fucking kill you." I quivered with rage.

"You don't seem so sure anymore. No, I don't think you will. You will witness." Morrick said and I felt a sharp pain in my neck. I didn't see him grab the syringe, but by the time I realized what had happened it was already too late and my barrier rune had faded. My faith in the rune left me the moment Elijah collapsed. The room started to spin and my vision clouded. The last thing I heard before everything went dark was a solitary, sinister whisper.

"*Witness.*"

29 THE HARVEST

My body felt heavy and my eyelids felt as if someone had glued them shut. My mind started to break through the smothering darkness, and I could make out the sound of humming computers and the cold touch of metal beneath me. I flexed my hands, but could barely move them. Something was tight around my wrists and was digging into my skin. It felt like plastic.

"Vale! Wake up!" Elijah's panicked voice reached me. The feeling in my whole body started to return and I was finally able to open my eyes. Blinking several times to clear my blurred vision, I scanned the room for Elijah. He was about thirty feet away on the other side of Morrick's grand machine. I met his gaze through the glass, struggling to get free from the chair he was bound to.

The machine thrummed with life and glowed with brilliant light. On the main platform were seven chairs and seven IV bags, all filled and hooked up to seven familiar faces. Kaito, Esteban, Liv, Ember, Lucien, Felix, and Eliza sat incapacitated, surrounding the center where Morrick stood.

"Ah good. Both of you have come too, at last. You were out for a few hours. I was beginning to wonder if I needed to start breakfast." Morrick held himself tall as he spoke. Blood and scorch marks still remained where Elijah shot him, but Morrick seemed completely unharmed.

"Fuck you and fuck your breakfast! You never cared about any of us! You just needed us as pigs for slaughter!" I found my voice and struggled against my restraints.

"Hm, perhaps I *am* selfish for living past what the universe originally allowed me, but the truth is that all the good I've done has greatly outweighed the bad. After all, who is going to miss a couple of strays, outcasts, and runaways? No, the world is better off with me in it, young Vale. I will be more merciful in your death than I'm sure you and your lover would have been toward me." Morrick offered, stepping down from the platform and pressing a few buttons on a keyboard.

I glanced over to some of the screens and next to pictures of all seven Travelers were heart monitors. I guessed Morrick wanted to make sure his cattle were alive and healthy until the moment he devoured them. Elijah looked weirdly calm compared to his voice only moments ago. He kept his eyes on Morrick and didn't seem to move at all save for small twitches coming from his arms.

"You okay, Vale?" Elijah called out to me.

"I think so. You?"

"I'm fine." He said and flicked his eyes downward or rather, behind him, as if he was attempting to tell me something. That's when I noticed a small pool of blood collecting on the floor underneath where his hands were tied behind his chair. What the hell was he doing that was making him bleed?

"Everything seems to be in working order. Normally there are ancient Alchemical rituals of transferring one's life force and abilities to another, but I found that to be inefficient these days, with the kind of technology at our disposal. If my hypothesis is correct, I won't just receive another century from this harvest, but several. It has become quite bothersome to hunt down more gifted ones as humanity advances. Especially in this age of communication, it is incredibly hard to cover up such an act as the Harvest. My 'Time Machine'," Morrick said, ironically and flourished his hand toward the glass cage. "will make it so I won't have to do this ritual for nearly another millennium." Morrick lectured and retraced his steps back onto the center of the platform.

He took a moment to look at each of the Travelers. "Thank you, my children. You will now join the others within me, and we will do incredible things for this world. One day the scientific communities will embrace our genius, but for now it's just us who work tirelessly in the shadows. Let us begin."

Morrick ended his monologue of madness, took a deep breath, and removed his goggles. With a flick, he tossed them off the platform. At the snap of his fingers the machine clicked and hummed louder. Glass shutters slid down, sealing the platform off from the rest of the r oom. Beneath Morrick's feet was a circle of runes that I instantly recognized from the Alchemy book, but this configuration was d ifferent. It was more intricate, more advanced.

Out from one of Morrick's pockets he pulled a scalpel and with one swift motion he sliced open his palm, squeezing blood into the carved runic crevices. The runes filled with his blood as he dropped the scalpel. It clattered onto the floor and Morrick outstretched his arms as white wisps from each Traveler reached out toward him.

"That's it! I can feel you pouring into me!" Morrick shouted, laughing, his eyes closed, and his face pointed to the ceiling.

That's when I saw Elijah jump from his chair. His plastic

restraints fell to the floor, and in his bloody hand he held a long shard of glass. He reached me and immediately got to work on the zip tie around my wrists.

"You're bleeding." I said.

"I know. I got the glass from the foyer floor. Just before I blacked out I managed to slip it into my back pocket. Cut up my ass and hands a bit, but it worked out...There! Let's get the hell out of here!" Elijah grabbed my hand and yanked me toward the elevator, smearing blood onto my skin.

"What? Are you crazy? We have to stop this! Morrick can't win!" I shouted, but the rumbling of the machine nearly drowned me out.

"No, Vale! This is insane! You saw how fast he spoiled our plan. You saw what he can do. We don't stand a chance!" Elijah argued.

"Normally I would agree with you, but did you forget about my backup plan?"

"You never told me or Liv! We really shouldn't even be discussing this, Vale! Please, I don't want to lose you!" Elijah begged, tears welling in his eyes. My heart lodged in my throat, but I swallowed hard. I pulled his neck and rested our foreheads together before whispering into his ear.

"This will work. It has to. We don't have a choice. Trust me, okay? I love you, Eli." Quickly, I revealed the workings of my backup plan. Pointing at a mop in the corner of the room and at his pool of blood, I reached into my bag still strapped to my back, and handed him the book of Alchemy. "Understand? It needs to be perfect to compete with Morrick's runes." I reiterated the importance of this plan.

"Got it. Just be careful. Buy me at least ten minutes, at which point I will wait for you on the platform. Vale...we both better pray this works."

"*Believe* and it will."

Elijah nodded. I nodded back, kissed him, and with no time to waste found the main power box to the whole lab, and started flipping switches.

Instantly, the time machine lurched to a halt and all the computers flickered and died. The lights overhead went out and were quickly replaced with blinking red, reserve lights. Elijah already hid somewhere in the shrouded lab and I moved back toward Morrick's machine, standing tall.

"Hey Morrick, don't count me out just yet! It's only you and me now. Over my dead body will you take the only real family I've ever had away from me!" I hissed at him through the glass panels.

"Well I was going to save you until after the Harvest, but seeing as you are so impatient I can move up your appointment to *now*." Morrick growled and vanished in a spark of light.

All my reflexes reacted, and I Skipped to the foyer. As soon as I reappeared I crumpled a barrier rune, chewed it in my mouth, and swallowed it. "Expel." I said and a thick, strong blue aura layered my whole body.

Just then, Morrick appeared in front of me, his eyes ablaze with a new rage. His skin looked visibly smoother, a full head of brunette locks hung just passed his earlobes, his eyes were no longer cloudy, but clear pools of blue, and all of his scars and wounds were gone. He looked to have de-aged by several decades, and if I didn't know him I'd place him in his mid-thirties. The ritual still worked, but not completely. He felt slower than before and his Rip didn't have the same gravitational pull it once did. My interruption must have weakened him.

I spotted the gun laying on the floor and Skipped straight to it, but just as I reached it I felt a force hit my stomach. Morrick planted his foot into my gut launching me into the dining room. Flinching in pain, I focused in mid air and Skipped to the multipurpose room. I dashed from one part of the room to the next turning on lights, speakers, and projectors. I Skipped to the sound booth and turned the volume to max level.

Just as expected, Morrick followed my Rip energy into the booth, but I was already on the other side of the window and pressed play on Kaito's playlist. Rave trance music blared through the speakers, making the whole room rumble and the glass shake. Morrick covered his ears and crouched in agony, but instantly vanished and reappeared next to me. He threw a punch which connected to my left cheek and sent me tumbling to the ground, but not without my barrier shocking his whole arm.

"Ah! Damn you!" Morrick screamed and formed fire in his hands, throwing it down onto the sound booth control panel. The music glitched and sparked to a halt. Morrick continued to throw fire all around the room and then turned to launch flames directly at me. I rolled out of the way just in time, as the bowling alley and arcade were set ablaze. I Skipped away before the fire surrounded me and reappeared across the hall in the gymnasium.

Slamming and latching the doors shut, I grabbed a Protection rune from my pocket, licked it, and stuck it on the door. "Protect me from those that mean me harm!" I shouted as fast as I could. The room was enveloped in a blue glow the same as before, but what followed was a great shaking throughout every wood panel and marble slab. A Rip tore through the air in the middle of the room and Morrick slowly stepped through.

Instantly the Protection rune activated and an electrical surge pulsed through his body. Morrick grunted in rage-fueled pain, but then began chuckling. He tucked his arms into his chest and, for a moment, I felt a force pulling me toward him. The gym equipment tumbled, rolled, and bounced away from the walls only to be jettisoned across the room as Morrick released a powerful shock wave from his body.

I was knocked onto my ass as the polished court was lifted and splintered into jagged points. Basketballs popped, their leathery remains scattered across the floor. Weights were wedged into the walls and mirrors were shattered into countless remnants of sparkling dust. I stood to my feet and dusted myself off, staring Morrick down.

"Seems to me like you need some fresh air. Let's slow down and smell the flowers, M orrick." I challenged and Skipped directly into the greenhouse. Without a second to lose, I ran over to the sprinkler valves and turned all of them on to full power. Torrential rain fell from above and soaked all my clothes, but created a misty shroud to hide in.

I heard the pulse of Morrick's Rip appear somewhere among the flora. "Vaaaaale." Morrick spoke in sing-song. "It's rather rude of you to destroy my house like this. Don't you want to be part of something bigger, boy? You have a grand destiny with me! Without me, you are lost. Society has discarded you in every way. You are a freak to them and I don't only mean your ability." Morrick taunted me as I hid within the mist and foliage. "Ah, I sense it in you. You revealed part of yourself, didn't you? And they rejected you, didn't they? Poor, lost Vale."

He wasn't wrong, but...No! I couldn't allow him to get in my head. I had to keep this fight going for the sake of Elijah and for the sake of the others. Maybe, just maybe, I could end Morrick's madness tonight. His kingdom of dark science and lost souls would come crumbling down.

"You're just an ancient fossil, Morrick and your soul has rotted to the core, festering inside that dressed-up corpse you call a body. This ends only with one of us dead, and it won't be me!" I shouted back through the rain. There was only the sound of water hitting the leaves and collecting in a basin below the metal grates.

"Such pretty words. I believe you are a word-smith, correct? How quaint, Vale, but all the flowery language in the world will not save you now. Nor will it change my mind. As for who will survive tonight...*you will try*." Morrick snickered, his voice reverberating off the glass walls.

Staring through the artificial rain and out the glass panels, I focused on the dark forest behind the manor. I had never actually been in the backyard of Morrick's estate and I wondered what awaited me out there, but that would be my next stop. I peeked around a corner of brightly colored flowers and large leaves. Only water and mist wafted across the metal pathway.

"Looking for me?" A voice growled right behind me. Instinctively, I threw a punch toward Morrick's side, but he caught my arm in his. I threw my other fist at his face, but he caught it in his hand, restraining me. Morrick lurched back and threw his forehead hard into mine. I flinched and attempted to release myself from his grasp, but he clutched me tighter. Stars exploded through my brain, and I regained my composure quicker than I expected. I gazed up at Morrick's drenched, madly grinning face and I rapidly returned the favor, head-butting him directly on his nose. With a roar, Morrick's hold on me was released as he screamed and held his nose. Blood poured from his nostrils into his hand and mixed with the water below.

"You no-good, fucking child! Look what you've *done to me!*" Morrick shrieked and seized my shirt in his hands pulling me through his Rip and out into the backyard. With a hard shove, Morrick tossed me to the ground, dirt caking my skin. I stood up and prepared myself for another attack. "Welcome to the center of my Labyrinth, Vale." Morrick sneered.

I glanced around to find tall hedges surrounding us and four metal gates that were sealed shut. In each corner of the area was a suit of armor equipped with a sword, as if to depict them as guardians of the maze. Beneath us was a spiral pattern made from cobblestone and pink granite. There was nowhere to go, no way out...except up.

"*Magnetize.*" Morrick said, sticking his hand out to one of the suits of armor. A sword released itself from the knight's iron grip and flew directly into Morrick's outstretched hand. He spoke the word again and retrieved a second sword which he tossed in my direction onto the ground. "Pick it up. We will resolve this with honor, like gentlemen." Morrick stated, settling into a fencing stance.

I picked up the sword, twirled it in my hand once and gripped it like a baseball bat. I took the first move, Skipping behind him and swinging the sword at his back, but Morrick vanished before my blade could connect. He reappeared a few feet away to my right and made a mad dash at me, attempting to stab. My body reacted, deflecting his blade three times with mine. Morrick countered by kicking me in my chest, causing me to land on my butt, my sword flying out of my h and. Morrick magnetized it to his free hand and though I tried to scoot away it was not enough. Morrick's blades were on me in a scissorlike fashion mere inches from my neck.

"Any final words, Little Mage?" Morrick grinned wide, the full moon shining down on us in all its brilliance. Smoke could be seen rising from the manor and upon scanning I realized the flames from earlier had reached the green house which gave it plenty of fuel. My guess was that the water system was not strong enough to quell the raging alchemical fire.

"Yes, actually." I smiled. "Your house is burning." I said and Morrick turned, gasping at the rising smoke and the death of all his precious plants. I took this distraction as my chance to reach into my pocket where I knew a Wind rune would be, crumpled it up, and swallowed it. "*Fly!*" I called out and instantly my body soared upward into the moonlit sky. Just as my legs passed Morrick's blades he managed to cut me. I winced as blood started to trickle out, but it was only a minor wound.

"So you want to take this to the skies, do you? Fine with me." Morrick spat, his nose still red from blood, but the flow had slowed. He vanished yet again and reappeared several feet away from me floating in the sky. The vast forest opened up beneath us and I could see endless mountains and dark woods. How did Morrick keep casting runes without drawing them, or even speaking at times? Was he just that powerful or was I missing something? There was nothing on his person or his clothes that looked runic, and the only energy I felt from him was that of a Skipper, save for the Wind rune that allowed him flight.

"You seem confused, my boy." Morrick snickered. "How could I be flying without using a rune? Easy. When you have a photographic memory, like yours truly, Alchemy becomes second nature."

That was it. A sharp memory. A vivid imagination. If *intention* and *belief* are what drove Alchemy, then what could the creative mind of a writer do with it? My eyes darted around frantically trying to think of a solution, when my mind landed on Elijah's handgun still laying on the floor in the f oyer. I closed my eyes to focus and reached my hand out to the manor. I attempted to recall the rune for Magnetism in my mind.

"Hahahahaha! What is the Little Mage trying to do? Will you Skip away again, because I can assure you that I will never stop hunting you. This ends tonight." Morrick laughed into the night and I could feel his Rip start to open.

Motion slowed, as if time were coming to a halt. The rune of Magnetism appeared clearly in my mind, but I mixed it with the rune of Binding. Visibly, in my mind, the runes danced and melded to create a completely new, original rune. I felt the metal of the gun being pulled to my hand until finally, I heard a distant shattering. A heavy object landed in my grasp. The handle of the gun felt warm from the fires, but just as it touched my skin I snapped my eyes back open to face Morrick. He vanished, and was emerging behind me. The pull of his Rip gave him away. Faster than light, I Skipped back down to the labyrinth, aimed down my sights, and took my shot.

The handgun jolted to life, belching a red aura as the bullet soared directly at Morrick, connecting with his left shoulder. Morrick's whole body seized up, causing him to drop his swords as well as making him to fall more than twenty feet to the ground. There was an audible crunch when Morrick hit the ground; his screams of anguish filled the trees.

"My legs! I can't feel my legs! What have you done to me?" Morrick shrieked, unable to move from the Binding rune fused to the bullet in his shoulder. I never thought him capable of sorrow, but surprise struck me as tears flowed from Morrick's eyes.

"You did this to yourself!" I shouted back. I never wanted to hurt anyone. I felt immense dread coming over me. I just completely crippled a man and soon he would die by my hands. I knew I had to follow through to save the others, but by saving them will I be lost?

I touched Morrick's unwounded shoulder and Skipped us back into his lab where Elijah had just finished his role in the backup plan. We landed in the center of the time machine where Elijah drew a rune of Reversal in front of each of the Travelers' chairs, in his own blood using the mop. He did just as I had instructed and now stood by the computers.

"Finally, Vale! You took a little longer than ten minutes so I started to worry. Holy shit...What did you—" Elijah started, but I cut him off when he noticed Morrick writhing on the ground in defeat.

"I did what needed to be done. I stopped him. Now, where's the on switch for this machine?" I asked and Elijah, having already restored the main power, pointed at an LCD screen that read: Start Sequence. I gave it a harsh poke and Morrick's machine came to life, but this time something was different. Green energy began flowing from Morrick back into the seven Travelers. Where wrinkles and gray hairs had formed now morphed to colored follicles and smooth skin.

"You are a childish fool, Vale! This world needs me! It will perish without my genius!" Morrick grunted through his teeth as he managed to sit himself up, but was still unable to move. His face started to droop and his hair grayed. "And there is another thing..." Morrick's voice became dark and he strangely smiled, looking down at the floor. "*Skipping...will destroy you.*"

Morrick started to laugh, but winced from the immense pain of his blood loss and splintered bone. "The more you rely on it, the more of your own life you give to the void."

Morrick flopped down on his back, weakly chuckling up at the lights as the last of his energy drained from him. His body completely shriveled, his bones disintegrating into dust. It was over. Thank God...it was over.

"We...*We did it.*" Elijah breathed as the machine shut down and the glass shutters lifted. The others were waking, and struggled with their restraints.

"He's gone, but there's still the fire and we need to get out of here." I said, rushing around the control panels and back up to the platform. Elijah stayed close behind me. We both worked together to release the Travelers. They were all groggy from the drugs Morrick fed them, but were coherent enough to stand. "Everyone grab hands and hold on tight. I know things are fuzzy right now, but do as I say!"

Hands clasped hands, some supported each other by the shoulders, and we formed a circle. I focused as hard as possible to open my Rip to everyone. I felt gravity pulling me, and Skipped out to the front water fountain. The release of transporting everyone left me with a blistering headache, and blood dripped from my nose. I went to touch my nose but realized I was still holding Elijah's gun. My stomach lurched and I vomited on the ground. The weight of everything came crashing down all at once and consciousness swiftly escaped me.

I awoke and jolted upright. I was surrounded by familiar faces who all looked ecstatic to see me awake. They were all here in Elijah's room. "What? How did I get here?" I asked as I held my still-aching head. I rubbed my temples and focused on their voices.

"Elijah watched over you until all of us came to from the drugs that bastard Morrick pumped into us." Lucian said.

"He also told us what you did to bring us back and to stop Morrick. Vale...You're incredible." Eliza doted.

"I don't know about that. He wasn't who I thought he was. I can't believe I..." I started, but stopped as a knot formed in my throat. I covered my face.

"Morrick fooled us all, Vale. If you didn't do what you did we would all be dead. You are not at fault here. Don't do that to yourself." Ember consoled me.

I rubbed my wet eyes and sniffled as my dread subsided. "What about Langdorf Manor?" I asked, remembering the smell of dense smoke.

"Completely gone. Esteban and I made sure of it so no one stumbled upon it. Only problem is now there is a fire in the Maryland Black Hills that firefighters are attempting to put out, but there will be nothing there for them to find." Felix stated, rubbing the back of his neck.

"You really showed that pendejo not to underestimate young people." Esteban slapped Felix on the back and gave me a thumbs-up in approval.

"I wanted to try and save some things, but the others wouldn't let me. The only thing that we managed to leave with was Morrick's fortune in his underground safe. We moved it to a secret undisclosed location, but you're family Vale and that goes for you as well, Eli. We'll be able to take care of each other." Kaito explained and grinned shyly at me and Elijah who sat next to me on the bed.

"Wow! That's...*wow*." I said and swung my legs over the side of the bed.

"Easy. I just patched up that leg wound. Don't get up too fast." Elijah stated, as he caressed my back.

"Wait, where's Liv?" I asked.

"Present." Liv said as she moved from behind everyone else.

"Oh dang, I couldn't see you behind Felix, you're so short!" I joked, but it was true.

"That or Felix is just a giant." Liv jabbed back and playfully shoulder-shoved Felix. Everyone chuckled in unison. "I'm glad you're alright, Vale. Thanks, by the way. I'm a little embarrassed I went down so easily, but I'm glad that ass-hat bit the dust...no pun intended." Liv clenched her fists and her cheeks turned red.

"There really isn't any need to thank me, guys. Everything I did was on a whim. In other words, I had no clue what I was doing and at any moment I thought we were all going to die. Maybe that's what kept me going. I wanted to prevent that from happening at all costs." I stood up and spoke plainly. I stretched and cracked my joints.

As I relaxed, I spotted my bags in the corner and realized we were in Elijah's room. I remembered the fight with my parents. I couldn't go back there, not as I am. I no longer had a home here in the armpit of California.

"So what now, Vale? What's your plan?" Lucien asked. For the first time in months, I felt like I could think straight.

"Well, I was hoping I could go wherever it is you all are going. We can start over somewhere and be each other's family." I suggested. When the words came out my heart and mind completely felt at peace with the idea.

"A wonderful thought!" Ember shouted in approval.

"Yaaaaassss! The Travelers have an eighth member again

and this time they aren't a maniac bent on killing us." Eliza said ecstatically.

"Eliza!" Ember glared at her in disapproval.

"What? Too soon?" Eliza shrugged.

"What about it, Eli? You going to join your man on this new adventure." Liv elbowed Elijah in his side and chuckled, but when he didn't immediately answer the room went silent.

"Can we talk privately, Vale?" Elijah asked, his voice as serious as it has ever been.

"Um, sure. Guys, give us a minute." I said, grabbing Elijah's hand and Skipping us to Morro Bay beach where we went at the beginning of the semester, where this all started.

The morning sun of All Saints Day shone brightly and illuminated the sandy shores. The waves moved steadily and glittered magically. I smelled the fresh sea air and the only presence was that of seagulls. A gentle misty fog floated around us and stretched several yards out on the ocean.

"Remember our day here, Eli. It was the trip that started this all. It's when my true self, as well as my love for you, came out of the closet. So much has changed in such a short amount of time." I said sincerely, eyes fixed on the horizon.

"I want you to stay." Elijah said.

"What?"

"You heard me. I don't think you should go with them." Elijah's face was stern and he felt firmly planted in place.

"What do you mean? They're my family. They chose me. They actually care about me or did you suddenly forget what my parents said to me? They basically kicked me out." I rebutted.

"I didn't forget, Vale, but they are still your parents and you are the one who left. They 'basically' kicked you out, but they didn't."

"Are you serious right now? They don't love! Not really! What am I supposed to do, live with you and your dad? Oh wait, except he wouldn't be okay with gay sex happening under his roof either. So why don't you just come with me, Eli? Imagine the life we can have together? We don't even need to finish school. We have everything we need." I begged, but as much as I tried to convince him to see things my way he was immovable.

"I can't just leave my dad. Believe or not, we actually have a good relationship and he is coming around to the whole, 'me dating guys' thing. Plus, I actually *want* to finish s chool. I want to graduate and…I was hoping you would be my date to the senior prom." Elijah blushed and locked eyes with me, hope and tears welling up. His hands locked with mine, his thumb caressing my fingers.

My mind played back the memories of the past few months. From the very beginning when I set foot on this beach to the moment I Skipped everyone out of that burning manse, Elijah has been right there. Either in person or on my mind, he has been there to remind me of the logical choice and to support me. Elijah was my oldest friend. He taught me how to stay on my bike, instead of on the pavement with scraped legs. He got me into all sorts of music I wouldn't have bothered to listen to otherwise. He distracted me with countless pre-teen adventures and activities that broke me out of my shell, and he was partially how I discovered that I wanted to be a writer. It made me question whether or not my feelings for him started recently, or if they've been there all along. When he first came out as Bi, I recalled feeling something inside me do flips, a piece of me that, at the time, I decided to shove down because of religion.

All the sleepless nights.

All the whispered conversations.

All the major revelations in our lives.

Elijah was there for it all.

Before I knew what was happening, I was embracing my love in my arms. Our lips interlocked as I caressed his back, and he traced his fingers through my hair. The warmth of the autumnal sun kissed our cheeks, and just when I was about to run out of air, I remembered to breathe through my nose. We reluctantly separated our mouths, and inhaled the salty wind as we smiled at each other. I took in his face, his every flawless pore, his thick, dark eye-brows, and the black stubble lining his upper lip and chin. Elijah was right, I was being ridiculous. I needed to think this through. I was almost done with school and it wasn't too late to get my grades up. There was still a big chance Elijah, Lauren, and I could all go to college together in Colorado. As much as I cared about the Travelers I did not know them nearly as well as those who I grew up with, and who still love me.

"Prom sounds...amazing." I sighed.

"Really? You mean it?!" Elijah exclaimed, tears misting his eyes.

"Absolutely. I don't know what I was thinking. I may be fighting with my parents right now and last night will haunt me for a while, but I shouldn't be taking it out on you or any one else who clearly loves me. I can't run away from this...from us." Sincerity flowed out of me and Elijah hugged me so tightly I thought my joints were going to pop out of place. "Can't... breeeeathe!"

"Oh sorry, handsome!" Elijah laughed. "I'm just...so proud of you." He held my face, rubbing my cheek as he looked into my eyes. I did the same and used my thumb to wipe away his tears.

"Things are not going to be easy for a while, and my mom will probably have loads of questions."

"But you won't do it alone." Elijah reassured.

"Thank you, Eli."

"Now can we please have some breakfast? I'm starving!" He said as his stomach let out a loud rumble. "We can invite the Travelers too!"

"Ha! Of course you are. That's a great idea. Hold onto me." I agreed and prepared to Skip.

"I'll never let go."

30 HOME

Winter.

A season of togetherness. A time to draw close with our loved ones, forgive past transgressions, and seek the warmth in each others' hearts. I was reminded of those facts as I gazed down the busy streets of Denver, Colorado. Twinkling Christmas lights illuminated nearly every inch of the sidewalks as pedestrians passed, tightly wrapped in their coats and scarves. Beyond the frost-bitten city streets, wind swept and snow laden mountains lined the dark horizon.

Elijah and I stood wearing our University of Boulder hoodies in a long queue that traced the side wall of the Bluebird Theater. The marquee read, **"Christmas Eve Show: Cigarettes After Sex!"** Our favorite band as of recently and one that lulled us into the throws of romance instantly with their alternative-indie melodies.

We huddled close to each other, our hot breath flowing from our lips with each word. I clutched onto my phone, the screen lit, and the camera on in an active video call. Mom's bright cheeks and crimson lips cheerfully chattered over the phone speakers. "Are you being safe out there, Vale? We miss you."

"Of course, Mom. You don't need to keep asking that. We're just waiting in line for a concert." I explained, rolling my eyes.

"Oh I know, but you will always be my baby boy and a mother has a right to worry about her child." Mom wagged her finger at the camera. She took a sip of red wine as her eyes widened. "Oh! What time will you be here tomorrow?"

"I mean, I can come anytime, because..."

"Oh I know, honey, but just because you can 'Zip', or whatever you call it, doesn't mean I don't need to plan. I still don't understand why you insisted on moving all the way to Colorado when you could just live at home and save money." Mom trailed off on a tangent.

"Oh, I don't know? How's Dad? Still not opening up after a year?" I muttered. Mom was quiet and then sighed.

"I see your point, Vale. Your father will come around. Please be patient." She begged. "We almost lost you, after all. I just want you to be okay. *We* want you to be okay."

"I'm okay, Mom. I promise. Eli and I will be there first thing tomorrow morning. Maybe I'll take us to Ireland or something after we open presents?" I offered. I wanted to keep the peace with my parents, for however long it took them to finally be accustomed to their new-and-improved son.

Just then, the line of concert goers began shuffling forward and a tall girl with full, dark curls appeared with three steaming hot chocolates in her hands. "Some hot chockies for me and my favorite guys-oh! Hi Mrs. Dagwood!" Lauren chirped as soon as she saw my Mom on the screen.

"Hi sweetie! How was the end of the semester?"

"Oh it was great—"

"Oh Mom, sorry. We have to go. The venue is letting us in. I love you! Merry Christmas!" I interrupted as we rapidly approached the front doors.

"Oh okay. You kids have fun! Lauren! I expect you here

tomorrow too! Merry Christmas!" Mom pointed a finger through the phone and blew air kisses at us.

"Byyyye!" The three of us said in unison. The call disconnected and I let out a big groan up to the sky.

"C'mon, Vale! That's progress." Lauren nudged my shoulder.

"I know. It's hard to be patient with them. I wish they would just catch up already." I moaned.

"They will, but forget that for now. Let's hurry up and get some good spots. It's standing room only in there." Elijah grabbed my shoulders from behind and pushed me through the doors.

The show was about to begin. The stage was set. The crowd buzzed and murmured with anticipation. I lifted my hot chocolate to my lips when a sudden stinging pain shot through my right hand. I winced, and stared down. My heart jumped as the skin on my hand wrinkled and writhed in an unnatural way. And as fast as it begun, it stopped. My skin was smooth and stood still around my tendons and bone. I swapped my drink to my other grip and flexed my hand into a fist as Morrick's last words echoed in my head.

"Hey, you alright?" Elijah wrapped his arm over my shoulders, shaking me out of my silent panic.

"Of course." I smiled, his amber eyes melting me into his touch.

The lights in the venue dimmed and the crowd cheered as the band came on stage. They played their song, "Nothing's gonna hurt you baby" and I swayed in Elijah's arms. I looked to my left to see Lauren singing the lyrics and she caught my gaze. She pulled us both in for a side hug as we allowed the music to wash away our anxieties.

Uncertainty shrouded my mind for a moment, but these two were my light out of the fog. My lighthouses on a cape near a treacherous sea.

They are my home.

About the Author

Corey has been writing poems, short stories, and full length novels for nearly two decades. He grew up in the Central Valley of California where he dreamed of magical adventures, new worlds, and great purpose. He generally has an interest in Fantasy, Sci fi, Horror, and YA stories. Corey has a degree in Film from San Francisco State university and used his skills on various film projects and on the streaming website Twitch. There he goes by the name King Corey Bear, where He runs his own growing community of viewers and friends. Corey often enjoys playing narrative based video games, especially scary games. If something can legitimately scare him then he knows it's good. Corey is in his early thirties and currently lives happily with his Partner in the San Francisco Bay Area surrounded by their many collectibles.

You can connect with me on:

🌐 https://linktr.ee/KingCoreyBear